Distorted Mirrors

Beyond The Wallace's

Carey Anderson

ISBN-10:0692493484
ISBN-13:9780692493489

DEDICATION

I would like to dedicate this book to all of my honorary Rough Riders. To those who have supported me from the beginning. The readers who read Volume I and decided to learn more about the Wallace's. This is dedicated to each person who has said to someone else, "have you heard about the Wallace's?" And the readers who have taken the time to leave feedback that I can grow from in the form of reviews and ratings. Without you I'd wonder if my voice was even being heard. Also, I would like to thank my Rough Riders who have been there with me from the beginning listening to my stories over the phone, looking over my shoulder as I hand wrote doodles to entertain them. The ones who checked their emails daily looking for the latest chapter of my rough draft. And those who reread my stories as much as I do. I could never thank you all enough for how you've gone above and beyond to support me and help me along this journey.

To every person who's ever been in a "relationship" where they wondered why their partner didn't love them, or what the hiccup in their relationship was. There's always three sides; to every story yours, theirs, and then the truth. Just know that as long as you live in your truth your happy ending is just around the corner.

Cover by Cover Couture (www.bookcovercouture.com)
Photo Copyright: art studio / shutterstock
Photo Copyright: Art of Life / shutterstock
Photo Copyright: Audy39 / Shutterstock

Join me on Facebook –
www.facebook.com/careythewriteranderson

Twitter - @CareyTheWriter

Blog - http://careyanderson.blogspot.com

Website – http://www.careythewriteranderson.com

ACKNOWLEDGMENTS

I would like to thank my baby-girl who is my life's ultimate expression of a dream realized. Thank you for sacrificing mommy time so that I could have the time to work some things out on paper.

I would like to thank my Soul Sistah #1 who has been my captivated audience since middle school. Without your love, support, encouragement, and FIRE I never would've completed Volume I or II, etc. Thank you for bringing me laughter when I couldn't get outside of my head.

I would like to thank my Sister-In-Law for taking time out of your busy family life to humor me with a read through of my latest thoughts and expressions. (SS1 & SIL THANK YOU for the trip to St. Helena where we spent the day lost in my imagination. I will never forget it, and it was exactly what I needed. THANK YOU!)

I would like to thank my dear cousin for reassuring me that my little hobby was relatable and entertaining. You are definitely a speed-reader, thank you for taking time out of your busy life to be entertained by my imagination.

I would like to thank last but not least Mrs. Laverne Dyes! Mrs. Dyes the day that you read my short story to my class changed my life. Thank you for giving me a positive outlet for all the angst going on in my life. You have forever changed my life, I am so thankful to have ever known you.

<u>**Mirrors**</u>

When I was a little girl I used to stare in the mirror. I used to wonder if the reflection staring back at me was as horrible to everyone else as it was to me. I'd dissect my brown skin, almost pudgy nose. The beauty mark on my cheek that I inherited from my mother.

Sometimes I would cry so HARD at the disappointment of the image that I beheld. I don't know what I hoped to see each time I looked in the mirror. I used to pray and ask God to make me beautiful when I grew up. I would cry so hard begging him to show me mercy and somehow change the image I saw before me for the better...

Chapter 1 ~ Boys will make you feel ugly

I had a boyfriend my freshman year, but we broke up. I actually dumped him (sad face). He was cute.... kind of, but he always had these big stories that didn't add up. In the end my head always turned for the upper classman Steve. I didn't feel it was right to continue in my relationship if I found myself really liking someone else. My poor boyfriend was hurt when I broke up with him, but I felt it was the right thing to do. I didn't approach Steve or make my silly crush known to him, not then anyways.

My sophomore year, suddenly there was this guy. When I saw him I said out loud that he was cute. Little did I know the next day my world would change. This guy had already noticed me and he liked me. **ME!** I was so excited! For the first time ever someone I liked, liked me. I snuck to the carnival to be with him. I would go see him on my way to work. I found a way to be with this boy whenever I could be. One day a girl approached me stating that my boyfriend was on her line constantly trying to holler at her. I mean, the disappointment of a stupid guy was no new territory to me. But this one hurt! It hurt really badly! I remember I put my chin on my desk telling myself not to cry, as I listened to her provide her proof. After school I found my boyfriend, and I confronted him with everything she said to me. He said they were just friends, and he was not interested in her. I told him to prove it by telling me everything he just said but in front of her the next day at school. Sure enough the next day like he told me the day before he told me exactly the same way. I felt so vindicated. So.... So.... SPRUNG! Our "relationship" continued until that summer when he dumped me because he got caught cheating on me by a so-called cousin. His reason for cheating was because I didn't put out.

At this point I honestly felt like beauty is in the eye of the beholder. Who was I to say what beautiful was and what beautiful wasn't?

Chapter 2 ~ And then there was him

My graduation was pretty standard. They called my name my family cheered me on as I got my diploma. My family came back to my house and we had Costco cake and punch as I opened my graduation gifts. I wore my cap and gown all night long. One of my cousins asked me if I was going to take it off at some point and I told him no. I was proud of myself for my accomplishment. My parents were proud as well, but I hadn't shared my news yet. I only told my little sisters and I made them promise not to tell the others. I got accepted into the University of California, Davis. My GPA earned me a partial scholarship. The day before I got my job acceptance letter. Everything was falling into place. Over the summer I planned to work hard and save up for an apartment for the fall. My parents bought me a little car the year before when I got my license just like they did for my brother when he got his. Going to school wasn't going to be the issue for my parents although some people thought it would be. No, the issue would be that I wanted to move out during this time. My parents just moved to this big and beautiful house in Oakland after all of our time in Richmond Ca. Each of us got our own rooms after all the girls had been crammed into the same room since the twins came. Terence was still there so it's not like it was going to be a waste to have so much space now. Now they'd have a guest room.

That Sunday after service I told my parents that I got into UC Davis and they smiled for me. Then I told them about the job I was going to be starting the next day. At first it was all smiles and good times. Then it was one too many times where my family wasn't together at service that my father pulled me to the side to talk to me. He was trying to appeal to my heart and stress the importance of staying on the straight and narrow. I couldn't hear him though. I had all these ideas about how my life was going to be as soon as I moved out. Finally I'd meet a guy, go out on dates, have sex, and then I'd marry this guy and live my version of happily ever after. This did not match up with my parent's ideas for my life.

Armed with my summer wages I found a small studio apartment in Crockett, this little town right before the Vallejo Bridge. My school was still about a thirty-minute drive from my place, but my job was in San Francisco. I drove to the bus stop in Hercules and then took the bus to the Bart station in El Cerrito and then took Bart to the city.

Freshman orientation was like exportation into a whole new world. I had a list of required literature in my hand and no idea of where to go next. "Why don't you have a sign posted or something? How am I supposed to know where to go?" A girl fussed out loud. Our eyes met and I smiled, "you're just as lost as I am?" I nodded yes. "Good then we fail college together." She walked up to me and showed me her list of needed books for her classes.

Some guys heard my dramatic panic attack, and he told us where to go to get our books. He told us to get used books before we bought new ones. Then he suggested that we go to Berkeley and try stores out there first.

I turned to my new friend who was too happy to search closer to her home. "I'm Tracy by the way."

"Nicole, nice to meet you. You want to go together?"

"Sure you want me to follow you?"

She was thinking, "Do you mind following me? I need to give my mom her car back. I'll give you money for gas."

I followed Nicole to her place on the El Cerrito and Albany boarder. She lived within walking distance to the Bart station. She invited me inside her apartment to meet her mom. Her mom was in her bedroom getting dressed for work listening to music. She knocked on her door and then she went in. Then they came out. Her mom was very nicely put together. She was the same average height as Nicole. Nicole had her mom's eyes, but her mom's lips were fuller and her skin was a deeper chocolaty hue. Her hair was braided in small corn rolls across her head just like Nicole. "Hello I'm Allison King."

"Tracy Thomas, nice to meet you." We shook hands.

As she pulled her hand back she scanned me up and down. "Very cute outfit. I like how you combined your studious look with a more casual feel."

I smiled, "thank you." I hate when females do the scan and say nothing. That's how lots of fights started at my school with females doing that.

Nicole smiled, "I like your earrings, I don't think they'd look good on me."

"Thank you," I touched my ears to remember what I was wearing. "I think they would look good on you. If they look good on me they would look good on anyone."

Nicole's mom smiled then she excused herself to finish getting ready for work. As Nicole and I walked down the stairs a guy was walking towards us. He smiled at us and then he kissed Nicole's cheek, "you leaving?

"Yea, I gotta get books for school. This is my friend Tracy. Tracy this is my mom's boyfriend."

"Hello." He smiled, "let me know if you need money."

"Shoot I don't have to leave to tell you that. I need help if you're offering."

He smiled real big and reached down into his Jean pocket. He pulled out his wallet. He gave her a bill, but I didn't see what it was. "Let me know if you need more, I'll go to the bank. Nice to meet you Tracy."

Nicole got in the car excited. She said she really liked her mom's boyfriend. She said he's been with her mom for a long time. She said she hated the boyfriend before this one, when I asked why she just shook her head looking out the window. I tried to imagine what it would've been like if my parents weren't together and my mom had different boyfriends trying to find mister wonderful. My life wouldn't have been so rigid, and maybe I could've experienced a few things before now.

Then I feel bad for thinking like that. I mean, it's not like I didn't look at my friend's lives and appreciate my virginity most times. One friend got pregnant over the summer from middle school to high school, she graduated with an almost four year old and I don't know how many abortions after that. Or my friends who were looking for love and they let every possibility in, and when he turned out to be nothing that hurt.

There was this one guy that I really liked. In my mind I called him a triangle head, cause his face was shaped like one, but boy did I like him. He was a complete bad boy. Driving underage going to juvenile hall all the time. He even kissed me in front of my cousins one time, but ask him what my name was... Yeah, go ahead stand me in front of him and ask him what my name was. Even better ask him if he ever kissed me, and he'd have to think real hard about it. I was such an after thought that one time he was trying to get me to put out and when I couldn't he took my so-called friend in the room and she did. She put out so much that she forgot not to take life in. I can't remember if she had an abortion or she miscarried, but that was a baby that never breathed the breath of life. Yea moments like that I was glad that my virginity made me gun shy and held me back. But I'm tired of this life.

"Tracy? Hello Tracy?"

"Huh? Sorry, what were you saying?"

"If you park in the garage I'll pay for the parking."

Food was calling us, but there were so many choices. I told Nicole to pick cause I could go for them all. She picked this hot dog place. When I looked at my hot dog I was not impressed, AT ALL! But then I took a bite! OH MYLANTA! It was delicious! The bread was fresh, and slightly toasted. The fresh onions gave me flavor. Everything was delicious and I fought with myself to stick to just one hot dog. I wanted another one just because it was good. As Nicole and I walked down the street there were students everywhere moving into dorms, getting to know the area, everything. There were cute guys everywhere, but I didn't look hard enough to entertain any of them. They were all looking at Nicole anyways. Some of them she would encourage and others she would reject and return to sender. After awhile she looked at me and rubbed my back. "You plan on remaining a virgin until you get married?"

I got so embarrassed, "you can tell?"

"Saying hi wont get you pregnant. It's when you say *HELLO!*" Then she winked at me. I hung my head lower, "girl being a virgin is nothing to be embarrassed about. Just be careful, cause these wolves will sniff you out. Then you become a challenge and your virginity will be the trophy. Stay on guard."

****

There he is again, I always see him on the Bart while I'm on my way to work in the city. One morning I saw him actually checking me out. I also saw him trying to spit game at a girl who was not interested. He wasn't my type, wasn't ugly just not my type of fantasy for sure. Still it was nice to have someone notice me.

I focused on my book and got as much reading in as I could on the Bart then I rushed down the San Francisco streets to my job. I work as much overtime as I can especially on the weekends. Everything cost so much. PG&E, Telephone, Water, Food, Gas, Car Insurance. A couple of times I had to let my insurance lapse just to make ends meet. My parents call me to see how I'm doing, but then they try to encourage me to come back to service. Even if I wanted to right now, I can't. I just don't have the time. School is heavy and I got to focus, work is work, and then I have my social life. Nicole spends the night at my place so much she has a toothbrush, scarf, and pajamas here too. A couple of times I've spent the night at her place with her even.

It was getting late and I wanted something sweet but I couldn't put a taste to it. Nicole and I went to the store and then she followed me around as I went up and down the aisles trying to think of what I needed. As soon as I saw the fresh pears there it was. I grabbed four pears, blueberries, and blackberries. Butter, flour, and most important Homestyle Vanilla ice cream. Nicole was clueless as to what I was going to do. I told her to turn on a movie and give her brain a rest while I created a dessert for us. As my cobbler baked Nicole came in the kitchen area and sat on the floor with me in front of the oven. She said it smelled delicious. When she asked me what it was, I shrugged and said a cobbler if we had to call it something. Nicole wiped her mouth as I took the bubbling cobbler out of the oven and let it rest on the stove. We tried to go back to studying but the aroma kept stealing our concentration, and then Nicole blurted out. "FOR THE LOVE OF ALL THINGS HOLY! DO WE HAVE TO WAIT ANY MORE? I CAN'T TAKE THIS!" We laughed and then we made our bowls of cobbler and ice cream. I watched Nicole, as she tasted it first. Her eyes rolled in her head then they got big. She sung my praises as she ate, and then she got seconds. The butter, the cinnamon, the flaky doughy crust! The tart berries were balanced and given texture by the pears. I was in heaven my own doggone self. With our second wind we finished our papers and then we knocked out.

"Would you like to sit down?" The guy was gesturing towards the open seat. I smiled, thanked him, sat down, and went right back to my book. "That must be a really exciting book."

"Not especially, it's for school."

"Oh! A college girl, what school you go to?"

"UC Davis," I wished he'd let me read.

"Have a good day brainiac." Then he got off the Bart.

Somehow that became the name he gave me, and daily he'd try to say something to me. One night I was able to stay and shut the call center down. I was too tired to read so I just looked out the window, even when we were in the tunnels; I looked out at the nothingness. I was trying to think up something to eat at home. Nothing there even sound good. I didn't have much money to splurge with so I kept trying to think of something creative and worth eating. "What you doing on this train brainiac?"

I tried to smile, but I was too tired. "On my way home after a long day."

"Did you eat yet?"

"Nope, I was just trying to figure out what I was going to do."

"I normally have dinner at Denny's right by the Bart, you want to come?"

"Pass, I don't know you."

"Well how else are you going to get to know me if you don't come out with me?" I didn't say anything, "it's my treat."

That was music to my ears. I agreed to meet him there; I wasn't giving him a ride. I didn't know him. I waited for him in the front, and he asked me how I got there so fast. I shrugged but I didn't answer. My stalker finally introduced himself as Mancel, but he told me to call him Celly. When he started exhibiting flirtatious behavior I got nervous. Was this supposed to be a date? When he asked for my phone number I felt kind of obligated to give it to him so I did.

Chapter 3 ~ Really?

Celly only caught me at home whenever Nicole was over it seemed at first. I talked to him a few times over the phone, that didn't really phase me much. It was the times he caught me on Bart and got me to talk that started to capture my attention. Celly kept saying he wanted to see me so Nicole suggested a double date with her and her man Dajuan. I don't know why I felt the need to keep reminding her that Celly was not my type. We agreed to meet at a little cafe in Berkeley. After fifteen minutes Dajuan was tired of waiting and ready to eat when Nicole asked me which one was the guy. Celly was walking towards us with a guy who looked familiar but I didn't know why. Celly introduced his friend Brian to the table then he asked the waitress for an extra chair. Brian looked at me then he looked away. "Why do you look familiar?"

"We ride the same Bart train in the mornings."

Celly was kind of loud and he definitely had to be the center of attention. Brian kept quiet mostly and only spoke up only to cosign some of the things that Celly said. After we ate, Nicole shot me a look so that I saw that Brian paid for our food, we went to the movies. Brian paid again. Celly kept hugging me and telling me he was so happy to finally see me again. On the way home Nicole asked me if I liked Celly and I didn't really know. I kept shrugging and saying he was fine. Celly stayed on my phone after that. He kept trying to figure out how to get to my place. Most times I was studying and I couldn't have him over and other times I would ask him to meet me somewhere. Whenever we went out Brian came with him, and Brian always footed the bill for us. When I asked him about it, he said that he gave his money to Brian to hold for him. So Brian would pay for our things, but with Celly's money. Our first kiss wasn't a great kiss, but it wasn't horrible either.

After a month Celly was confessing his love for me so much that I felt like a jerk for not responding in kind. I sat myself down and had a long talk with myself. No one was beating down my door to date me or even get to know me. This wonderful life I envisioned after leaving my parents house wasn't happening. I wasn't attracted to Celly but that was no reason to ignore him or disregard him as if he was nobody. He wanted to shower me with everything that I said I wanted from a man. I told myself to get over myself and open my heart.

Chapter 4 ~ He said

My name is Steve. I grew up in Richmond California. My parents divorced when I was very young and both of them remarried. My parents married young and my mom says she tried very hard to make things work, but my dad cheated on her and one time he hit her. I don't know how true the part about him hitting her is. I try to be unbiased in my opinion, but I know how difficult my mother is. I know they divorced because of her. She's the reason we could no longer be a family. If my father was as horrible as she says he was then how come all three of her marriages after him failed as well? Some how she always tries to come back to my father even if she's the woman on the side. My father remarried and has been married to that same woman ever since. I've seen some of the things my father has done and I know he isn't a saint, but my father never abandoned us. My mother would make it very difficult for my father to see us and spend time with us. She didn't care about how much she hurt him or us. There were three of us. My oldest brother, my older sister, and then me. Our brother got sick and after many years of fighting to live he died when he was sixteen. I was about ten years old, my mother sunk into her depression even more when he died. She forgot about me and my sister and somehow we had to be the adults. We went to school came home cleaned, cooked, and did our homework. We were left to figure out how to survive on our own. My mother should've tried harder to save her marriage. Maybe if she would've fought harder they never would've divorced. Maybe if they never divorced my brother never would've gotten sick. Once my brother got sick I would sit and talk to him. He became my best friend. I would tell him everything and even though he couldn't always respond he understood what I was going through, what I was feeling. My sister was always too busy being momma's baby to care. She was and still is my mother's favorite. I remind my mother too much of my father. Seems she can't look at me without seeing my father's face. After awhile of trying to cope with my mother's depression I decided that I couldn't take it anymore, I asked to go live with my father. When I told him why, my father went to court and was awarded custody of my sister and I. In my father's home there was structure and discipline. My job was to go to school and get my education, I did my chores, and then I could relax and be a kid. It took some time for my stepmother to grow on me. At first I believed all the horrible things my mother said about her. Then I grew to see that most of it wasn't true. Nobody is perfect, but I grew to love her very much. And I liked the relationship she has with my father. In the end she was loved and cared for just like we were.

I was given my mother's eyes. Which just about makes me blind, an exaggeration. But my prescription is pretty strong. So since I was little I've needed to wear some pretty thick glasses. Kids would call me nerd, and when that show *Family Matters* came out, people loved to call me Steve Urkel instead of just Steve. I hated the similarities. The glasses, the dorky clothes, but I was never as annoying as Steve Urkel. I mostly kept to myself and had mental fantasies of all the beautiful girls around me. In my mind I made love to them daily and multiple times a day at that.

In high school I learned that I had to take control over the things I could control. That's when I started working out. All the guys on Tv would have amazing girls falling all over their selves just because they worked out. The guy didn't have to be all that good looking just built and girls would fall at their feet. As my body started to transform so did my image in the eyes of girls. They started to notice me and suddenly I wasn't as much of a nerd as they deemed me to be. At the end of my sophomore year I got fitted for contacts and that summer I went from being the little guy to growing a little over a foot taller. The growing pains were no joke it hurt so badly, but it paid off in the end. Junior year was a new year for me. I lost my virginity almost immediately. Girls looked at me differently and lots were willing to do anything to have my attention. **Me**! Mister can't get a girl to say hi, now had to beat them off with a stick. On the outside I was all the new me, on the inside I was still the same kid with the glasses who sat in the corner and went unnoticed unless someone wanted to make fun of me.

My mother would say men are dogs and all these things, but she never warned me about how doggish women could be. It only took a couple of heartbreaks for me to understand that everyone was playing games, so I played along as well.

A lot of girls I only slept with once, and then they'd disappear. No biggie to me cause I already had them. The others would hang around for more. I let my moves and conversations with my best female friend be my guide to learn what to do. My bestie told me that I had to switch positions and I had to keep the girl guessing at how I was going to come at her. Shannon was the first girl that I took from someone else. She had a boyfriend when we met. She swore up an down that she was in love with him, the more she talked the more she reminded me of my mother at times. We were just friends at first and we worked at the same shoe store in the mall. Shannon came to work upset because this girl was always trying to get to her boyfriend. I pretended to listen, pretended to care. I even subtly convinced her that her boyfriend was cheating on her. I didn't expect things to escalate like they did so fast. I didn't expect to get her when I got her. I wasn't prepared or covered, but the situation caught us both by surprise and we were in the stock room going at it one night after closing. A month and a half later she came crying to me saying that she and her boyfriend broke up and she thought she was pregnant. I didn't think anything of it until she said if she was pregnant it was mine. I wish I could describe the anger and betrayal I felt in that moment. I didn't trust her and I didn't believe her. She said her ex would not give her the money to get rid of it. So when she went to Planned Parenthood and got confirmation that she was pregnant. I gave her everything I had to get it taken care of. My mother told me not to trust females and I felt like my hands were forced. When I had to go without lunch or any of the other treats I like to treat myself to, I got angry. Shannon was playing games and probably got the money from her ex but wanted my money as well.

I stayed covered after that especially with Shannon who was all over me even though she wasn't technically my girlfriend. Even when I had girlfriends, I still saw Shannon on the side. We were "friends" so there was no harm in that.

Chapter 5 ~ Then He Said

Women always seem to think that if they give it up, then they've given you something special and you're supposed to be their slave after that. So I feel it's my job to get them before they get me. Whenever my movies show me something new I normally try it on Shannon first. She is so stupid and sprung it amazes me. If you ever would've told my pre-contact wearing self that I would have girls throwing their selves at me like this, I never would've believed it. I know that as long as I stay in the gym then the girls will keep coming. Sometimes I still get lonely though. Sometimes I still feel like no one cares about me. Oh and then its the references to my "size" that hurt too. I know I was not "blessed" but that's another reason I work so hard to be good. Seems like the first insult out of a girl's mouth these days is not that I'm a nerd like it used to be; now it's how I'm lacking. One girl said this and then I turned her out. Had her on my line begging for another hit.

I want to be loved, appreciated, and valued just like everyone else. I want to feel taken care of again. For now, I'm enjoying the revolving doors of females.

****

I just got home and my phone was ringing. I looked at the clock and it's almost eleven thirty I was tired from the session I just had with Ms. Newbooty. That girl was flexible and a lot of fun. "Hello?"

"Steve!" It was Shannon and she sounded panicked. "I'm pregnant."

I exhaled, "I'm not going to play this game with you again Shannon. You got me the first time. I'm not falling for this again."

"This is not a game Steve, I took the test and it's positive."

"You said you were on the pill."

"I missed a few and I thought I could make them up."

"I'm not giving you money again. I don't even know if that baby is mine."

"Steve!" She started crying. "You are the only man I've been with since me and Yussef broke up. How could you say this to me?"

I exhaled, "you could be lying. I don't believe you. I'm not giving you another penny. You will have to figure out how to make whomever else you've been sleeping with pay this time."

"I'm keeping it."

"Why? I know it's not mine."

"It's yours Steve, I'll prove it any way you want."

"I don't want any babies right now, and especially by you. You need to stop playing and tell the truth." Then I hung up on her. I didn't have time for games.

Nine months later my office received paper work from the child support office. Fortunately my friend in payroll told them I didn't work there. I told her about Shannon and how she was trying to game me.

I'm not ready to be anybody's father. Shannon nor those other two were going to trick me into thinking that I owed them anything. My friend always has my back and tells the child support office I do not work there. I make sure to bring her flowers regularly, and we never bump without a condom.

Chapter 6 ~ What is Done

Tracy

So I have a boyfriend now. Whoopty-doo! I mean I like Celly and he's constantly trying to convince me of how much he loves me that it makes me feel like a shallow jerk for not responding to him. So I dig deeper and I try harder. I eventually ended up caring about him as well. Celly spends a lot of time at my place. He even has the nerve to act neglected when I need time to study. Despite him I keep my grades up and try to spend time with Nicole as much as I can. Sometimes I just need to get away. When I finally gave in and slept with Celly it was out of obligation. I had to get drunk just to go through with it. It wasn't magical, fun, or anything like people try to make it seem. He made it seem like I was wrong because I was never eager to have sex with him. He kept telling me there was something wrong with me because all of his ex's loved sleeping with him.

I lied to Nicole and told her it was amazing. I thought Celly was right and there was something wrong with me. He got so tired of trying to make sex good for me that he would literally go in just to get off. I tried to talk to him about what I was feeling and he would always blame me for not responding. He even turned on porn and told me to take notes. It was interesting at first, but then every time he got mad at me he would turn those movies on. I started hating those movies, I wasn't some porn star wanting and willing to satisfy his every command. One night while he was drunk he told me that he was disappointed in me. He said with a body like mine I should've known what to do and how to do it. I was so hurt and insulted by his comment. All this time I thought he was in love with me, when in fact he was always telling me he was in love with my body. His head always turned towards any light skinned girl no matter what she looked like. I wasn't even his type with my rich brown skin. Celly had me stressed out. He was always at my place, with him in my space my bills went up. He always had some excuse for why he couldn't contribute towards my bills. He was jealous and a coward. After a year of dealing with his nonsense and feeling completely broken down I had enough. My job gave me a small promotion out of the call center. My new position was structured as a Monday - Friday gig and around my school schedule. That gave me the weekends to study as hard as I needed to. It didn't feel like complete freedom yet. I had to get away from Celly for it to feel truly free. I found a cute little one-bedroom apartment still in Crockett, but on the other side of town. No more basement living for me, and I would have a bedroom that didn't include a stove and a refrigerator. Celly and I got in a fight, an argument if you will, about something dumb. He actually acted like he was going to hit me. I called my brother in tears cause I was scared. My brother Terence and my little sisters came over and they helped me pack up my place in an hour, it wasn't like I had a lot of things. Then we moved me across town. I changed my number and I said good riddance.

My parents let my little sisters come over from time to time. I missed them so much and they would catch me up on everything happening at home. They told me that Terence was going to propose to his girlfriend. Tara said for a minute it looked like they weren't going to get married. Amy flipped out when she found out she would never be able to have kids. She didn't want Terence to go without children just to be with her. My adorable brother told her that he loved her more than having children right now. He told her they would spend their time on this side getting to know and appreciate each other. They would have eternity on the other side to fill the earth and subdue it. Tia asked me why I was crying and I told them that was so romantic and true love. I wanted a man to love me like that. I wanted to feel valued and appreciated. The girls didn't understand what I meant, but they were younger and eventually they would get on my level.

****

I ran into my ex from high school. We talked for a little while. We even made the physical connection. At first I was wondering why I was uncomfortable. That was when I realized that he was longer than Celly. Longer, but still a waste. There was nothing exciting about laying with him. He didn't like a lot of things and it was kind of like, "I brought the dick now you work your magic on it". Eventually I learned that he was seeing someone and it was no point. I had already did this in high school I was over it. We parted ways peacefully.

Chapter 7 ~ *When Fire Meets Ice*

Tracy

I thought the things Celly told me were true. I was broken, I was frozen, and I had no idea of how to fix me. Being lost in Celly-land I had missed out on so much. Nicole had an ugly breakup with Dajuan. It was so ugly that her friend Sonya had to come and help get him. Nicole said she was not going to be taken for a fool ever again, and she would never promise loyalty to a guy who wasn't giving it back.

That's why when she met Hubby she didn't think anything more of him than he was cute. Hubby was hilarious and a good guy. He was always dressed and groomed just like she liked, but she was carrying so much pain it was hard for her to applaud him like she normally would've. He would bring her flowers, and call her just because he wanted to hear her voice. One time she was cramping, and he brought Midol, chocolate, wine, a hot water bottle, and a movie to my place just so he could hang out with us. I could see how much he liked Nicole, but she kept shrugging it off. She even went out a few times with Dajuan as she called herself backsliding temporarily. She didn't hide any of this from Hubby, which I thought was bold, but he seemed to take it, talk it out and then they would move on.

Hubby wasn't innocent, and his side adventures would surface from time to time. But they were doing this weird thing where they would talk it out. They'd come to each other with their nonsense and somehow stay together. The moment Nicole realized she was in love with Hubby it broke her down for almost a week. She was sick to her stomach at the idea of him being so imbedded in her soul. Personally I would've been overjoyed to have that in my life.

Nicole and I were indulging in some retail therapy at Ross. We were finding the best stuff and they were all deals. "Didn't you go to Kennedy?" The male voice asked me.

I looked up and it was "*The Shirt*" is what me and a girlfriend called him. We didn't want to say Steve cause then people would be all up in our conversation and then rumors would fly. I smiled, "yes I did. How have you been?"

"You know who I am?"

"Of course I do. We took driver's education together."

Steve stood there talking to me like we were old friends. My insides were screaming at me. He was still so fine! I like Steve because he was down to earth, and he didn't carry himself like he thought he was all of that. The conversations I had with him were real conversations about real stuff.

Steve

I can't remember this girl's name. I remember her face, but her name escapes me. I was actually approaching to talk to her friend when I realized I might know her. Her friend walked away so I kept talking, then my boy walks over. I didn't introduce him because I can't remember her name. Sensing my predicament he reaches out to shake her hand and introduced himself. "He's so rude, I'm Topaz, an you are?"

"I know who you are, you went to Kennedy too. I'm Tracy, and that's my friend Nicole." She pointed to her friend who was a few racks over concentrating on her shopping. Her friend waved without looking up at the sound of her name.

"Tracy, I'm going to get going. Let me give you my number." I wrote it down, "call me when you can."

When we got in the car my boy laughed hard at me. He kept telling me I was on fire when I was talking to her. I didn't think there was anything different about the way we spoke, but he seemed to think so. He said he could tell I didn't remember Tracy's name. I laughed as I said I was going over my mental Rolodex and I wouldn't have picked Tracy as her name. He said he would've called her foxy brown or something like that. Then he started drooling over all of her curves. Her body was cool, but it only made me think of Shannon. I mean I'm not that much of a breast man; I could care less whether they're big or small. I love butt and legs. Fortunately for her she seemed to have that too. My rotation was starting to dry up so it was going to be nice to add a new face and name to the list.

Tracy

I love talking to Steve over the phone. It doesn't even bother me when he mentions sex. I guess that's his way of letting me know he's interested. I am curious about the stuff he talks about, so I listen. Whenever that awkward pause comes we normally get off the phone right after. So I try to keep the conversation going as long as I can just to keep him on the phone. He works in the city too; he works for a mortgage company. He said he was tired of school and he may go back later, but for right now he was enjoying his break. I didn't share that once I got my AA I got another promotion at work. My financial situation was starting to look better and better.

I casually asked Steve what kind of dessert he likes and he said he loves cookies. He hinted around wanting to take me out and so I suggested that he come to my house for dinner. When he came I had fresh baked cookies cooling on the counter. Steve smiled really big and I saw him relax.

Steve

This girl made me cookies. Now this I liked, I only mentioned to her once that I loved fresh baked cookies and she went ahead and made some. At first I thought they were store bought, which is ok too. But the irregular shapes suggested otherwise. I had to have one before I sat down to eat dinner. I took one bite and my mouth watered. She stared at me to tell her whether I liked them or not. I slowly chewed and once I cleared my mouth, I picked her up and kissed her in complete gratitude. At first she was surprised by my kiss but then she got into it. I expected her to stop me as the kiss kept progressing and progressing, but she shyly went along with me. I carried her to the couch and I went in. Tracy may be inexperienced, but the man who was here before me left space. I got nervous thinking that she wouldn't feel me, but she started moaning. I wasn't expecting to go here, but those cookies got me caught up. As I laid there, I couldn't help but wonder if this is what she normally does.

Chapter 8 ~ *The Honeymoon Phase*

Tracy

I couldn't help it I was embarrassed. I did not mean for this to happen the first time he comes over my place. I bet now he's going to think that this is just what I do. I don't want him to look at me, but I don't want him to leave. I laid there not saying a word hoping that he would say something. He asked me if I had just gotten my hair that was all over my head now, done. I told him I had gotten it done yesterday. He said it smelled good, I thanked him. After a little while he asked me what I made and I told him I made chicken fried steak, and mashed potatoes, with green beans. Then his stomach grumbled. I sucked it up and I told him to come to the table. Now only wearing my long shirt we sat. I saw Steve looking at me as I passed him his plate to take to the table. "Your body looks even better than I thought it would."

I smiled, "thanks. I still want to come work out with you at some point."

We sat at the table completely calm as we ate dinner and talked a little in between bites. He seemed like he was thinking, but then he would throw another compliment my way. He stared at me when I told him that those cookies were homemade and I didn't write down a recipe for them. He asked me how I could do that without writing down measurements of key ingredients. I shrugged and said it was a gift. He said dinner was good, and then he stared at the cookies. When he said he loved cookies he wasn't kidding. When he put the first one in his mouth he stared at me again. He dang near put himself in a sugar coma eating half of the rack right then. I only had a couple with some milk. I asked him if he wanted me to take him home and he said in the morning like he had plans for those cookies. I thought we might go again that night, but we slept uninterrupted. In the morning I awoke to him finishing his cookie and rubbing my butt. I had to remind him to get his condom, I wondered if that was a test or not.

Ok so I wasn't tripping last night, he doesn't reach that far which is new. I held on to his butt trying to push him in as far as he would go. Then he switched positions and got behind me, I definitely felt him this way. And since he was smaller he didn't have to be all that gentle. Nonetheless, I had a good time. He said our sex life would get better. I took that as a promise.

Steve

Tracy's cool, but her good girl act gets on my nerves sometimes. She don't understand half the things I'm trying to show her. Like I hope she don't think she's my woman now, cause I never asked to be with her. And if she starts to get all high and mighty cause she's in school and I'm not, I'm going to have to put her in her place. If it wasn't for those cookies, I would've hit it and quit it. This girl can bake her but off. Sometimes for fun I'll think of something I want and then she creates it. Last time I told her as she picked me up that I wanted a banana cake. She frowned for a minute like she was thinking, and then we went to the store. The bananas on the floor weren't ripe enough. I thought she was going to use that as her excuse for why she couldn't do it. But she found someone who worked there and asked them if they had any ripe bananas in the back. The person came out with six very ripe bananas. She told Tracy to come through her line when she was ready for them. Tracy got other stuff and then the cashier gave her the bananas for free stating that they couldn't sell them to her like that.

When we got to her place Tracy set everything out on the counter and then she started walking back and forth. Next thing I know she's mashing and mixing. I was on the couch watching TV while she worked. When she put the cake in the oven she sat at the table working on her homework. She kept sniffing the air. I asked her how long did she put the timer on. She ignored my question and went back to her work. If that cake burns I'm going to be pissed. I

had my mouth all ready for something that tasted like bananas.
Tracy was writing and then she shot out of her chair and into the
kitchen. I could hear her checking the cake. When she sat down
she went back to her work and then a few minutes later she was up
again. She let the cake cool a little in the pan then she turned it
over on to the rack. I peeked into the kitchen it didn't look or smell
burnt from here.

She went back to her work. Then she poked holes in the cake, then
she poured glaze over it. In my mind that didn't look impressive.
Then she took icing out of the refrigerator and poured it over the
top in a way that made the cake look like a store bought cake and
not homemade. Then she went back to her homework. I waited as
long as I could in the living room then I decided to get an apple
from the kitchen. I stood there staring at that cake. I couldn't
believe she pulled it off. I started kissing on her as she tried to
focus on her work. I had to have her, she tried to tell me to wait but
I couldn't. I asked her if she was on the pill yet. I told her a couple
of months ago to get on something cause I was tired of using
condoms. We had a dumb debate about hormones and what they
do to your body. She had a point when she said she naturally had
mood swings and she was afraid of how hormones would affect
her. She is so dramatic and when I sense the drama in her tone, I
stay away. I told her we had to do something cause I was tired of
condoms. I told her condoms were only for when you didn't know
the person. I knew this girl was turned out and as long as I break
her off she wasn't going nowhere. Another Shannon if you ask me,
but this time I wasn't messing this up by getting her pregnant.

Chapter 9 ~ What goes Up

Tracy

I looked at the clock and it was almost ten o'clock. He said he was
coming at eight. I wondered if the bus ran that early and he said it
did. He was convinced that he would get here in time. I took a big

disappointed breath and I made my way to Walnut Creek to go hang out with my cousin Marie. Steve was supposed to come with me, but it appears that he has decided to blow me off yet again. I haven't really gone anywhere in public with Steve in some time now. Whenever we go somewhere he sees someone he knows. He never introduces me, which makes me feel like he's embarrassed to be seen with me. I know I've gained a little weight since we started, I told him I wanted to work out with him. I met him at the gym one time, the whole time he was telling me how he wanted to peeled my sweats off with his teeth. It was a whole flirt session and no working out. After that he said he couldn't have me in his space messing up his head. He said he needed to work out with someone who was serious about working out and not there to flirt with him. Excuse me, I came ready to work out and he swore it was time to make out or something. Nicole told me to pull back on baking for him; especially since the last few times he said he was going to come over. He asked for cookies or a specific cake and then he didn't show. I try to remember to bring the leftovers to work or drop them by my parent's house. Most times I forget and instead of worrying about what to eat for dinner it's easier to grab some cookies or cut a slice of cake and wallow in my depression. I felt so trapped; I had fallen in love with Steve. And it seemed like now that he knew he had me he didn't even care. Last time we *broke-up* he looked me up and down like he was taking in my weight gain, but he wasn't saying anything. That time, we didn't even make love. He said he was tired and he wanted to go to sleep. I wasn't tired so I sat in my living room watching TV. He came in my living room telling me to turn off the TV and come to bed. He said the hum of the TV wouldn't let him sleep. I looked at him like he was crazy; I rolled my eyes and changed the channel. He stormed back in my room violently throwing his clothes on the whole time mumbling this was why women couldn't keep a good man. When I asked him where he was going he rolled his eyes and stormed out the door.

Then I didn't see him for a couple of months. He didn't return my phone calls, it was like he vanished. I didn't realize we were breaking up when he left or I would've at least wanted to talk about it.

Eventually he resurfaced and wanted to act like nothing had happened. That he didn't leave me hanging for those months. When he came back he came back good, and as soon as I got comfortable he was gone again.

This time I made him chase me, I wasn't so open. He did work harder to get back in my good graces, but now here we are AGAIN! I'm getting tired of this. I wouldn't have said yes if I thought he was going to flake out on me again. I gave Marie a hug and kiss, then I said hello to her friends. Marie patted my hands cause she could tell I was upset, and then she did her amazing charming thing with the group. Everyone was coupled off except me. No one said anything to make me feel bad about it. Marie told the waiter to give me a pitcher of Mimosa's and a straw so that I could get on their level. Brunch was nice and I had a good time with my cousin and her friends. We made plans for the next Friday to have girl's night out.

I didn't feel like going home, so I decided to shop. Still uneasy in my soul I grabbed a King sized Snicker and devoured it like I wasn't full from brunch. As my chocolate fix worked it's magic on my soul I went shopping. I picked up 12's cause my 10's weren't really fitting me these days. I did an angry dance as the 12's weren't as comfortable as they should've been. When I picked up the 14's I told myself to suck it up and deal with it. Nicole and I had a plan to exercise by walking at the nearby regional park or down to the sugar factory along the shore and walking over to the park that way. Either way I was going to get moving and there was no need to worry about it. Meanwhile I needed to look good so that when Steve did show up I could make him feel bad for standing me up. I found some really good deals and then I took myself to the movies by my house just because I didn't want to go home. I called Nicole from the payphone and she was making dinner, she told me to come over. So I did. I came over and had dinner with Nicole and her mother, then Hubby popped by to bring her mother some roses as a "just because" he was thankful that she raised such a wonderful young lady. Nicole's mother was speechless as she said her children's boyfriends and girlfriends have never considered her before. She gave Hubby the biggest heartfelt hug. Hubby was going to leave, but now Nicole was bubbling over after seeing her mother so happy. I knew that was my cue to go home. I pulled up to my dark and cold apartment and told myself to suck it up and I wouldn't open the door if he showed up. I wasn't answering the phone without screening the call first so; I turned the ringer off and listened for the click of my machine.

Steve

When I woke up it was ten-thirty, I cursed at the realization. Karen popped up and looked at me like she was hung over. I told her I had to go, she wanted to tell me not to. But she couldn't get her lips to cooperate with her thoughts. I walked out of Karen's door and down the long Arlington Street to the little corner store on McBryde and I called Tracy from the payphone. She wasn't home, I cursed again. I continued my walk down towards San Pablo Ave as I debated whether I should go home or still go to Tracy's. When Karen busted an illegal U-turn a little ways ahead of me I told myself I'd call Tracy in a few days, give her a chance to calm down. I didn't want to argue about this cause what happened, happened and it's over. There's not too many more hoops this girl is going to put me through. ESPECIALLY as she's blowing up right before my eyes. Now, I'm all for the comfort of a Sistah, nothing will ever replace the softness and comfort of a real woman's body. But she's taking this too far. All she do is eat, cook, bake, and study. Talking about she wanted to work out with me. I don't need no woman relying on me for motivation to go to the gym. Sometimes I don't want to go my own self. I need someone who's going to motivate me to go when I'm weak. All she do is go to school, work, and come home and eat. She's not trying to do nothing with herself. I need someone I can be proud of when I go out, someone who conducts theirself like a lady.

That stunt Karen pulled last night wasn't cool. I'm not fighting over no female. She the one who walked in there with everything hanging out and then gonna look stuck when that guy stepped to her. I told her to sit down and stop switching in front of all these guys. What she do? She was enjoying the attention too much. Causing scenes and what not, I walked away from her, cause I didn't have time to be getting beat up by some drunk fool just so she could feel like a queen for the day. Karen came running out and overly apologizing. Karen has a pretty face, but not much else. BUT! She'll let you do whatever you want to her as long as you stay the night.

I was actually looking forward to relaxing with Tracy today. Watching a chick flick on her TV with her to make her feel special. I'm sure she would've made me something special just because I was there. I like when she takes care of me, these days it seems like she's the only person who cares. Karen and all the rest say they want a real man in their lives but they know nothing about how to keep one when they have him. Am I asking for too much, I don't think so. I need to be the King of my castle! I need to feel like there's a queen worth coming home to. Sometimes I think of Tracy in that space. I mean after all I did introduce her to my mother. I kind of wanted to see if they got along or not. My mother was passive with her, and when I talked to her later she told me to watch out for Tracy cause she was going to end up pregnant. The thought of Tracy having my baby didn't make me as sick to my stomach as I thought it would. But now that she's putting on this weight I pulled back the thought. She's one of those girls who will have a baby and never look the same again. I wonder if Shannon lost her baby weight or if she's a fatty too! I hadn't thought about her in a long time. I wondered what she had, and if she ever found the real father? I'm not buying that the kid is mine. I don't know why females always think it's ok to try to trap a man like this. Lying about babies that aren't even there sometimes. I don't make enough money to take care of nobody's babies. I can barely take care of myself.

As I sat in Karen's car and she happily drove me back to her place, I told myself I had to get a car. I can't continue at the mercy of rides anymore.

Chapter 10 ~ Green with Jealousy

Tracy

"Mirror, Mirror on the wall, tell me if he'll ever fall so in love with me or could this all just be a mystery? Ho! Ho! HO! If you're looking for love! It's right in your face!..." Kelley Price was singing my heart's song today. I should be on top of the world. I just signed my acceptance letter for yet another promotion at work. I was starting to get nervous and think that I was going to need to look for a new company, cause nothing was coming through for me. I graduate soon, and pretty soon those student loan payments were going to be due. I have my eye on a location in hilltop, I talked to them today and they're waiting for me. Crockett is cool and all, but it's so far out. This new position is going to move me to the corporate side of the house, and on occasion I can drive into work and actually have a parking space in the garage. Or I can walk to the bus stop right around the corner and let my car rest as I take the same bus to the Bart station and then to work. My new boss to be Becca has already sent out the email blast announcing my new position with their group. I am still starting at the bottom of the stack, but at least I'm moving up. When Becca showed me where I was going to be working she introduced me to the rest of her team. This lady, Shirley complimented me from my head down

to my toes. She said she loved my whole look. I should be on top of the world, but I'm not. One minute Steve is running hot and things are good, then the next minute he's completely cold. One minute he says he wants one thing from me, and then the next minute he acts ugly about it. Now that I'm a size 18/20 he just looks at me, or makes underhanded references to my weight. At one point I was finally doing it, I was running and it felt good. I was shedding pounds and feeling good about myself. Then he started complaining that I was never home. That I didn't cook, and that I was being lazy in bed when I could barely keep my eyes open. Between school, work, and working out I was zapped. I was almost out of school and graduation couldn't come a moment sooner. Now I'd only have to juggle him and work. Instead of being happy for me that I'm almost done with school he gets all huffy and then he started telling me how my credit is going to be ruined because I'm going to be in debt. I really don't know what he was trying to do with all that negativity. Ooh! And don't let us get going on a more intellectual conversation and I poke holes in his logic. He gets so mad at me! I let him slide on the intellectual stuff; he can sound like an idiot for all I care. I've learned to just let him talk. But when we get on the topic of God my soul won't let him say the things he tries to say. I may not know a lot, but I know God is real, and I know he loves us all whether we do right by him or not. I shut him down every time and he gets so mad, he's screaming and acting a complete fool. A couple of times I've asked myself if he really is this far gone or if it's that he can't stand for me to know more about or on any given topic?

"Or will he always love someone who can't SEE! YEA! YEA!" I held my chest as I tell Kelley to sing it for me. Suddenly I jumped almost out of my Bart seat as my CD skips and I realize my cellular phone is ringing. I look and smile as I see that it's Nicole. "Hey, what's going on?" I tried to put some pep in my voice.

"Eewwll! You need to come out with Hubby and I tonight. I told him about your promotion and he wants to celebrate. From the sound of your voice you need to get out."

I sighed, "I don't feel like going out to no club watching all you guys dance, while I sit on the sidelines watching. No thanks."

"Ha! That's what you get for thinking you know what we do all the time. This time his friend is having friends over for what they're calling a *Kick Back*."

"Nicole, what the heck is a kick back?"

"House party, their words not mine. It's going to be a cool little group, you should come."

"No, I'll pass."

"Tracy! Come on, you never want to go out no more. You need to stop waiting at home for Steve to show up. Go out and have some fun, and if he's there when you get home then ok. But you need to get out."

I didn't feel like being the big friend with Nicole and Hubby tonight. Neither one of them treat me any different, but I know other people see my weight when they look at me. I try to act like it doesn't bother me, but it does. I can't even focus to figure my way out of this. I know what to do, but for some reason I can't do it. Seeing Hubby and Nicole together makes me hurt. I start remembering how Steve and I used to be in the beginning. When he used to compliment my.... body.... The realization of again being a body sends me way off into left field. Nicole is trying to talk to me as I realize I'm about to miss my stop. I rushed towards the door and I just made it, but my jacket got caught in the door and I fell. My phone flew out of my hand, my CD player hit the ground. I knew for a fact something cracked inside. My purse was secure on my shoulder. The train operator opened the doors after witnessing my fall to release my jacket, as people on the train and

39

on the platform belly laughed at me. The operator asked me if I was ok, over the loud speaker. The only thing hurt was my pride. He held the doors open until the station agent came up to make sure I was ok. I told her I was fine and I picked up my things. Of course the call is still going, anything to eat up my minutes on my phone. "Nicole I just fell off the train in front of everybody. I'm in no mood to be laughed at anymore tonight."

"Are you ok? I could hear people laughing over the phone."

"SHUT UP!" I laughed a little and so did she, "I'm fine. But I'm no fun tonight. I promise to celebrate with you and Hubby another time. I gotta go sign my new lease and take care of some business tonight anyways. Tell me all about it later on."

I made it to Hilltop in thirty minutes I was so happy. I walked into the leasing office with a huge smile. I told the guy I was the person he spoke to over the phone today. He showed me the end unit that was available and I absolutely loved it. It was a one bedroom and the bedroom was huge. I had a nice sized walk in closet and a good-sized living room. Off of the balcony there was even a small storage area. I signed my lease on the spot to move in, in thirty days. I felt very good about this move. I was moving to a nice looking apartment that was centrally located. My little putt-putt raised it's head and said it could not go on any longer. I was hoping to get one more year out of her, but I understood that she could no longer continue on. I slowly drove around the corner to the Hilltop AutoRow and then I slowly drove by as I attempted to see which dealership looked the most promising. I parked my car and pulled out a piece of paper. I ran the numbers in my head, my move-in deposit and first month's rent was going to cost me so much. Paying someone to move me was going to cost me so much. Moving my bills over was going to cost so much, and after everything in order to continue living and not dipping into my savings I only really comfortably had $500 to put down on a new car. I sunk a little in my chair, and then I told myself I could do this. I thought of my cousin who's always about her business. I decided to ask for so much for my trade in, they could only tell me no or counter with something else. Considering the counter I decided to up my trade in amount and hope that they landed on my ridiculous original price. Armed with my bank statements and my new job offer letter I stepped out of my car. The salesman came up to me very excited to meet me. I knew he wouldn't be smiling by the time I finished with this deal. I guess since I was stepping out of a bucket he thought I would go for the lower end cars. I pointed to the beautiful car right outside the sales floor. It sparkled at me and begged me to take it home. I walked around the car and I took it in. It was fully loaded with every possible feature a car like this could have. The guy seemed like he was cautioning me instead of doing his job as a salesman and trying to sell me up. Now I let Steve run all over me, but the buck stops there. I took the car for a test drive and then I knew the car was mine. Since it was later in the evening I knew they weren't going to waste my time going back and forth forever. I was very stern with them, I told them I had nothing but my trade in, and I didn't want to pay more than a ridiculously low amount monthly. The sales guy kind of looked at me like yea right as he took my application information in the back. It was quiet for a minute and then the sales guy came back completely willing to work with me, but still trying to get every nickel and dime he could from me. I stuck to my guns though and I walked out of there with my BRAND-NEW, fully loaded, reasonable monthly payments car. Oh and they threw in a FULL tank of gas to get me on my way. I went home, wrote up my thirty-day notice. I gave it to the apartment manager and then I wanted to go for a ride. I took a deep breath and I drove to my parent's house. They were having company, celebrating my brother's upcoming nuptials. It dawned on me that I hadn't returned any of Terence's calls. I didn't mean to blow him off; my life has just been so all over the place. The girls came out completely excited about my car. I could tell my parents wanted to see the car too, but they had to stay for their guest. Terence and Amy said they liked my car.

Then I took my sisters for a ride. I turned up the music loud as we bopped down the highway. I showed them where I was moving to in a month. They both got excited saying that now they could come by Bart to spend the night at my place. I told them to please come and see me. I told them how much I missed them. They begged me to come back in when I dropped them off, but I couldn't. I went home excited about everything.

Steve

When I pulled up to Tracy's place it was completely dark inside like she hadn't even been home. I told her about leaving her place completely dark, but as usual she don't listen. But I guess she figures as long as she keeps packing on weight she don't have to worry about anyone breaking into her place. I don't have a cellular phone cause I don't want to be reached when I'm out. If I'm not home deal with it, but moments like this I wished I had one. When I was getting ready to pull away a car came sparkling down the street even in the dark. When it pulled into Tracy's spot I sat there for a minute looking at her. Oh I see, I see what this is. I got a car, so now she has to go get a newer and better car. This is not a competition. She's the dumb one wasting her money trying to keep up with me. She got out of her car so proud asking me if I liked it. I shrugged and said it was a waste of money. Her smile weakened as she said she got a really good deal on the car. I rolled my eyes then I said I had to use the bathroom; I didn't want to be out here anymore. The manager hurried out of his apartment calling Tracy as he hurried. "I told the owners that you put in your notice and they offered to make you a deal to stay. Are you interested or do you have a new location already lined up?"

Tracy's eyes darted at me as she spoke to the guy, "I already have a new location. Tell them that I am truly honored that they would want to keep me."

"Are you kidding? You are drama free and you pay on time. You're a landlord's dream tenant. I'm going to miss you." Then he hugged her.

"What's with all the touching?" I barked.

"Calm down, this young lady has been through a lot. The only drama she's ever had while here has been around you. Don't let my orientation fool you, I was middle linebacker in high school and I will break you down right here in front of her. I don't like you, never have, and I never will." Then he hugged Tracy again and walked back up the stairs like I wasn't nothing.

Tracy hurried to the door to open it, and then we got into a huge fight. I told her I wasn't helping her move cause I doubted that she knew how to pack and I didn't feel like dealing with it. I went in so bad on her that her tears just made me angrier. As I was about to leave, I realized that I was wrong. Plus, I didn't know where she was going. I wanted to tell myself that I would be fine without her in my life. But the truth of the matter is that no one, not even Shannon could ever take care of me like Tracy does. Even when she's mad at me she still pushes her feelings to the side to take care of me. My own mother could never do that. My stepmother would do that, but never my mother. I hate that I'm addicted to this woman who has given up on herself. Why does my stuff always have to be run down and raggedy? Why can't I meet a woman who has the whole package, good career, good credit, nice spot, knows how to cook and clean, knows how to take care of her man, and wants to be as healthy as I am? Tracy may have a lot of that but the complete package she is not. I walked back in Tracy's room where she was curled up in a ball on her bed crying hard. I apologized for laying into her so hard. I went for every sensitive spot I knew she had. She didn't say anything she just laid there crying as silently as she could. I got on the bed and I kissed her cheek, her real tears made me feel like garbage. If she truly forgives me, she'll let me sleep with her. When I kissed her lips, she didn't return my kiss, still I forced my tongue into her mouth. As I touched all over her

43

body, Tracy mildly tried to fight me off. She's way stronger than this, so she's just trying to make me work for it cause after all she is supposed to be mad at me. Tracy loves me more than she could ever be mad at me. I put a condom on and she was as dry as the desert, she just needed a minute, she'd get into it. Tracy laid there with her eyes closed, probably trying to hide how much she enjoyed my touch. When I finished she rolled over to her side with her back to me and continued to cry. I rubbed her back; I started explaining that I needed her not to be mad at me anymore and that I knew I overreacted and I was sorry. Then she suddenly turned to me with blood shot red eyes as she very angrily asked me how I could do this to her. I frowned at her, she was over reacting. She said I was the one person she trusted to stop when she asked me to. My mind went blank as it registered what she was accusing me of. I put my hands up in surrender and then I dressed and hurried out of there.

Chapter 11 ~ Forgiveness

Tracy

I didn't answer my phones all weekend. I only got out of the bed to use the bathroom then I went back to bed. Sometimes I didn't even realize I was crying as tears streamed down my face. Why does this happen in every relationship I'm in? Why do I make men do this to me? I couldn't stop crying and I didn't want to face daylight.

It was Monday morning and I couldn't move. I didn't call Nicole to tell her I wasn't going to school. I just laid there. I called in to work and then I rolled over. Just before noon there was banging at my door. My heart was pounding cause I thought it might've been Steve and I didn't want to see him. Then there was tapping on my window. I could see Nicole's form through my blinds. I got up slowly and then I went to the door and unlocked it then I went back to my bed. Nicole hurried to my room with worry in her eyes. She looked around my room then she stared at me for a minute. She sat on my bed on top of the covers; she put her arms around me and rocked me. I cried all over again. She asked me if I was ok and I shook my head no. "I should've went with you."

"We're not going to live in the world of regrets. How badly should I have Hubby hurt him? Kneecaps? Permanently handicapped?"

I squeezed her back, "I'll be ok."

She eyed me, "he got you in here disconnected from the world and you're trying to tell me he walks away unhurt?"

I don't know why I felt the need to protect him or make light of the situation. "You know me, I'm so dramatic."

She looked at me with no smile, "did he hit you?"

"No," I could say honestly. "Nothing like that. Things are going extremely well for me and I think it was system overload for him."

"I'm sure you think that's the better answer, but there's something wrong with all of that. He should be happy for you and supportive."

I know she's right, but hearing her judge him makes me want to defend and protect him. "I'm not saying anything right."

"Who's car is parked in your spot? Where is your car? I almost thought you weren't home."

I forgot all about my car. "That's mine. I got it Friday night."

"It's beautiful! Congratulations!" Then she looked around my room. "Get up get dressed lets go eat."

As soon as she said it my appetite seemed to return to me and my stomach gurgled. "Ok, where do you want to go?"

Nicole smiled, "The Dead Fish!"

"That's pricey!"

"My treat."

"How? I thought you were still looking for a job."

"Hubby! Duh!"

I popped up, "he's here?"

"Outside in his car. I thought Steve might've been holding you hostage in here. I brought backup." She smiled.

"You guys wanna ride in my new car?"

"Of course, is it ok if he comes inside, while you get ready?"

"Yes. I'm going to jump in the shower real quick." When I stood up I felt heavy, not in weight but in spirit. "I'm moving in a month. I'm going to have a bathtub again after all these years. I can't wait." My basement apartment and this place only had showers.

I drove us down the long street to The Dead Fish restaurant. I had the best restaurant lasagna ever! I had a cocktail with my meal, but Hubby and Nicole kept throwing them back.

"You know what we need?" Nicole said very tipsy. Hubby and I looked at her, "banana pudding. Do you like banana pudding?" She asked Hubby.

He shrugged, "I guess so."

Nicole gasped, "Tracy please make him some pudding so that he can understand. He has no idea of what's about to happen to his mouth."

I took the two drunk kittens to the grocery store. Hubby paid for what I needed then we went back to my place and I made pudding while they spoke outside. It wasn't until Hubby started uncharacteristically slurping that I realized how red both of their eyes were. Hubby asked for more, I got a little more then I watched them devour the rest of the dish. Hubby said he loved my sauce. Nicole laughed and told him it was pudding. Hubby then proceeded to make us laugh. I laughed so hard I had tears running down my face and a pain in my side. My friends stayed overnight with me. They were just what I needed to be okay.

****

As the movers brought my furniture and boxes in, I unpacked the important stuff. I was in the kitchen when I heard knocking, "hey! Hey! Tray! Tray!"

I was excited to see my sisters who decided to surprise me. I introduced them to Nicole and Sonya. A little after Nicole and Sonya left Tia asked if some of their friends could swing by for a minute. A few kids from their old school got a ride over. They stayed for a little while and then they left. My sisters hung out longer then I took them home. I got so excited when I walked in the door. It was time to unite with my bathtub. I filled my tub with my bath milk and salts. I lit candles and I brought a bottle of wine into the bathroom. I could hear the hallelujah chorus as I sunk into my steaming hot water. Oh how I've missed you. I let my mind go blank for the first time in a long time.

Steve

Every time I think to call her I don't know what to say. I honestly didn't think she would flip out on me like that. I guess I was too eager; I should've waited for her to kiss me back. I know this is not the end for us, I just don't know how to get around this. This can't be the end of us.

Topaz went to go holler at a female while I sat back mindlessly chewing on pizza, trying not to think about Tracy. I love that girl even if I hold admission of my love for her hostage. I know I'm just afraid that she'd realize she has some kind of power over me. The girls who walked in caught my attention. That's Tracy's friend, what's her name. I mentally snapped my fingers trying to remember her name. I waited to see if Tracy was going to join them, and after so long I realized she's not coming. As long as I make my presence known then they'd run back and tell her they saw me. BINGO! Now she's thinking about me. I walked over and her friend looked at me like she was trying to place me. "Ladies."

Tracy's friend said hi, but not in a tone that said that Tracy had bad mouthed me, which means she still loves me. I held in my smile. The other two girls smiled at me like they could eat me up. Again I held back my smile. "Steve." Tracy's friend said.

"Sit down, sit down." One girl said, "Steve's your name?"

"Yes, and you are?"

"I'm Sonya." She smiled at me.

Tracy's friend touched Sonya, "that's Tracy's Steve."

"Oh!" Both of the girls said in unison. Then the other girl flashed me a look that said she's coming for me as soon as she thinks no one is watching.

I turned my eyes; it still puzzles me when females act like that. If I was sitting here with my glasses on and clothes that covered my body none of them would even look in my direction. Tracy was the only girl not to react when she saw me in my glasses. The first time I wore them in her presence she looked at me like she didn't see them. When I brought them up she said she liked them. It was little stuff like that. "Why is that a big Oh?"

"It's not Oh, it's just *oh*, like we know who you are now." Sonya said.

I started talking about nothing, hoping to make them laugh, while the other friend stared at me giving me wanting eyes. I guess its true that in order for another female to want you they have to know that others want you. Where was all this attention before? I didn't stay too long, but long enough that I was satisfied that Tracy would definitely hear about this. When their pizza was ready they left. A minute later the girl who stared came back inside alone. She walked up to the counter and she asked for pepper and cheese. Then she stared at me. So I walked over to the counter. "Steve." I put my hand out.

She smiled, "Kamony. Steve are you Tracy's boyfriend?"

"You're Tracy's friend, shouldn't you know the answer to that?"

She smiled bigger, "Tracy and I are just acquaintances. She's their friend, not mine."

"Interesting disclosure, what's up?"

"I want to be your friend."

This could be a test, "can you do me a favor?" She nodded her head yes. I wrote my number on a napkin. "Can you give Tracy my number? I recently got a cellphone and she doesn't have the number. "

Tracy

Nicole let herself in with her key. Sonya had the pizza. Kamony had the drinks. "Girl guess who we saw at the pizza place!" Sonya announced before they were in the door good.

I didn't feel like playing the guessing game but I asked, "who?"

49

"Steve!"

Nicole and Kamony stared at me for a reaction. I gasped, "what did he say?"

"A bunch of nothingness." Nicole watched me.

"He was talking about me?"

"Nope he didn't mention you."

"Actually," everybody looked at Kamony as she reached in her back pocket. "He asked me to give you his new cell phone number." She held out a napkin with writing on it.

"When did that happen?" Sonya looked at her with a crazy look.

"When I went in for cheese and peppers." Sonya kept staring, "chill out. He came up to me at the counter and asked me to give it to her so I am."

I took the napkin, "thank you."

Steve

Text from unknown number: what you doing?

Me: who dis?

Unknown: an admirer

Me: stop playing

This is either Tracy or that girl I gave my number to. Tracy would just say who she is, I think.

Unknown: can you keep a secret?

Me: stop playing

Unknown: can I trust you?

Me: stop playing

Unknown: I'm serious

Tired of this game I call the number. "Hello?" I didn't recognize her voice.

"Look, I don't like people playing on my phone. If you grown act like it and speak your peace. Otherwise I don't have time for games."

"Sorry, but I can't stop thinking about you."

"Who is this?"

"Kamony."

"I don't know no Kamony."

"You gave me your number a couple weeks ago."

"At the pizza place?" I held back my smile.

"I thought I told you to pass it on?"

"I memorized it first, I hope you don't mind." She tried to sound innocent.

"Heck yeah I mind." I figured she'd do something like that. "What do you want?"

"You!"

"Stop trying to get me caught up."

"I promise this is not a setup, I'll never tell."

"Tell what?"

"Tell what happened when you came over."

I sucked my teeth, "stop playing." I needed to play my cards right. I'm going to get Tracy back. "I gotta go."

She said a disappointed ok and we got off the phone. I went to bed early and I woke up at a quarter to midnight. I was up dressed with my keys in my hand. I called the number back. "Hello?" She said dragging herself out of sleep.

"Where you live?"

"You're coming over?" Excitement jumped out of the phone.

"Duh! I don't believe you aren't trying to get me caught up."

"I promise!"

"Where you live?"

I stayed on the phone with her as she directed me to her apartment not too far from mine. She told me to give her five minutes when she invited me into her room. She ran out to the bathroom, while I looked around her room looking for hidden cameras. I listened for her to be on the phone. Then I noticed her phone on her pillow. I guess this is real. I stood in the middle of her floor when she came back in the room in a robe. She smiled at me, "can I trust you?"

"For what?" Then she kissed me. "What are you doing?"

"Ssshhh! This will be our secret." Then she opened her robe and kissed me again.

I left a few hours later tired and satisfied. When I got home I was missing Tracy though.

Tracy

Shirley and I were having lunch at this little cafe spot. I was forcing myself to eat this salad that wasn't doing it for me feeling depressed. Shirley was telling me a story about when she was younger and I was trying to remain focused on her. "Can I sit here?" I looked up and it was Steve. He was watching me for a reaction.

"Sit honey, sit." Shirley smiled at him, and then she looked at me. "You know him?"

"This is Steve." I exhaled; suddenly I didn't want to eat another bite. I sucked in my stomach and said a silent prayer that I hopefully looked decent.

"How come you haven't called me?"

"This is my friend Shirley."

They shook hands hello, "I was supposed to help you move."

"You said you didn't want to."

"I didn't say I wouldn't. You know I'd do anything for you."

"Aw!" Shirley gushed.

"Stop acting like you not happy to see me. Give me a hug."

I got up to hug him and he picked me up squeezing me. I expected him to say something about me being too heavy or something, but he didn't. He asked me what time I got off work. When I said I got off at four he asked Shirley if she got off at the same time. When she said yes, he suggested that the three of us go out to dinner. I looked at him wondering if he got a promotion cause he didn't make very much money. I've seen his paychecks; I've even done his taxes for him. He said he would meet us right outside of my building. He kissed my cheek and walked away. Shirley went on and on about how handsome Steve is. Of course he wants Shirley there cause he knows I won't say anything in front of her. He did look really happy to see me though. He's never hugged me in front of people before either.

After work when Shirley came down, there he was, waiting for us. Shirley got really excited about a restaurant as we walked and she asked if we could go there. Steve said he couldn't afford it and she said if he covered the appetizer she'd cover the rest. I wanted him to say no, but he agreed. I had a couple cocktails and then Steve promised Shirley he'd make sure I made it home safely. He followed me to my place. He hurried and parked then he came to my car. He looked me in my eyes as he asked me if he could kiss me. I said yes and he kissed me the way my heart had been begging him to for a long time. The way he used to. When we were done he put his arms around me and kept gently kissing my cheek. After that night we were inseparable for a while.

Steve

I shouldn't have answered the phone. When I saw that it was my mother I should've let it roll over to voicemail, but I answered like an idiot. My sister told my mother that Tracy and I went over my father's house a couple weeks ago. My sister told my mother that Tracy and my stepmom got along really well. My phone was dying so I called my mother back from Tracy's house phone and I put my cellphone on the charger. When Tracy heard I was talking to my mother she went back to making my cookies in the kitchen. I got off the phone frustrated. I walked in the kitchen as she was putting the first batch in the oven. I snatched the refrigerator open looking for something. When I opened the freezer there was a bunch of pints of the same flavor of ice cream, "English Toffee?"

"No!" Tracy reached for the door. "Leave my ice cream alone."

"You got all this ice cream and I can't taste a little bit?" I said getting a spoon. Tracy leaned against the cabinet as she held herself. She watched me eat it like she knew how good it was going to be to me and she was dreading it. This ice cream was so good I stretched my eyes at her. "Oh I see how it is!" I said as I ate a little more.

"Stop!" She said helplessly.

"I'll buy you some more. How you gonna hold out on me?"

"You don't even like ice cream."

"Fat people always know about the best stuff." As soon as I said it Tracy walked away. I stood there eating the rest of her pint trying to calm my nerves. I had to smooth this over before my cookies burned. Tracy was in her room taking out her bath junk. "Hold on, before you start soaking your life away. I need to know if you want to go over my mother's house for dinner with me?"

"I'm sure you don't want to show up with a fat person!" She pushed past me.

"Tracy! Don't do this. You know what I meant. You know what you look like. I'm still here aren't I?" She slammed the bathroom door shut. I let her sit for a little bit then I undressed and I squished my way in the tub with her. "Don't be mad at me. I'm sorry!" Then the smoke detector went off. I got out of the tub annoyed. I turned off the oven. I opened the window in the kitchen and turned on the ceiling fan in her dining area. I took the battery out of her smoke detectors cause they wouldn't shut up. When Tracy got out of the tub, I hugged and kissed on her until she came out of her funk. She finished baking my cookies and when we were waiting for my mother to open her door I noticed the box of cookies. She handed them to my mother as soon as she opened the door. I was **HOT**! How she gonna give my cookies away? My grandmother and auntie were there as well. Both of their eyes stretched when they saw Tracy. When Tracy was in the living room my auntie asked me how long I've been a chubby chaser. I told her I wasn't. I told her Tracy wasn't my girlfriend, cause she's not.

Chapter 14 ~ How Could You Call Her

Tracy

Steve's been moody since we went to his mother's. It seems like every time we take two steps forward something always pulls us apart. I tell myself not to focus on him, and to just be patient. He needs time to grow. Hubby's still growing with Nicole, but at least you can clearly see them growing together.

"You ready?" Nicole asked her mom. We were having a pamper day with Nicole's mom. Hubby was footing the bill. When we got to my car Sonya and Kamony pulled up. Kamony rolled her eyes at me and immediately started sulking. I looked at Nicole cause I thought I might've imagined that. "What's wrong with you?" Nicole snapped.

"Nothing. I didn't realize other people were going to be here."

"Little girl you need to pick your lip up cause I'm coming and you better act happy about it." Nicole's mom said.

"Oh naw! Not you Ms. Allison. I just don't understand why every time I want to hang with my oldest friends; she gotta be there too. "

"Nicole I don't have to go. You guys can go have fun." I said not understanding why Kamony had a problem with me.

"Kamony you can go home. My man specifically set this up for my mom, Tracy, and me. You and Sonya were add-ons."

Sonya looked at Kamony like she was trying to figure her out. "I'm happy Hubby said I could come. I don't know why you're tripping."

"Maybe you should ride in Sonya's car since you acting funny." Nicole said.

"But I barely got any gas. Kamony you can walk to the Bart station if you can't get it together." Sonya said opening the back door to my car and getting in. Kamony huffed and then she got in the car. I stood there looking at Nicole. I told her she needed to get her friend. Nicole said she was going to talk to her. We went to the nail shop and got our pedicures. I didn't even look in Kamony's direction cause I don't know what her problem is. She seemed to mellow out after the pedicures, but how could you not calm down with people rubbing on your feet? I talked everyone into trying this Sushi place in El Cerrito that I go to from time to time with Steve. I don't eat sushi, but they have a teriyaki bowl that I always get and I was definitely in the mood for. When we pulled up to the restaurant Kamony sucked her teeth. Sonya asked her what was wrong with her. She sunk in her seat and looked out the window. "Kamony, you are the party pooper for real today. Cut it out before you ruin my good vibes." Nicole's mom snapped.

"Sorry Ms. Allison."

The lady recognized me when we walked in the door. She asked me where my boyfriend was as she looked at my group. I told her it was a girl's pamper day. Two of the other servers slowed down when they saw our group. All of them have waited on Steve and I, cause like I said we come here all the time. They were looking at us and almost laughing. Our server sat us at our table and then she gave everyone except Kamony a menu. We asked for another menu and she said she would bring it. Sonya shared her menu with Kamony who found what she wanted really fast for someone who's never been here. Maybe she knows her sushi that well. I shrugged it off. When our waitress came back to take our order she wasn't even apologetic about Kamony's menu that she completely forgot about. Normally she's really good about her service. She made sure she brought me my mango ice tea without me having to ask for it. When she sat down my glass she rubbed my shoulder and smiled a pained smile at me. We placed our orders and then the waitress brought out everyone's drinks. She was very specific about which soda went to Kamony. "How often do you come here? I mean she knows what to bring you without you even ordering it."

I smiled, "I guess that's why Steve likes little mom and pop places like this. You're more than just a number here."

"Or they know that you're a walking advertisement for good eating in here." She chuckled.

"WHAT IS THAT SUPPOSED TO MEAN?" Nicole blurted completely pissed off.

I started counting backwards from 100, she better hope I don't make it to 20. At 69 they brought out our food, but now I didn't have an appetite. Everyone's plates came except Kamony's; the waitress told her that her plate was coming. As I was calming Steve walked around the corner with my waitress. He stopped smiling when he saw our table. He walked over to the table saying hello in general to everyone and then he kissed my cheek. I noticed Kamony gripping her fork as she tried not to look at us. I looked at Steve and he wouldn't look in Kamony's direction. I looked at the other waitresses who were standing close to the kitchen watching us. I gestured towards my waitress and I asked her for a to-go box. Steve told me he'd come by my place later on tonight. Then he said goodbye to everyone and left. Sonya was looking at Kamony now with an irritated look. Nicole paid the bill and as we walked towards the car Kamony was beyond pissed. "You know, no one is forcing you to ride in my car."

"Shut up! Don't even talk to me right now!" Kamony said

dismissing me.

"Shut up?" Nicole jumped in, in my defense. "Kamony you can't ride with us!"

"Nicole! We've been tight since elementary school, how you going to choose her over me?"

"I don't know what your problem is. Tracy hasn't done anything to you."

"She gets on my nerves!" Kamony looked like she was about to blow a gasket. I started over at 100, when she started walking toward me in between 84 and 83. I dropped everything in my hands. I snatched her up by her shirt, which caught her by surprise, and I swung her around which made her fall. She tried to steady herself by grabbing me, which pulled me on top of her. I wasn't going to hit her but she punched me in the face. My head started ringing and I started boxing. I don't know what this girl's problem is, but I was tired of her taking whatever she was mad about out on me. Ms. Allison told me to get up so I did. Kamony was HOT! When she touched her face.

"STOP IT!" Nicole was crying.

"She's just jealous!" Kamony screamed.

Sonya shook her head, "Kamony. You didn't?"

"You fat pig! I'm not on the ground now. Try to fight me without using your weight to smash me! How in the world does Steve sleep with you?"

"Kamony! Stop it now!" Nicole's mom said.

"I can't stand her! She always..."

Nicole's mom looked so fed up as she grabbed Kamony by her

face. "I told you to stop!" Then she looked at Nicole, "I told you it was only a matter of time before her old ways came to the surface. Kamony you are so jealous of this child you can't see straight." Then she let Kamony go. "I hope for your sake the extent of your possessiveness stops at being jealous of how close Tracy and Nicole are, even though I doubt it."

"Go home Kamony!" Sonya said standing in front of me.

"Go home!" Nicole repeated.

Kamony was calling me every name she could think of. The waitresses came out and were picking up my stuff. They kept asking me if I was ok. I don't exactly understand why we were fighting but something told me I didn't want to know. I apologized to Nicole for fighting her friend. Then everyone got on my case for apologizing when I didn't do anything wrong they said she came at me.

Steve

I couldn't stop cursing! You could cut the tension at that table with a knife. Damage control! I gotta figure this out. I stopped at the gas station. My phone started ringing, it was Kamony. I thought about not answering. I took a deep breath. I barely said hello while Kamony was screaming and crying into the phone. She said she and Tracy got into a fight and my heart sped up. I was waiting for the part where she told Tracy about us. She kept going on and on about how fat Tracy is. Finally I had enough. I told her to meet me around the corner from the restaurant. There was some kind of girl code going on in there cause there was no reason for that waitress to take me to their table other than to bust me out.

I got out the car and when Kamony got close I started laughing. Her weave was all over her head and she had a knot coming up on her forehead. "Shut up! It's not funny!" She pouted.

"Looks like you lost."

"She fell on me, I should be smashed like a pancake. She has to be paying you. I don't know how you sleep with her."

I stopped laughing, "don't worry about what happens between me and Tracy. Why would you go anywhere with her?"

"I didn't know she was going."

"Why were you fighting?"

"I don't know, she grabbed me and threw me down then she got on top of me and started hitting me. I stuck her though."

I took a deep breath, "you don't know how to lay low. I can't mess with you no more."

"What? Over that fat girl?"

"That's all you can say about her huh."

"Don't act like you don't know she's huge! Go ahead and be weak, I hope she's paying you enough for this to be worth it." When I didn't respond she got mad. "You gonna retire me for that?" She got in my face, "what would your little dick self know about anything!"

At that point I closed my ears. If I'm so little and all the things she was saying why would she bother? When I got home I told Topaz what happened. After he stopped laughing at my description of Kamony's jacked up hair and face he told me to stop stringing Tracy a long and to stop trying to act like I didn't care. I didn't admit to anything. "If I had a woman down for me like Tracy's down for you, I'd be all over her."

I laughed an embarrassed laugh, "or suffocate under her."

Topaz didn't laugh; he looked at me for a long time. "Be straight with me. I won't tell anybody if you admit that you love her. So what if she's gained some weight, you lost your hair. She didn't make you feel bad about any of that. She still gives it to you when she knows you're running around on her. How many times she been mad at you and dropped everything to be there for you? She's a beautiful, intelligent, and good woman. I don't know why she loves you and lets you run all over her like she does. If you don't wise up one of these days a cat is gonna come along and not care about the extra cushion, then what you gonna do?"

So basically he's telling me he's feeling Tracy? Yeah right! Who would deal with her other than me? I looked at my roommate who was waiting for my answer. "I'm not gonna lie to you. What do you want me to say?"

"Keep pressing your luck like this and she's going to move on."

I decided to lay low for a little bit; if I came around right now it may look as though I'm admitting to something I'm not. Besides I met this new girl who looked promising as if she could be everything I need.

Tracy

It's been about a month since I've heard from Steve. I'm tired of being depressed about him. Shirley is constantly telling me to hang in there and that Steve really does love me, and that I need to hang in there with him. Sometimes I think he pays her to cheerlead for him as much as she has his back.

Nicole groaned as she hit the pillow. "No! This is exactly what he expects me to do. He knows I ran over here to you. I pour my heart out and then you talk me down. By the time I leave here he knows I'm going to be open to getting back together. NO! Tonight we're going out. Get dressed!"

I lowered my eyes at her, "so it doesn't matter that I want to stay in?"

Nicole jumped up, "I'll make it up to you later. Get dressed."

I huffed and then I got in the shower. I stood back and looked at my jeans, heels, and black top. I kept taking deep breaths trying to feel good about my appearance. I did look pretty cute, but I'd rather stay home. "Where are we going?"

"Reggae on the Bay, you've heard of it?"

I frowned, "no."

"It's in Alameda."

On the way to the club Nicole told me how Hubby popped up on her while she was having lunch with Dajuan. I got on her case about holding onto Dajuan when she has Hubby. Then she told me about the chicks that she's caught Hubby with. She said he wasn't innocent, but they had been doing well, then she messed up. I asked her what she was afraid of. She said she was afraid of ending up like her mom. In love with a man who turns her out and breaks her heart. I told her to stop selling herself short.

When we walked in this club I sighed then we went to the bar. I got my drink then a guy was standing to the side trying to get MY attention. When I looked at him he called me to the dance floor. I was SHOCKED! I was SURPRISED! I was... I was... IN HEAVEN! I danced with this guy for a long time. When I went back to Nicole she was sitting at a table with Hubby. I gave him a hug and asked him where he came from. He just smiled and said I looked like I was having fun. I smiled real big as chocolate from down under took my hand and led me back to the dance floor. This club had big girls and everyone else on this dance floor. Mister chocolate was a freak though, and when he tried to grab my breast I walked away from him. I didn't make it to my table before someone else asked me to dance. I'm all for dancing and letting off some steam. But mister chocolate was all over me. He kept trying to lick my cleavage and I was turned off. This new chocolate was a lot of fun. We freaked a little, but we danced. I thought I was tripping when I thought I saw a familiar form float past me. When I saw it again I knew that déjà vu feeling. I moved my partner in the direction of the form. Then I saw Tia winding some guy down almost to the floor. Tara wasn't too far from her breaking some guy's back who couldn't hang. Clearly they've been here before as they perfectly executed these island dances as if they were second nature for them. Since Tia was closest I stared at her until she saw me. "Hey Tray-Tray!" She gave me a sweaty hug. Tara came over and did the same. Neither one of them even seemed concerned that they were underage in this club. When we eventually sat down both of them produced IDs with my picture. I laughed so hard I couldn't believe that worked. "We have news!" Tara said excitedly.

"What's up?"

"We got in to NYU!"

"You're going all the way to the East Coast?"

"You gotta come visit us." Tia said stroking my hand.

I ended up having the best night at this club with my sisters while Nicole and Hubby sat over to the side talking out their issues. I gave my number to one really nice guy.

Steve

That was a complete waste of time. That girl was crazy and too possessive. It was only fun in the beginning. Indigo was beautiful and smart, and unfortunately crazy. She runs with equally crazy females. One of her friends liked to stare. I don't remember her name, but it's water under the bridge now.

I frowned at the phone as I hung up. Tracy hasn't been home and she's not picking up the phone when I call. I shook off the thought; she wouldn't hook up with someone.

****

"Where have you been?"

"Huh? Hello?" I could tell she wasn't awake.

"I'm coming over, unlock the door."

"But what about the muffin people?"

I started laughing; she was talking in her sleep. "I'll keep them away, unlock the door." When I got to her place the door was locked. I called her again, "Tracy, come and unlock the door."

When Tracy opened the door now in a sleep walk trance. I stood there staring at her for a minute. She lost a little weight, she looked good. I instantly got excited. She got back in the bed and went back to dreaming. I anxiously took my clothes off and got in the bed. My hands went all over her new body. When Tracy woke up for real this time she lightly screamed when she realized she wasn't alone. I laughed and told her about both of our conversations and that she let me in the door. When she said she would be right back I tried to kiss her with everything in me. I knew she wanted to go put that thing in and I didn't want her to. It's not like I could afford to have a kid, or that I even wanted one. I just wanted to be skin to skin and throw caution to the wind, after protecting myself from that crazy girl. I could trust Tracy, not those other ones. I kept kissing her, and then she said she had to pee. I let her go and then I waited. When she came out I was all over her. She wouldn't let me in without a condom. Irritated I rolled over and went to sleep. Now she wanna talk, now she wanna know what's wrong. I didn't feel like talking about it so I didn't. In the morning I had to go in, I was too pent up not to. I told her she needs to learn how to satisfy her man and stop worrying about the small stuff.

Chapter 13 ~ Dancing Partners

Tracy

Reggae on the Bay had become one of my new hangout spots. The girls would come over on Friday after mom and dad said they could come, and they'd spend the weekend with me. A few times we got Marie and her friends to come. We were having so much fun, and as an added bonus all that dancing was making me shrink. I talked to that guy a few times over the phone. He would tell me that I was so pretty, but I'd change the subject when it seemed like he was trying to talk about sex. Eventually he learned to only call to make sure I was coming to the club.

Now that Steve's back my clubbing life has come to a halt. He doesn't want to go, and although he doesn't stop me from going we're arguing about dumb stuff because I went. Steve was talking to his mom on my phone when he told her to hold on. "Hello?" Steve cut his eyes at me. "Who's this?" Then he frowned, "Tykeith? Hold on." He clicked back over. "Mom, I need to call you back." Then he handed me the phone.

"Hello?" My heart was pounding.

"I guess ders no point tin askin' ya where ya been. How long he been back?"

"For a little while." I was nervous and embarrassed. Steve looked like he was about to pop; he was burning me with his eyes.

"Call me when dat busta disappears again." He was annoyed, "take care Tracy."

"You too." Then we hung up.

"Him too what?" Steve said as nonchalantly as he could.

"Take care."

That was that, Steve didn't ask anything else about my friend. I got served up daily for a while. Things were good.

****

"Tracy why do you act like you can't come over or interact with us?" My mom looked hurt.

"Cause," I acted like that was an answer.

"Cause what? We're still your parents and we love you very much."

My eyes filled up with tears. "Just cause mom."

She gently picked up my hands. "Tracy, you're my first baby girl. We love you very much and our family isn't the same without you."

Great! Now she's got me over here snotting and crying. I came over for my sisters' high school graduation not to feel guilty about my life. I don't want to hear how much they love me every time I see them, making me feel horrible. Every time I want to bring Steve he disappears. I love him so much but we feel stagnant. The other day while I was in the shower he was talking about getting married, he said if he didn't make me happy I could just divorce him. He was kind of mumbling and when I asked him what he was saying he walked out the bathroom very fast, and then I heard the front door. He didn't come back for days and then he acted like he didn't know what I was talking about. I tell myself not to worry about getting married, even though I can tell that any day now Hubby's going to propose to Nicole. He's very open with everyone about how sprung he is. Nicole goes into an all out excited spazz out when she thinks about possibly marrying Hubby. They've been doing so well.

"I love you mom, I'm just going through something's right now."

She put her arms around me and kissed my forehead. I took deep breaths, and when that didn't work I excused myself to the bathroom. When I came out the bathroom my dad was looking at me like it was his turn. All he said was, "sweetheart," and I screamed and ran back in the bathroom. I sat on the edge of the tub crying. They wonder why I don't come around? Stuff like this! They're trying to make me feel guilty about my life and I don't appreciate it. I know they love me, but I'm in love with Steve. He needs this time so that we can be sure that when we get married that we're ready. Meanwhile I'm waiting on him, and being around my parents makes me feel guilty. They love me, no doubt about that, but this guilt trip is so unfair. When I came out the bathroom I asked them to stop telling me they loved me. To stop pretending like they're ok with my life. They defied me and told me they loved me as they hugged me and cried. My mom told me to stop staying away. I told them I would try to do better.

We cheered my sisters on at their graduation, and then we went out to dinner. My sisters came home with me and we prepared for their *secret* party in El Sobrante at this community center off in the cuts.

We didn't want a calm and reserved party. We wanted everyone to come and feel comfortable about being at the party. We invited all of our cousins around our ages and their friends. I made individual cakes for the girls and then we had a bunch of seven up and sock it to me cakes. We had pizza, soda, and chips. My biggest expense was the rental of the center, and the DJ.

I invited Steve, but he said he wasn't coming. Tara said she invited Tykeith. Marie grabbed my arm when we spotted Tykeith coming. I wanted to run, but she had my arm and he was looking. I was looking for disappointment in his face about me gaining all my weight back. He didn't seem to notice. Tykeith and I talked for a while and then we went out on the dance floor once he moved the conversation towards sex. I kicked off my shoes and we were living on the dance floor. Then I had that feeling like someone was watching me.

Steve

I was at home bored with nothing to do and no money to really do anything. I called Tracy and then I remembered that her sisters were having their little party. I decided to go and surprise her since she always wants to talk about how we don't go anywhere. I could see her being excited that I was there. Maybe we'd stay for an hour then we could go back to Tracy's. As I drove around the driveway I could hear the music. Good thing they weren't in a residential neighborhood, I could see the police being called behind all this noise. I found a parking space and then I followed the music. No one in this party looked familiar, a good thing. The only people who were sitting looked like they were only breaking to catch their breath. There were some people standing along the walls drinking punch and engaged in conversations. I went over to the punch bowl and got some punch. I was scanning the huge crowd of people on the dance floor when I spotted Tracy and some guy dancing. They weren't freaking but this was not a family member with the way they were dancing. I stood there watching for a minute when Tracy finally looked around and saw me. I could hear her gasp from across the room. She told her partner something and then she hurried over with a nervous smile. A couple of guys noticed and watched her approach me. I pulled back my attitude. "You said you weren't coming." She gave me a hug.

Her dancing partner came over, "you must be da boyfriend dat took her away." He extended his hand for a shake.

"Boyfriend?" I gripped his hand like he gripped mine.

"Oh well shoot! I know ya not her brother, let's finish our dance." He put his hand out to Tracy.

"Um!" Tracy looked stuck and her watchers were watching.

"Tracy, come on." He took her hand and took her back to the dance floor.

I stood there irritated for a minute. I walked out the door. I was almost to my car when Tracy called out asking where I was going. I told her I was going home. She begged me to stay. I looked at the guys who were close behind her watching me. I asked her who they were and she said they were her cousins. I got in my car and drove away.

Tracy

I wanted to cry. "Who was that?" My cousin asked me.

He didn't embrace the label so what was I supposed to call him? "A *friend.*"

Both of them frowned at me, "that ain't your *friend.* But you gonna be goofy about it so what's the point. Let's go party."

Tykeith was saying bye to my sisters. Then he gently took my hand and led me close to the door. "I've got ta go, but I need ta say sumting. Dat's who ya left me hanging for? Some guy who can't claim ya?" He opened his hands. "Ya got ta long road ahead of ya child. He don't love ya by now, he not goin' ta love ya ever. But it's ya choice. Ya choose him, he choose everybody else. I can't watch this, they'll deport me fa killin' him." Then he hugged me and kissed my cheek. "I can't even joke with ya 'bout da sex we never had. Ya know how ya get." He smiled.

I smiled, "we could be friends like we have been." I liked Tykeith but not like he pretends to like me. I mean he's nice and yes he may kind of like me, but every time I talk to him he brings up sex. We could be talking about jet skis and or the ocean. Some how, some way he would throw sex into the conversation. Now I'm all for talking dirty when appropriate, but he don't really know all that much about me. I didn't feel like he was trying to get to know me all that well.

"Ya don't get it. I like ya; I want ta be witcha. I want ta be da one making 'dem eyes roll back in ya head." I didn't say anything to that. "Have a good life Tracy." He hugged me then he walked out the door. My cousins came back and led me to the dance floor. I tried not to think about Steve. I didn't want him to feel like I invited him to watch me dance with some other guy. I did my best to enjoy the party. When the party was over, my sisters and my cousins my two dance partners came back to my house. My heart sped up when I saw Steve's car in the visitor parking by my apartment. My sisters and I got out of my car. Steve was walking towards us when he saw my cousins. He pursed his lips and then he walked back to his car. He started his engine as I approached him. He slowly pulled out of his spot. He rolled his eyes at me then he drove away.

"He better be happy we're only here for the weekend. Tray-Tray you need to get away from him, he's bad news."

"You didn't even say hi."

They looked at me sarcastically. "We're men."

"I know that," I rolled my eyes feeling irritated.

"When a man tells you a man is up to no good, you listen."

I looked at my sisters, "please tell them that he's normally really nice and that tonight was an off night."

My sisters smiled at me but they didn't speak.

Steve

That was a waste of a perfectly good night. I don't know who that girl thinks she is, but she needs to be thankful that I waste any of my time with her. "What's wrong with you?" Topaz was on the couch with a girl.

"Females play too many games. Tracy invited me to a party just to be there with some other guy. You always rallying for her, how you explain that?"

Topaz excused himself from his company and followed me down the hallway. "Do you claim Tracy?"

"No!" What kind of question is that? He knows I don't claim that girl.

"Then she's free to do whatever and whomever she pleases. Unless you're willing to put some kind of claim on her she can do whatever she wants. You need to quit playing before that girl gets some kind of self esteem about herself and finds herself a real man."

"I am a real man!" He was now getting on my nerves.

"Not when it comes to Tracy. You always punk out. Then you wanna act like she's always the one who's wrong. Just leave her alone."

"I thought you were my friend, why you always defending her?"

"As a friend I'm telling you the truth. You're wrong."

If I didn't think so before I know it now, he wants her.

Tracy

I looked at my self in the mirror. I loved the look of my braids. My last perm left me with chemical burns in my head and my hair had gotten really thin. I've been braiding my hair for the past almost year, but it's time to let these braids go as my edges need a break. Too much tension I think. I've been online watching everyone take care of their natural hair, gassing me up to attempt the unthinkable with my own hair. I spent all day taking down my hair, and then I took out the scissors. My eyes glazed over as I parted my hair and started cutting the straight ends. The first cut hurt the worst. I literally stood there crying for five minutes cause I could not go backwards and I regretted that first snip. My straight hair was thin and beaten up. I took a moment of silence as I stared at my Afro in the mirror. I got in the shower, washed and deep conditioned my hair. The hair on the top of my head went to my brow line. I took a deep breath, I could do this. I picked up my homemade oil mixture and whipped Shea butter. I used peppermint as the baseline for each of them. Seems like I forgot about the cutting of my hair as my scalp started tingling in the most glorious way. My hair smelled and felt GREAT! I wondered if Steve would hate my hair. I gave myself a lecture for caring what he thought. I hadn't really talked to him in the past couple of months. I was getting ready for bed when my house phone rang. I thought it was Steve so I almost didn't answer. "Hello?"

"Tracy! It's Allison!"

I sat up, "Ms. King?"

"Allison, baby can you help me? Nicole is in jail and I'm trying to come up with her bail money."

My heart dropped, "of course! I'm coming to your place right now. Give me five minutes."

"Ok baby, drive safely." Worry was all in her voice.

I got dressed in record timing and I ran out the door. I flew down the freeway to Ms. King's place. She was waiting by the curb with her purse. I asked her what happened and she said Nicole beat up Kamony. I gasped, I mean I didn't like Kamony but I didn't want my friend in jail, especially behind her. I asked why they were fighting and she didn't know. I just got another raise at work and it was a big deal. This raise put me in the serious comfort zone. My tax guy told me to consider buying property cause I'm going to get taxed like crazy. Even after taking extra taxes out of my check like he told me to I could afford my life within reason. I have a nice cushion growing in the bank, my future down payment for whatever I buy. Ms. King could have it all for my friend. When we got to the police station they told us her bail was $1,500. I pulled out my Checkbook. When Nicole came she still looked mad, but why wouldn't she? As soon as she got in the car she went off. She said Hubby told her that the last time they all went out together Kamony was pushing up on him. She said she called Kamony and Kamony didn't call her back until today. Kamony wouldn't talk over the phone so Sonya and Nicole went to meet her. She was there with two other girls. She said Kamony didn't deny pushing up on Hubby cause she was still mad about everything that happened the last time I saw her all those years ago. "So I asked her why she was acting funny with you. She said she didn't appreciate how we had your back instead of hers. She said we shouldn't care about her doing Steve as long as he wasn't one of our men."

I slumped, "she was sleeping with Steve?"

"She made it sound like she still is. Then she said she stopped caring about me and Sonya cause we chose you over her." Nicole started shaking her head. "Then she tried to jump me with her friends and I had to remind her of why she never wants to fight me. Sonya fought one girl and I concentrated on Kamony. The police came and they arrested me because I was the aggressor. It's my word against hers."

"They didn't arrest her?"

"Yes, I told Sonya to leave as they were pulling up."

As I started to pull away, Hubby's F150 pulled up next to me blocking me in. He jumped out of his truck demanding to know what was going on. "Hubby baby calm down, follow us to my place and Nicole will explain." Ms. King said. When he got back in the truck we saw someone's head in the window.

When we got to Nicole's place a woman got out with Hubby. Nicole said it was Hubby's mom. She hurried over to Nicole faster than Hubby and she tilted Nicole's head gently so she could see her face. "Are you ok baby?" She looked at Nicole with so much love.

"I'm ok, you should see the girls I was fighting."

She put her arms around Nicole and squeezed her tight. "Hubby! Did you call Drew?"

"Momma! I don't know how to take care of my woman now?" Hubby had his arm around Ms. Allison.

"I want those idiots locked away! How dare they ever raise their hand against my people." His mother said.

"So I'm going to call some guys to handle some dumb females?" He looked at her sarcastically.

"You could call Sasha and Tanisha, you all are just as close." Hubby's mom said.

"Sasha lives in LA and Tanisha is the one who called me." He said annoyed.

"I was wondering how you knew cause Nicole told me not to tell you." Ms. Allison said.

"Woman! Why can't I know?"

"Can we talk about this inside? Why we out here in the dark?" Ms. Allison said.

"Hold on," Hubby jogged back to his truck. He got something out and then he chirped the alarm. As we walked up the stairs Ms. Allison and Hubby's mom talked like two old friends. As I walked in the door Hubby stopped in front of me. "Thank you for always being there for my baby." Then he put an envelope in my hand.

"What's that?" Nicole asked staring at the envelope like I was.

"The money she posted for your bail... PLUS! A love offering for always having my back."

"Your back? She's always got mine!" Nicole came and put her arms around me. "I'm sorry girl." She was talking about Steve.

I chewed back the hurt I was feeling over Steve. "You know I got you guys back. Somebody deserves a happy ending in this story." When we got inside Nicole told me she liked my hair cut, then she had us laughing as she told us about the fight. One by one everyone would stop laughing from time to time and stare at the smile I had plastered on my face. I was trying my hardest not to reflect the hurt on my face that I felt in my heart. When I got in the car to go home I finally opened the envelope, it was full of cash. The $1,500 that I posted for bail was there as well as an additional $3,000. The paper inside said, "thank you for always having my back."

When I got in the bed I finally let everything out. I cried really hard until I fell asleep.

Steve

Tracy don't answer her phone. I've gone to her place and she don't answer even though her car is parked outside. What gives? "Hey stranger!" The lady from Tracy's job said.

"Hey how are you?" I stood to give her a hug.

"I'm concerned, what's going on with you and my girl?"

"She's avoiding me." I said honestly.

"Well you need to try harder, that girl is so in love with you. She's so depressed without you."

"Then why isn't she taking my calls?"

"She knows about you and that girl kimono." I didn't say anything, I just stared. "I've been trying to explain to her that when she has a young handsome strong man like yourself, these little girls will always try to snatch. She's got to have faith in how much you love her to get through this whole thing."

I lowered my head, "I do love her." I never admitted that to anyone except Tracy in moments that I couldn't stand not to tell her. "Is she hurting really badly?" I watched her eyes as they softened on me.

"She's hurting, but she loves you child. You gotta go smooth things out with her."

"How? I don't know how to fix this." More truth.

"You've got to be persistent. Let her know you love her and that you can't live without her. Let all your walls come down, make yourself vulnerable."

"Okay." None of that sounds good to me. What if my vulnerability somehow makes Tracy think she has the upper hand? When I couldn't stand this truth session anymore I changed the subject. Shirley happily told me stories about when she was young and all the "fun" she used to have. She kept referencing how good-looking she was when she was younger. To the point that I felt obligated to tell her that she was still beautiful today. I wasn't in the mood to talk to this lady anymore, but she was telling me everything. About the men that Tracy works with, her promotion that now requires Tracy to interact with vendors. Shirley said a lot of them of were men and male or female they sing Tracy's praises. I asked a bunch of questions about the men that Tracy worked with. Then I'd ask Shirley questions about herself whenever she seemed bored just to keep her engaged. Shirley was spilling over with all the information she could about Tracy. I asked her to be my eyes and ears on the frontline.

Chapter 14 – Love's In Need

Tracy

Sniff! Sniff! Hubby and Nicole were on either side of me harassing me. They loved the smell of my peppermint oil. I don't say anything anymore cause the kiddies seem to be fueled on by my request for space. I stopped mixing and then I looked at both of them. Nicole smiled then she slowly backed away pulling Hubby with her. I put my hand down like I was ready to mix again. Hubby acted like he was going to break away and come back. I raised my hand a little; if they came back I wasn't doing it *no mo'*. I was making a three-tier cake for Nicole's brother's anniversary party. The top tier was triple chocolate fudge with a ganache filling. The second tier was lemon, with a lemon curd filling. The third was a carrot cake. The chocolate cake was cooling on the racks. The lemon was almost out the oven and I was almost done with the carrot to put it in. Hubby slowly backed away with his hands in the air. I quietly chuckled to myself they act so silly.

Sometimes I go on autopilot when I'm in the kitchen. I've been so lonely lately. My sisters are enjoying life across the country. Marie has a new man, and Hubby's going to propose any day now. I sit at home alone a lot. I bake, I eat, I look in the mirror and I cry. How come I don't have anyone? Is this what my life is going to be? Forever alone! Nicole said no, but guys didn't pay me attention before. Now that all this weight is here it's even worse. I'm so tired of my life tired of being me. Maybe I should try being like someone else.

I took the lemon cake out and I put the carrot cake in. I iced the chocolate cake and then I put it in the refrigerator to set. Then I started cleaning up. Nicole and Hubby were in rare form today. All love pats and wrestling moves. They disappeared to the bathroom at one point; I rolled my eyes in complete jealousy. They didn't have to do all that here. "TRACY!" Hubby scared me.

"What?"

He smiled, "what kind of cat you like?"

"What difference does it make?" I moved around the kitchen.

Hubby put his arms around Nicole. "I got friends, they want good women. How come you never want to come out with us?"

"Never is a bit extreme."

"Ok, hardly ever."

"I get tired of being the third wheel."

"You're not the third wheel with us." I didn't say anything I kept moving around my kitchen. "Wait a minute! How come I never met your last boyfriend?"

"You saw him."

"Seeing a cat and meeting him is two different things. You ashamed of me or something?" He had a point.

"I don't do blind dates." I said.

"Why not?" He sighed.

"The disappointment. In order to get someone to agree to something like that you have to build up the person to be special. Then you meet and they're just ordinary."

Hubby sucked his teeth, "so what if he's just an ordinary guy. You got something against ordinary?"

"I was talking about me."

"Tracy you are not ordinary." Nicole interjected.

"Neither one of you are. You are good to my woman and me. If you were ugly I wouldn't say nothing."

"Hey!" Nicole laughed.

"I'm just being honest. I'm telling you Tracy you need to get out and meet people. Your future baby daddy is around the corner."

"Then I'll stay put. I don't want a baby daddy. I want a husband; shoot I want to be in love too. Maybe I'll get a little dog, something that will love me back when I give it love. Someone to come home to."

Nicole frowned, "don't become that lady just yet. Do you really want to pay for a sitter when we go out?"

"Like Hubby said, I never go out anymore anyways."

"Seems like you stay home to wait for someone." She raised an eyebrow.

"I stay home to hang out in my bathtub. I don't answer the door when he shows up."

Nicole sighed, "it's only a matter of time before you two are back together. You could do so much better Tracy."

****

"Look who it is." Shirley smiled as she nodded to Steve who was standing in line with his back to us. I shook my head in disappointment. "I'm going to invite him over."

"Don't!"

"You two need to talk even if you're not going to be together." Then she stood up. "Steve!"

Sometimes she gets on my nerves.

Steve

WHAT DID SHE DO TO HER DOGGONE HAIR!! I turn my back for a minute and she's chopping stuff. Doesn't she know that cutting her hair off draws attention to her face? Some hairstyles only look good on thin faces. Ugh! She's gotten bigger! I almost want to run in the other direction. I walked over like Shirley and I discussed. "Tracy," I nodded at her.

She looked up at me with innocent eyes, "Steve."

I took a deep breath; one look and I didn't care about everything else. I wanted to kiss her and be all over her. "Why have you been avoiding me?"

"You were sleeping with Kamony."

"I didn't know you knew her. We weren't in a relationship."

Tracy looked hurt; I almost wanted to take it back. "So what is there to talk about? Stay off my phone."

I pulled out the chair and sat next to her. "Doesn't mean I don't miss you. It's like we had nothing."

"I don't want what we had, I need more."

"I'm too young to offer more."

"Your age is a cop out, you're older than me."

"Tracy you know how I feel about you. I don't care about anyone like I care about you. I'm just not ready to offer you more right now."

"Then leave me alone." She turned her body away from me.

Her little turned off attitude was surprisingly turning me on. "I can't leave you alone. Don't you think I've tried."

Tracy sucked her teeth and then she walked away leaving her food. Shirley smiled at me; I couldn't believe she was acting like this. I hurried out my chair and ran behind her. She was power walking back to the office. I ran in front of her and then I kissed her. Right as she started to melt into the kiss she pulled away and tried to hurry away from me. I grabbed her hand and I sincerely said, "please." Then I pulled her back in to finish our kiss. I know she can't resist me but I give her an A+ for trying. Tracy put her arms around my neck as our kiss went on and on. Her hair smelled like minty freshness. Maybe I like this hair after all.

Tracy

"Is this just a silly game? That forces you to act this way? Forces you to **SCREAM** my name! Then pretend that you can't stay. Tell me who I have to be! To get some reciprocity! No one loves you more than me! AND NO ONE EVER WILL! NO MATTER HOW I THINK WE GROW YOU ALWAYS SEEM TO LET ME KNOW IT AIN'T WORKING! IT AIN'T WORKING! IT AIN'T

WORKING! AND WHEN I TRY TO WALK AWAY YOU HURT YOURSELF TO MAKE ME STAY! THIS IS CRAZY!" Lauryn was singing my heart's pain for me.

I feel so! I feel so! So.... DUMB! I was crying on Marie's couch. She was rubbing my back as she told me I deserved better. "Tracy, when you're ready for a good guy you will put yourself in the position for a good guy. This is not your prince."

"I love him," I got mad at myself for sounding so weak.

"He's got you backed into a corner. Why did you let him back in?"

"I was lonely."

Marie rubbed my back, "I know what you mean."

"You broke up?" I sat up to look at her. Her eyes were watery. "I'm sorry, I didn't know."

"How could you? It's not like I told anyone." She turned the music down.

"Why not?"

She shrugged, "was kind of hoping we'd get it together and I wouldn't have to tell anyone. I'm starting to think this is permanent."

"I hate men, what are they good for?"

Marie turned off the music and looked at me like I was crazy. "You don't know what they're good for?"

"Sex isn't all that!" I huffed.

She frowned then she felt my forehead like she was checking for a fever. "Sex is glorious when it's done right." She smiled to herself,

"I've had GREAT sex." Then she bumped me. "Men have a purpose, it's when we start relying on these kids in men's clothing that gets us all twisted up." She went to the kitchen and poured more wine in our glasses. "Let's take a trip. This will be our empowerment trip."

"Ok!" I got excited.

We decided to go to Tahoe for a long weekend.

On our trip we had an AMAZING time. Marie invited some of her friends.

*Well this is where I exit this story stage left. The rest of my story picks up in Volume I of the Wallace Family Affairs. That's where I meet my love, but Steve.... **You'll see....***

Steve

Curiosity wouldn't let me walk away. This white girl had stars in her eyes for me. I've never had one and I wanted to see if anything was different. At first it surely did seem like it. She was at the gym more than me, she cooked different. Her natural smell was different. Kissing her was different. Looking at her grey eyes as she appreciated me was different. Wet hair every morning *DIFFERENT*! The looks from my beautiful Sistahs as they watched us was different. It wasn't like they watched with the intention to steal. It was like they crossed my name off the attractive list. I don't know why I started feeling like that nerd in glasses again. When I brought her home Topaz just stared at me. When she left the next morning he asked me what I was doing. His hovering was getting on my nerves. If I'm wrong let me be wrong, he's not my father. "You don't even like her."

"Why are you saying that?" How did he know?

"I was watching you. You're self conscious about everything she says, you're not comfortable."

So what if he was right does he sit back and judge me now? Annoyed I went in my room, and then I left.

This girl had everything except genetically brown skin. Then I saw it, that thing that always made me drop a female. She wasn't looking out for me. I was just her trophy. I backed away slowly. When I finally thought about calling Tracy she wasn't home. I decided to go to the mall to get some more clothes for work when I spotted Tracy's car. I parked as close as I could to her then I pulled out my phone.

Now it's time to focus on me. Understand where I'm coming from and my side of the story. In the next story I'm going to tell you the truth about everything. Not some made up fantasy.

Carey Anderson

Distorted

|Chapter 1 The Waiting Game

I have been with this woman for years! Years! All she ever did is gain weight while we were together. Then she meets this other fool and suddenly she goes to workout. She don't bake no more, and she's even changed the way she eats. I suck it up when she gets off the phone with me for him. Ok, ok I'm lying I don't suck it up. I usually throw a fit or call a stand in just to blow my top. I didn't tell my roommate about this little hiccup in Tracy and I's relationship. All he's going to do is plague me with a bunch of "I told you so's", and stuff like that. So I try to keep it to myself.

"A! Look who it is." Topaz smiled real big. "Is that Tracy?" He smiled real big satisfied with himself. She was with some guy. The idiot! There were four chairs at the table and instead of sitting across from her he sits directly next to her. He keeps touching her hands and I guess he's smiling at her, I can't tell his back is to me. Tracy's smiling at him and eating it all up. They look like they're coming from somewhere. Probably grabbing a bite to eat before they go back.... I swallowed... to her place. "Jesus! Tracy looks good! How much weight has she lost?"

I shrugged, "a lot!"

"You didn't tell me she cut her hair. It looks good on her." He smiled at me. "Look at the poor sap. I mean, I'm not gay but that is a good-looking brotha! What you think? You think he's hung?" He looked at me as if I would answer that. "Oh never mind. We'll be able to tell by her walk."

"Why are you talking?"

"Oh snap! You know they say Mexican food is an aphrodisiac! Somebody's getting their back blown out tonight!"

"Stop!" I couldn't take anymore. "He can have her if he don't mind putting in all the work. There's a lot of stuff you don't know about her. You need to know what you're talking about before you start talking."

Topaz faked surprise, "Steve! Don't be a hater. You weren't all that into her anyways. Good thing he came and took her off your hands huh?" He smiled at me as if he thought I was going to respond to that. "We should go say hi."

I took a deep breath to calm myself. Topaz was going to play this dumb game by himself. Topaz stood up and walked over to their table. The guy turned his head and looked at Topaz before he was all the way to their table. Topaz smiled and nodded, the guy nodded back. Then he gave Tracy a hug. I watched as she proudly introduced the guy as her boyfriend. A label I would never allow. The whole scene made me mad. I got up and walked out. As I was walking out Tracy and the guy looked at me. Topaz better be happy he was driving cause I would've left him.

He took his time talking to them and then he casually strolled out with the biggest grin. He stood there smiling as I cursed him for playing games.

****

"So that's your little boyfriend?" I tried to sound upbeat.

"Little? Could you hate on him any harder?" She laughed, "why didn't you come say hi?"

I know how to play this game. Tracy loves me; she's going to come back to me. That pretty boy won't win, Tracy and I have history. She's been in love with me for how many years? Even though she's lost weight for him and she wouldn't do it for me, I know she's still in love with me. So I'm playing best friend now. I call her every so often to check on her, see how she's doing. I wait for her to complain about him so I can gradually steer her towards me. Only thing is she doesn't complain. When I ask her questions about him she changes the subject. She don't say much about him. "I don't care about him. I can say hi to you whenever I want." I took a deep breath to pull back my attitude. "My mother asked about you."

"Why? She never liked me."

"My mother doesn't hate you." I was lying but so what.

"Doesn't mean she liked me either."

"As long as I want you it shouldn't matter."

"Want-ed!"

"Want!"

"I got to go." Tracy said dryly.

"Can we have lunch tomorrow?"

"I don't think that's a good idea."

"WHY?" I didn't try to cover my irritation.

"Steve you never wanted to be with me. If you wanted me you would've had me. It's not fair to talk to me like this now. I'm happy, please respect that, and be happy for me."

"We're friends Tracy."

"I gotta go." Then she hung up.

****

I had a long day and I was looking forward to my workout to let off some steam. When I stepped off the elevator a woman looked at me and smiled. She was beautiful, then the guard pointed to me. Her eyes narrowed and she walked seductively up to me. "Steve Turnage?"

"Yes." I said looking over her form.

"I got something for you." She smiled and handed me an envelope. I took the envelope and her smile dropped. "If you don't show up you will go to jail!" Then she turned on her heels, "stupid deadbeat father! As if I would ever!"

It was a child support court summons for Kamony Johnson; I didn't even know her last name. My blood boiled! I told that girl I wanted a blood test and she wasn't getting a dime until I knew for sure. Shannon didn't even push the issue this far.

****

"Your Honour, I asked Ms. Johnson numerous times for a blood test since she told me she was pregnant and she constantly refuses."

"Ms. Johnson is this true?"

"Yea!"

"Why would you deny him his right to a blood test?"

"Because he's rude for asking. It was fine with him to lay raw with me. He didn't even try to pull out or anything. He was all lost in the sauce your Honour! I'm pretty sure Mr. Turnage knows how babies are made. He didn't need confirmation that I was clean. His money means more than his life!" To say Kamony was mad would be an understatement. "My daughter looks just like him. She don't even look like me!"

"Mr. Turnage, do you think the child looks like you?"

"I've never seen it your Honour."

"That's a lie!" Kamony blurted.

"Ms. Johnson?" The judge gave her the floor.

"My sister sent him a picture when he refused to come to the hospital. AND! He saw my baby when she was six months old."

I frowned at her, "what? Now you're lying!"

Kamony caught herself from cursing me out in the courtroom. "Now you don't remember?" She laughed showing her irritation. "I was with my then boyfriend, he was holding her!"

"Your Honour how am I supposed to know that the child some other man is holding is supposed to be linked to me?"

"You stared at her!" Kamony cried and crossed her arms angrily.

Now I remembered. The baby did look just like me. The whole thing was unnerving. The little girl looked like me but more like my dad. I could see Turnage all over her. However, she was the same complexion as the guy who was too proud to hold her. She wasn't as brown as me, she can't be mine! "Oh! I still need a blood test."

The judge looked at Kamony, "Ms. Johnson is the child here today?"

"No sir. Why would I bring her to this? He don't want her, and he don't care about her!" Angry tears fell.

I almost felt bad for her. ALMOST! She was the one who came after me. She was the one who kept calling me back when I was done with her. If she didn't want a baby she could've told me to stop like Tracy always did. I hate when females try to act innocent like we do something terrible to them when they know the consequences just as much as we do. "Ms. Johnson and Mr. Turnage I'm sending the orders for the DNA clinic in to the downtown Oakland office tomorrow. Ms. Johnson your appointment will be..." He looked at the clerk who was typing away on a screen. She wrote information down and handed it to the judge. "2:30. And Mr. Turnage your appointment will be.... At 4."

"I can't make it at that time is it possible to push back?"

The judge looked at his papers, "according to our records you don't work. So there should be nothing holding you back. Am I right?" I mumbled under my breath. "We will reconvene in three weeks. The results of the test will be revealed at that time. You are dismissed."

Kamony hurried to the embrace of an older woman. The woman rubbed her back as she kissed her forehead and told her how well she did. Irritation filled my chest as I immediately thought of Tracy and how good it felt to be nurtured by her. I wished she was here right now.

****

"99.99009 percent chance that Steve Turnage is the biological father of Richele Turnage. Mr. Turnage's visitation will be determined during mediation. You are required to pay child support and provide health insurance for the child. Your case will be moved to the Contra Costa County District Attorney's office. Ms. Johnson the court findings will be on record in that office. Hopefully you two will come to some sort of agreement that is in the best interest of the child." The judge said some other stuff but I couldn't focus. I felt trapped and tied down. I felt like I was going to be sick. I needed Tracy in the worst way right now.

When he dismissed us that woman hugged Kamony again. Kamony turned to me, "do you want to meet her now?"

The room was spinning, "I can't today. Can I come by?"

"I'll make dinner if you come on Saturday."

"Fine, what's your address?"

Kamony's eyes burned me, "it hasn't changed."

"Okay Saturday at two."

I sped down the freeway and to Tracy's place. Her car wasn't there, so she must've driven into the city today. I got comfortable in my seat. Steve Turnage YOU ARE THE FATHER!!! My heart kept speeding up. After a couple of hours my stomach started grumbling. I went through a drive-thru and parked while I ate my snack. I can't believe that girl had that baby to get her hands in my pockets. I tried to calm my nerves. When I pulled into the parking lot by Tracy's place she was walking towards her place with Pretty Ricky! I wanted to run them over!

****

Kamony looked very pretty as she opened the door. She had the biggest smile as she excitedly said hello. I didn't know what to do so I brought a teddy bear and some flowers. How are you supposed to act when you meet your daughter for the first time? "Are those for me?" Kamony was too excited.

"No, this is for Richele."

Her smile dropped, "what is a little girl supposed to do with flowers?"

I shrugged, "I don't know. Same thing you would I guess." I smiled, "I was going to bring her candy. But I didn't know if you'd let her have it."

"Oh well you went the safe route." She closed the door. "Have a seat and I'll bring her out." She pointed to the couch. Kamony disappeared and then she returned with a little girl on her hip. "Richele, this is your daddy." The little girl smiled at me then she hid her face. "Say hi baby."

"Hi," she said in the littlest voice that made my heart melt.

"These are for you." I put the bear and flowers in her arms.

"Tank chu." She smiled at my gifts.

"Here let me put these flowers in water for you. You can stay here." She put the little girl down, and then she disappeared into the kitchen.

The girl looked like she didn't know what to do. I put my hands out for her and she slowly and cautiously walked towards me. I picked her up and I sat on the couch with her. Kamony was right, Richele was all me and nothing like her. I made the bear talk to her, he even sang to her. When I looked up Kamony was crying with her arms folded across her chest. I told her to join us and we played with Richele together. We ate dinner like a family. Kamony wasn't a great cook, but it was decent. We put Richele to sleep together then we went back to the living room. Kamony was looking in my eyes, looking for some sudden rush of parental epiphany to wash over me. I didn't want to feel like a complete jerk so I gave her what she wanted. I gave it to her all night long. I left early in the morning.

|Chapter 2 The Crack in the Pot

I knew it! I knew if I just remained patient eventually...

Eventually! Tracy would come back to me. Tracy and Pretty Ricky broke up out of nowhere. She was so heartbroken and sad. It annoyed me but I had to look at the bigger picture. My woman was back and she was improved. Although I felt she lost enough weight she was focused and determined to lose more.

"Hello?"

"What time are you coming? Richele is almost ready."

Shoot! I forgot this was my Saturday. "I'm not going to be able to make it."

"WHY?"

"I forgot, I got something to do today."

"Or someone!" She spit.

"I'll try to come by later."

"What is going on with you? You've been so absent minded.........
lately." She started breathing hard, "did you get back with Tracy?"

"Yes," there was no point in lying about it. Pretty Ricky was wining and dining her. I can't expect her to be ok with sitting in the house. Plus there was no reason to hide her anymore.

"Why do you always lose your mind over that fat girl? When is she going to meet Richele?"

"I'll come by tonight, we can discuss it then."

A slight rise in her voice, "ok."

"Let me talk to Richele."

She put her on and I told Richele I would come to put her to bed.

Kamony was more hurt than anything, but what did she expect?

Tracy and I went to the Farmers Market. She likes to go from table to table, booth to booth. Tracy and I were looking at these purple bell peppers when someone walked up on us. "Hey Tracy."

We turned around and Tracy said an excited hello to her friends from the restaurant that time. "Hey, you guys remember Steve." She smiled.

"Steve." They said politely, but you could tell they were going to hate on me as soon as I wasn't around.

"How's Drew?" The girl said looking at me.

"I don't know. I'm with Steve."

"Don't you know Kamony?" She asked me.

"Who are you?" My insides turned into fire. I hadn't decided how I was going to tell Tracy about Richele yet.

"Sonya."

"Sonya, you need to mind your own business."

"Steve are you coming to my wedding?" Nicole asked me.

I looked at Tracy, "do you want me to go?"

Tracy put her arms around me as she smiled, "of course I do. I was going to invite you myself." Then she looked at Sonya, "thanks." She spit at her.

Nicole bumped Sonya telling her to relax. Tracy kept her hands on me.

****

I was walking in the mall when I recognized the shape in front of me. I remembered those curves from the first time I saw them. She hadn't changed a bit. I'm assuming that was her son with her, he was begging her for some overly priced shoes and she was telling him no. I couldn't see his face, but he had my walk. I forced the lump in my throat down and I ducked into the sunglasses shop, pretending to admire their inventory. I was glad to see that Shannon didn't give up on life and blow up after having the kid that she's tried to pin on me. I'm pretty sure if she saw me, my office may get another submission to garnish my wages. Even though she was saying no, he remained persistent until she caved and walked into the shoe store. I wanted to see the kid's face, just because he walks like me doesn't mean he's mine. As I stood there waiting for a glimpse of the kid's face. I asked myself, what difference would it make if I saw the kid's face? I told myself there was no need to shop in this mall today and I turned on my heels and got out of there as fast as I could.

I drove around the corner to Tracy's. She was still in her workout clothes and she was preparing her chicken to go into the oven before she got in the bath. She really has gotten the hang of cooking healthier and the flavors have been good. One look and she was asking me what was wrong. I told her nothing was wrong. Her surprisingly curly hair had grown a couple of inches and since it was wet from sweating it was throwing her peppermint fragrance even stronger. Her clothes were wet and sticking to her. I wanted to lick the salt off her neck. I asked her when dinner would be, and she said forty-five minutes. That meant she was going to go soak in her favorite place to dwell. I asked her if she wanted some company in the tub. She smiled and then she told me no, she kissed my cheek then she quickly went to her bedroom. She shut the door and then she emerged with her robe and a new loofah sponge. She went in the bathroom and shut the door. I counted to fifty after I heard the tub water turn off and then I went in the bathroom. She sunk as low as she could and had the water as high as it would go. She was pouring water over her head when I walked in. "Steve! Come on!" She tried to use her hands to cover up.

"Come on yourself, I've seen everything you have why you acting shy now?"

"I'm not ready for more yet."

"Oh come on Tracy, this would be the perfect time." I put my hand in the water like a submarine searching for her hidden treasures.

Instead of looking like she was into it, Tracy looked a little panicked. "Steve please." She said weakly.

Her small little plea made me feel like garbage. She reminded me of a time when I didn't listen. I instantly felt irritated and out of control. I kind of scared myself, because I didn't want to stop. Her fear made me feel like the strongest man in the world. I have complete and total power over her, and I loved the feeling. I told myself not to abuse the power. So I backed up, and sat on the tub watching Tracy nervously bathe herself. I could tell she got out of the tub faster than she intended to. She went in her room and locked the door as she lotioned up and put something on. She tried to be upbeat and happy when she came out the room, but even Stevie Wonder could see how red her eyes were. She was in that room crying, and I don't know why. I stopped like she asked me to. After we ate dinner, I kissed her forehead and then I told her I was leaving. Normally she asked me to stay or tried to give me a reason to stay a little longer. Not today, today she was ok with me leaving. I told her I'd call her later.

|*Chapter 3 Well Hello*

I went to the bathroom before I found my seat. I sat on an aisle seat and I people watched. Women at weddings are so desperate,

watching a couple vow forever makes the others realize what
they're lacking. I'm sure I could hit any single female in this place.
I took out my phone and I texted Tracy that I was here. Then Pretty
Ricky walked in with his date. I thought he knew who I was cause
he looked directly at me like he was trying to figure me out, but
then I noticed that he looked at each person like that. So I looked at
this cat, yeah he's pretty but so what. He has to have money, which
would be the only thing he has over me. Shoot I'm not ugly, I
workout, I just don't have a lot of money. Child support is killing
me too, if those others ever found out about Kamony I'd be
working just to pay child support. Tracy is so desperate to have me
back that she doesn't seem to mind footing the bill most of the
time. This is definitely a new development in our relationship. I
don't know how much of this dieting I can take though. She's
absolutely the smallest I can tolerate. I was thinking about slipping
her some butter in her sleep, but then she said she reached her goal
weight. I kind of miss her old size some times. Shirley said that the
men in the office are always looking at Tracy, but she doesn't pay
any of it attention. I know she's had a lot of fun shopping. When I
come to her place she's hanging up another piece that she bought.
Shirley said sometimes Tracy spends her lunch shopping looking
for deals. I wonder how much money she's making these days. My
thoughts were wondering all over the place until a pretty lady
walked past me. As I started to scan the room, I hoped this
wedding started on time. I hate waiting forever for the wedding
party to get their stuff together.

The officiant moved to the front of the room and asked everyone to
take their seats cause we were going to be starting in a couple of
minutes. I smiled as I looked at my phone, the ceremony was on
time. The groom walked his mom down the aisle. She smiled like
she was so proud of him, and when they got to the top of the aisle
she kissed his forehead. A lot of people ooh'ed and aw'ed. My
mom would try to stop the ceremony, it wouldn't matter who I was
marrying. She hates me, and she tries to say it's because I remind

her of all these other people when the truth is I remind her of herself and she can't stand it. I watched all these pretty girls walk with their escorts. Even that girl Sonya looked pretty with her hair and makeup done. She wants me too, but she at least is trying to wait until she thinks it won't matter to step to me. The doors opened and Tracy and Pretty Ricky entered. She didn't mention that she was walking with him. It's not like it mattered, but I watched her body language. Tracy looked beautiful, and I could tell she felt it. I watched her eyes as she scanned the room as they walked. Pretty Ricky looked straight ahead, I imagined him dreading reaching the end of the aisle. Tracy's eyes smiled when she saw me. I guess I could get used to skinny Tracy, especially if she's going to look like this regularly. I thought about how many guys would be worshiping at my feet just because my woman is this fine. When Tracy looked at me I mouthed hi, and she mouthed it back.

When the wedding party left I stood and here came one of Indigo's girlfriends. Indigo and I dated for a while a few years ago. I can't remember this girl's name though. "Steve right?"

"Right. You are?"

"I'm Toya, Indigo's friend. Don't tell me you don't remember me?" She smiled.

"I just didn't remember your name. How you been?"

She looked around, "good. Are you going to the reception?"

"Yes."

"Ok, I'll see you there." Then she hurried away.

Then an Angel and her mother walked towards us. She could've been white, but I'm guessing she was walking with her mother who was clearly Latin. She was stuck up though; she threw her nose in the air as they passed. I shrugged, oh well. It's not like I didn't have my pick of the litter.

As I walked towards the reception hall Toya was waiting by the door. "It's not assigned seating, you wanna sit with me?"

"How you know I'm not sitting with someone already?"

"I know you're here with the girl who walked with my man." She seemed a little irritated about it.

"Pretty Ricky is your man?" I smiled, suddenly Toya became interesting. I figured she was just his date, but she's full on claiming him.

"Since we were kids." She sighed.

"Yeah, I'll sit with you." As she led the way I allowed myself to take her in. This girl is beautiful, NO! She's GORGEOUS! I've never seen chocolate skin done up so nice. Her body, I drooled! She has everything, the right amount of breast before they became too much. Big ole booty, thin waist. Her hair was long like I prefer, don't matter if it's a weave or not, as long as it looks good I don't care. When I saw her eyes roaming over me, I had to control myself. Never in a million years would a woman this fine look at me unless she's playing some kind of game. I decided to keep an eye on her. I would have to pat myself on the back if I ever had a woman like that. Pretty Ricky is just greedy.

Toya was conversational and light heartedly flirting with me nonstop. When Tracy walked in the room though, I got butterflies in my stomach. She can't run from me no more. I have to have her tonight. I was trying to get her heart back so I agreed to this no sex thing. I've had all that I can stand; I need to take that new body for a cruise. Pretty Ricky seemed wounded cause I know Tracy turned him down if he tried to holler. Toya may be pretty, but there's no one like Tracy. I know he's kicking himself right now, and I am applauding inwardly. He messed up and I wasn't letting her go for nobody. Pretty Ricky stepped out and Toya went after him, they were gone for a little bit. When they came back Toya's lipstick was gone, and she frowned a little like it pained her when she sat down. Toya's a freak! I like that! She also seemed to be attracted to my disregard for her. So if I played my cards right, she'd be trying to exchange numbers or something before the night was over.

Once Tracy pointed out the open bar, it was my mission to get her drunk. Every time she parted her lips I had a fresh drink ready for her. I told myself not to worry about the carbs associated with the drinks. I was getting laid tonight if it's the last thing I do.

****

Now she knows I'm sick, why would she leave instead of staying behind to take care of her man? Tracy got up this morning like she could actually get a work out in. It annoys me when she tries to over do it. Was she trying to show me up as if she's more dedicated to working out than I am? Someone pounded on the door, and it took me a minute to get up. I was still naked so I grabbed the sheet and wrapped it around my waist. I opened the door and it was Toya, she had coffee cups in her hands and she looked annoyed. "I saw your little girl friend get off the elevator, and when I get to the room my man isn't there. Do you know where your woman is?"

I was in no mood for her mouth, my head was killing me. "Don't come pounding on my door cause you can't control your man. Watch your tone when you talk to me!"

Toya stared at me for a minute like she was bouncing back and forth between responses. "I'm sorry, I just feel panicked right now. Things haven't been right between me and him since her, you know what I mean?"

"No," I knew what she meant but I wasn't going to let on that I did.

Until last night Tracy wasn't putting out, and her legs have always hung open for me. She was acting hurt and love struck too long over that fool. "Tracy is sprung stupid off of me, I don't need to worry about where she is or what she's doing. I don't care what your man looks like, there's only one me. She can't live without me!"

Toya stared again, "you know nothing about a woman's heart, but ok. Write your number down so that I can keep tabs on your girl."

"What?"

"From time to time I'm going to check in. If you say she's with you then she won't die. If she's not with you and I find out she's with Drew, I'm going to kill her." There was no joking in her face.

"He that good?"

"He's mine, does it matter?"

I wrote my number down, and then she left. I guess this weekend was productive after all.

****

"Steve?" The female voice was in tears.

I looked at the caller ID, I didn't know this number and I didn't recognize the voice. "Who is this?" I sat up to wake myself up. Tracy looked at me, "it's my aunt go back to sleep." I got up and walked into the living room. "Who is this?" I barked lowly.

"Toya, is Tracy with you?" She cried some more.

"Yes, we were sleep. What do you want?"

"Drew broke up with me on the way home from the wedding. He's not taking my calls, and I normally follow him out. He didn't come home after work and I don't know where he is. All the places he normally is he isn't."

"I told you, I've got my woman in check. You don't need to be worried about Tracy. Besides why would you be worried about where he is if he fired you?"

"Cause! We break up to make up normally. As long as she's out of the way, I know it's only a matter of time before he comes back to me."

"Well I guess he's coming back to you then cause my woman is in check." There was silence for a minute. "Look call me during normal business hours, don't call my phone late like this."

"I'm sorry, he just makes me crazy sometimes."

Tracy opened her door, "good night Auntie T. Kiss my grandmother for me and I'll talk to you in the morning." Then I hung up.

"Auntie T? Is everything alright?" Tracy asked half asleep.

"Everything's fine." Then I patted her butt.

****

Kamony was screaming at me. I stood there letting her go off. She was upset cause it's been over a month since I've come to see "Richele". If you ask me she was wasting time with this little show of dramatic emotions. I don't need this right now. Tracy is dramatic enough for ten people, managing her emotions is a chore within it's self. She's always freaking out and so insecure it's not even funny. You would think that losing all that weight would've gave her the confidence to take on the world. But, No! She's constantly looking for reassurance. I blame Pretty Ricky for this too. "Look, I told you my life has been crazy. You can stand there and argue with me about stuff that's in the past and I can't do nothing to change what's happened, wasting more time I could be spending with Richele. Or I can just leave and it will be even more time that passes before she sees me. You want to be the reason why?"

"Steve! Stop acting like I'm being unreasonable! You can at least call her if you can't be here physically. Richele has been crying and begging to see you. You haven't been answering your phone. Next time I'm just going to stalk your gym. You don't look like you've missed a workout in the last however long!"

I grabbed her wrist, "don't threaten me! I'll get here when I get here. You don't like it, take me to court. You're already taking all of my money making it dang near impossible for me to survive, now you're harassing me about the time that I spend trying to hustle up extra money. I have to get a second job doing anything just so I can support myself. You didn't think of that when you ran your butt down to the child support office to take me to court."

Why did I say that? Here she goes, "you wouldn't even acknowledge Richele! You've got to be kidding me right now. I don't care if you have to get two extra jobs you need to support your child. It's not like I have a roommate over here anymore. I can't do this by myself."

"You should've thought about all of that before you had a baby. Nobody told you to play hero and have it."

Kamony started jumping around. "How can you look at your child and then tell me I should've killed her? What kind of monster are you! You claim you love her in one breath and in the next breath you're talking about how she should be dead!"

"Kamony! You're too emotional. Calm down! I don't have time for this!"

"You don't have time for nothing! This isn't fair Steve! I did not make her by myself. Say whatever you want, you didn't try to prevent her being here. Keep messing with my heart and I'll mess with yours."

"What is that supposed to mean?"

"Exactly what I said!"

I rushed her and kissed her. This little angry fight scene had me so turned on I couldn't see straight. Kamony melted as soon as I kissed her. All she wanted was to feel like I cared. I served her up all over that living room. After I took a moment to catch my breath, I put my pants back on and I went in Richele's room where she was watching a movie on her bed oblivious to what was happening in the other room. She ran to me screaming, "Daddy! Daddy! Daddy!" Outside of Tracy, no female has ever been so happy to see me before. Richele followed me all around the house. Her mouth was going a mile a minute as she told me all kinds of stuff that didn't matter to me. Kamony cooked and followed me as well. We put Richele to bed together after Kamony read her a bedtime story. Kamony started crying when I told her I couldn't stay. She told me it wasn't fair and that my family was here. Then she told me she hated Tracy. I didn't say anything to dispute that.

When I got in the car I listened to my voicemail. Tracy called to check-in and say she was going to hangout with her cousin and she didn't know what time she'd be home, so she'd see me in the morning or so. In the next message Toya was in tears and begging me to call her back. So I did, she said she was pregnant and Pretty Ricky wasn't answering her calls. She said he's never ignored her like this, and she needed to tell him what was going on. She asked me where Tracy was, and I told her she was out with her cousin. She asked how I knew she wasn't with Pretty Ricky. I explained for the millionth time that I had Tracy in check, and that she would never do me like that. To pacify her I told her to be completely silent. Then I called Tracy on three-way. "Hello?"

Carey Anderson

"HI STEVE!" The group of females called out on Tracy's end.

"Ladies," I smiled. "Are you having a good time?"

"YES! Thank you for letting Tracy come up for air!" Someone said.

"Well I won't say you're welcome, I'm missing my woman right now."

"AW!" They all said in unison.

"Hey baby what's up?" Tracy said smiling through the phone.

"Nothing I was missing you. Where are you guys?"

"We're at this lounge in Walnut Creek, it's called 14. Have you heard of it?"

"No, but it sounds cool. Should I come rescue you?"

She smiled, "if you want to. You know I want you everywhere that I am."

"What if I said I'm looking at you right now."

Her smile got bigger through the phone. "Did you come to do me in the bathroom or something sir? Where are you?"

"I'm at home, I just wanted you to feel like I was there. I'll see you tomorrow."

"Aw! Don't get my hopes up like that. Ok, I'll talk to you tomorrow."

"Ok, I love you."

I smiled, "you know better than to say that to me over the phone. You're going to get it tomorrow."

When Tracy hung up, Toya pretended like she was vomiting. She said we were doing too much. I pointed out that if her man were there, Tracy would've freaked out, she's too dramatic not to. Then Toya told me to hold on and she called Pretty Ricky again. He sent her to voicemail. So she called right back, he finally answered telling her it was over. "I'M PREGNANT DREW! PLEASE!" You could hear his face crack through the phone. He asked her if she was sure, and she said she was. Then she asked him to come over, and he said he couldn't cause he was in LA. He said he'd be back in the morning. I understood the defeated sound in his voice. When he hung up he sound like he was about to break while Toya couldn't be happier. She said she was going to pick out her bridesmaids dresses next week, and she already knew what dress she wanted to wear. I'll never understand women. That man sound broken and beaten down, and somehow she was fantasizing about a life it didn't sound like he wanted.

"Toya! Stop!" She stopped talking mid-sentence. "I'm your friend, and I'm telling you as a friend. You need to slow down, he's not going to marry you."

She cough-laughed at me, "you don't know my man. He proposed last time; he'll propose this time. He's not as high profile as I would've liked my husband to be, but he's not broke. My momma will just have to deal with it."

"Your momma?"

"Oh yes, Madam Creole."

I laughed, "Madam Creole?"

"That's what her friends used to call her. I call her that when I'm being a smart aleck." She laughed, "she was always determined to have money. My father is supposed to be this big money guy that I've probably seen three times in my life. She tried to get him for child support and all that, but he wasn't going for it. She's always been against me being with Drew, I tried to tell her that she's not giving him credit. But it's whatever, you know?"

"My mom don't like Tracy, she always calls her the fat girl."

"Ha! Cause you know she's one cinnamon roll away from blowing up again. Fat city!" She laughed.

I exhaled, "I gotta go. Hopefully he don't make you have an abortion this time."

"Seriously, you're mad about me talking about her. You don't even care about her like that."

"I love that woman." I flinched at the admittance.

"Not enough to be faithful so it don't matter."

"Like Pretty Ricky is faithful to you!"

"He's changing, he's slowing down a lot. Which is why I know we're getting married. Besides! I was his first, I got him first and I'll always have him."

|Chapter 4 The Toya Affect

"I'M FREAKING OUT!" Toya was panicking; she was drawing attention to us. "HE HAD ME SIGN PAPERWORK! HE'S NEVER GOING TO MARRY ME!"

"Look either you calm down or I'm going to walk. Don't you have a girlfriend you can call with this drama?" I didn't like all the people looking at us together. I only met her here cause she insisted that she needed my help.

"Please! I'm too pretty to have girlfriends! Even with this belly!"

"Tracy has girlfriends."

"That's until she eats them." She laughed at her own joke.

"This is the last time I'm going to tell you. Stop talking about her!" I put bass in my voice to stress that I meant it.

"I'm sorry, it's just that I hate her so much!" She backed down.

"Your problem not hers."

"I don't have girlfriends." She said like the realization made her sad.

"What ever happened to Indigo?"

She made a face at me, "what do you think? Females can't handle having a friend as pretty as me. Their boyfriend starts dreaming about me. It gets ugly."

"What kind of paperwork?" I couldn't help her with that. I had a male and female best friend. So I went back to her original thought.

"It said we we're going to have joint custody of the baby. He's going to pay the rent for the apartment of my choice and all of my utilities, plus a car of his choice, and I would get some spending money."

"Sweet!"

"Sweet? I feel like he's lowballing me."

"How?"

"He never let me know where he works, but he went to college for crying out loud. He works hard, I know he can afford more."

"So let me get this straight. Just because you happened to catch his best swimmer at the right moment you think you're entitled to more out of his pockets? He could've ran from you, and left you to fend for yourself."

"Drew would never abandon his child."

"Is he sure the baby is his?"

She gasped, "This last time we were together I was faithful."

I smiled, "you're not always faithful?"

Her eyes sparkled at me, "no."

"What difference does it make now, you're all fat." I teased.

"I am not fat, the only thing swollen on me is this belly. Madam Creole makes me walk and walk and walk. She still believes that I can get someone better with bigger pockets."

"Is that all that matters to her is money?"

"It matters to everyone."

"What about heat, passion, and downright dirty sex? He might have money and want you to dance through so many hoops just to get five dollars."

She laughed, "that's what affairs are for. He's going to have them and I would be a fool not to have one or a few of my own."

"So why did you cheat on Pretty Ricky?"

"Because he loves me." She watched my eyes, "why do you cheat on the fat girl?" I frowned, "I mean your girl?"

"Because she loves me."

Toya smiled, "you understand what I mean?"

"I do, it's like you know that they love you. You know they will forgive you. You don't accept it though, you have to test it. I'm in Tracy's head. She could never love another man like she loves me. I'm first in everything she does. I know she gave up Pretty Ricky for me."

"Um! I came back that's why he dropped her."

"Here we go, how many times we gonna argue about this?" I smiled.

"Until you realize that I'm right and you're wrong."

We sat there smiling and staring at each other for a minute. "You are nothing but trouble, I can already tell."

****

"Hey Steve, I had the baby. It's a boy just like they told me. Call me back when you can." Her voice shook. "I feel so vulnerable right now. Drew's all about the baby, Madam Creole is all about the money. They even kind of had words behind it. Nobody's here for me, my aunt said she'll try to come by later, but I doubt it. I could use a friend right now." Then she hung up.

Her voice sound so sad and pitiful. That girl who had her entire wedding picked out in a week was gone. She's been so depressed that I've been happy to put a smile on her face. She's quickly taking the place of my ex-bestfriend Myeisha. Myeisha doesn't seem to have much time for me anymore. Ever since she saw me and Tracy out to dinner that time, she's been distant. We spoke once since then. The way she asked me if I was in love with Tracy was more like she was accusing me. Now that I've gotten into the habit of openly admitting my love it came out so naturally. Myeisha was disgusted, she spoke lowly almost mumbling as she told me off. I don't know why these females get jealous about me being with Tracy. The first thing they want to call her is fat, and that's all they can say about her. Myeisha doesn't answer my calls anymore. Good riddance! So now Toya's calling me all the time.

I called her back and we talked until Pretty Ricky came back.

"Who was that?" Kamony asked.

"Since when do you think it's ok to question me about my phone calls?"

"When you take thirty minute phone calls on my time."

"I'm here to see my daughter. I could take her to Tracy's if you gonna act like this."

Kamony looked like she was about to lose it. "I already told you, you will not take my daughter around her."

"What if I decide to marry her?"

Kamony turned pale, and everything in her dropped. "Don't." She said that like it took all her strength to get it out.

"I'm not saying I have a ring picked out, this past year since we've been back together has been great."

Evilness settled in her eyes, "why would you marry a fat girl?"

I walked in her face, "call her that one more time!" I dared her to defy me. "ALL YOU CAN SAY ABOUT HER IS THAT SHE'S FAT! I'VE GOT NEWS FOR YOU! SHE HASN'T BEEN FAT IN ALMOST TWO YEARS! NOT THAT IT'S ANY OF YOUR BUSINESS!"

"She's just doing that so you'll marry her. She's going to blow right back up. You have a family here, don't you know it's cheaper to keep her?"

"I don't have to worry about keeping you, I already got you for the rest of your life!"

She dropped her head and cried. "I hate you so much!"

I walked to Richele's room. I stuck my head in and she was still napping. I closed the door and then I looked at Kamony who was still standing in the middle of the floor holding herself. "Come here!" Then I walked in her room. When she followed me I closed the door and locked it so Richele couldn't walk in on us like she did before. She thought we were wrestling. I told Kamony to kiss me. She pecked my lips. I asked her if she loved me. She kept her eyes on the floor as she cried. I told her to kiss me like she loved me. She stood there for a minute crying then she kissed me with so much passion and want. I told her to undress and she did. Then I told her to undress me. Tears ran down her face as she kissed me all over as she undressed me. I told her to put the condom on me and she did. Then I told her to show me how much she loved me. I told her I wanted to feel it in every thrust. Kamony did her best to take everything she could from me that afternoon.

****

Ok so when I got off the freeway, my eyes quickly darted back and forth. I followed her directions exactly the way she gave them to me. When I pulled up to her building, I gasped. I've got to get me a uterus! I found parking on the street at a meter. It was two minutes until 6pm so I took my time about getting out of the car so that I can relax with the knowledge of my free parking. I walked back to her building and I buzzed her apartment. She didn't even speak she buzzed me in. She told me she was on the fourth floor, and to make a left and to walk all the way down to the end. This place was decked out, even the lobby was fancy. The elevator was so smooth; I didn't even realize I was moving until it dinged to tell me I arrived at my floor. The door was open, when I got to it. "Toya?" I stood in the doorway.

"Come in, shut the door." She called out from the kitchen.

This cat is supposed to be small potatoes? I wonder what she thinks a big fish is supposed to provide her with. Expensive furniture, rugs, artwork, girly stuff. This place was really nice. "I'm scared to touch anything, what should I do?" I called out.

She laughed, "hang your jacket on the coat rack. Leave your shoes on the shoe rack. Come in the kitchen and make yourself useful."

The wooden floors were so shiny they looked like they were covered in glass. I followed the sound of her voice to the kitchen. The outside wall from the counter up was all windows. And then floor to ceiling windows for the last few feet of the kitchen outside wall. She had an amazing view of the Bay. I stood there stuck for a minute as I took it in. Toya looked at me and smiled. When she came around the refrigerator I was disappointed to see that she was still carrying baby weight. "I thought you said you were all stomach." I smiled.

"SHUT UP!" She laughed, "I can't stand you sometimes."

"I'm not saying you look bad, but for someone who constantly talks about my girl's weight you would think that you would've made sure you snapped back."

"It's not as easy as I thought it would be, but I've been working out in the gym here. Don't worry; I'm going back to the old me. Madam Creole may literally strangle me if I don't. She's over Drew already."

"What did he do now?"

"He's just being unreasonable. It's ok; I'm going to fix his behind.

I'm taking him to court to fix him. He thinks he can control me."

"Well..."

"Well what?"

"This place is nice. If I was shelling out the cash for my mom to live like this, you better believe I'm controlling everything she does with it."

She cut her eyes at me, "the sooner everyone learns I can't be controlled the easier their lives will be."

"Calm down, I'm just telling you the truth."

"Money doesn't equal control!"

I laughed, "oh yes it does. But I can tell there's no point in arguing with you. You're going to believe what you want to believe."

She put her salad bowl on the counter, "stand up." I did. "Come here." I walked up to her face. She smiled, "you think we could pass for family?"

"HUH?" I was lost.

"I'm trying to think of how I can explain you."

I touched her ponytail, her hair had that just came out the shop look to it. I used to love the look and smell of it on Tracy. Now little miss all natural makes her own hair products and is becoming more and more earthy. I don't complain cause the smell of her peppermint intoxicates me, but I miss this too. Just straight hair fresh from the shop look and smell. "Why would you need to explain me?"

"Madam Creole is insisting that I get back out there and meet someone new. She still wants me to find my big fish."

"Why does she care so much?"

"Duh! So I can take care of her."

"Oh, right."

"So I figure we gotta come up with a plan to explain my bestie. No guy will accept us being close if you're just my bestie. However, if we're family they won't question us."

"Cousin T, huh?"

"Cousin Steve," she put her arms around me. "I like the sound of that."

"Wait a minute, hold on." I backed away from her. "What am I missing here?"

"Apparently everything. I'd like to have sex now. We can eat when we're done."

Her directness caught me off guard. I coughed and completely blushed. "What?"

"I know you're used to extra loving and it's been over a year for me since I got some. I'm over due."

"Pretty Ricky wasn't hitting it?"

"Only once in the very beginning of the pregnancy. After that he wouldn't even entertain me. I know he was seeing your girl still, but you were always making excuses for her."

"Why it got to be my woman? There are plenty of other females out there."

"Look! I'm getting bored with this back and forth. You've wanted me since the day of that wedding. I know it, you know it. I'm ready and you're acting gun shy."

I grabbed my shirt; "your aggressiveness makes me uneasy." I laughed.

"I know you brought condoms, come on." She turned and walked out the kitchen.

I stood there chuckling for half a second. I walked out the kitchen to see her standing in the doorway of her bedroom. I walked down the hallway taking in everything; this place was over the top for real. When I walked in her room there was mood lighting above her bed and the rest of the room was dark. You could see the remainder of daylight peeking out from behind the heavy curtains she closed. Toya was naked moving to the middle of her waterbed. I laughed and asked her why she had a waterbed, and she told me to come find out. I took off my clothes and she said I was beautiful, and then she told me to come. She took my condom from me then she kissed me. When she put that condom on me it was over. I loved this waterbed. We were all over that bed. Even though I was supposed to be going to Tracy's tonight, I still pulled a round two for Toya. No lies, No pretenses, No put ons! She knew what time it was and she was down. I knocked out so hard; I couldn't even call Tracy to tell her I couldn't make it.

Last night was good, better than Kamony any day. Toya's a freak for sure, but it was different than Tracy. I know Tracy genuinely loves me; Kamony wants to steal me at all cost. Toya only wants my friendship no gassing her up about nonsense. "Brutal honesty! Right now right here!" Toya sat up looking at me. Her hair was loose and falling so beautifully on her shoulders, and all over her head. "Tell me something, anything you haven't told her."

"I guess I can trust you, laying in this bed another man pays for, for you. You've got as much to loose as I do right?"

"Right." She kissed my lips, and then she licked hers like she wanted more.

"I've got kids." I expected her to act shocked or something, but she was waiting for me to get to the bad part. "I only claim one. And I only do that when I'm with her. As soon as the others told me they were pregnant, I told them to get rid of the baby and I bounced."

"Why do you claim the one?"

"She kind of forced my hand and made me come to court. I messed up one time telling her what building I worked in, in the city and she sent someone to serve me. I got to pay $200 a month in child support."

"Is that supposed to be a lot of money?" She moved her hands around the room.

"When you're broke like I am, it might as well be $200,000 a month. That's what it feels like anyways."

"Why don't you claim all of your kids?"

"For one I don't know how many actually were pregnant and how many were trying to game me. Or how many actually had the baby, and if the baby was actually mine." I exhaled, "I tell myself all the time, that if the others are mine the mothers would take me to court like Kamony did."

"Ka WHAT?"

I laughed, "Kamony."

"You still sleeping with her?"

"Yes."

"Why?"

"In her own way she loves me."

"Why not be with her instead of the fat girl?" I frowned at her, "get over it. She's the fat girl. That's what I'm calling her."

I exhaled, "I love Tracy. Kamony knew I was with Tracy when she came after me."

"Why do you love the fat girl?"

When I frowned, she rolled her hands like she was waiting for me to get to it. "She takes care of me. She's the only person to do that from her heart since my father."

"You got momma issues for real!" She shook her head. "Madam Creole is a piece of work herself. She never really liked Drew. She don't care who his daddy is or nothing she don't like him. I hate his family! They're judgmental and bullies. Drew can't stand up to nobody in his family, he lets his little brothers talk to me any way they please. His brother slapped my momma when I was in labor and Drew did nothing."

"What was he supposed to do? Sounds like she deserved it."

She lowered her head, "she's still my momma. He should've protected her. His momma, his aunties, cousins, you name it. It's like they all got in line to beat up on me."

"Why?"

"Cause I'm pretty." She laughed, "and they can't stand how much Drew loves me. I know they wished they could've said that Andre wasn't his. But he don't even look like me. He looks just like Drew."

"Speaking of the baby, when is he coming home? I'm not trying to get pushed out the window."

"He's with Drew all weekend." She looked around the room. "This was fun, I could get used to this."

"To what?"

"You are the perfect size for me." I waited for her to explain what she meant. "Some guys are too big! They get carried away and it's like they're trying to give you a hysterectomy. You can get as buck wild as you want and I like the feeling of not holding back for fear of being broken in half."

"How many guys have you been with?"

"More than you for sure? You really need me to count?"

"Um!"

"Get over it, cause I'm not going there with you. Just know that last night you tasted the fruits of all of my practice. I've been with a lot before you, and I'll be with a lot after you." My phone rang again. "She's going to be mad at you!"

I dreaded answering that phone. "You and Pretty Ricky going to get back together?"

"Maybe later on down the road. He's always going to come back to me. I was his first, I have that affect on him."

|Chapter 5 When Fat Comes Back

My father opened the door with his very casual smile. When he saw the cake he smiled really big. "Well hello Tracy! Good to see you. I already know him." He gestured towards me.

My stepmom was excitedly waiting as well. "It's about time you two got here!"

Tracy looked horrified, "are we late? Steve said 3:30."

Distorted Mirrors

It was about 3:15 when we got out of the car. My stepmom hugged Tracy, "we've been anxious for you to get here. Come in, come in."

My father took the cake to the kitchen, and then we sat in the family room drinking wine and talking. At the dinner table my stepmom started looking disappointed but she was trying to suck it up. When it was time for the cake Tracy asked for a tiny sliver. Where my parents cut modest pieces then they went back for seconds. "Tracy this German chocolate cake is melt in your mouth delicious!" My stepmom said enjoying her bite.

"I'm glad you like it. I don't bake too much anymore."

"Oh honey you're fine, you can let go every once in awhile. You've done a good job of keeping your weight down. Steve you better not give my girl no mess either."

"It's her choice, I don't stop her from baking."

My dad looked frustrated which means he was holding back, and now it was coming out. "Where's her ring? Son you keep dragging your feet and you're going to miss out."

"I honestly thought at some point you were going to reveal that you were getting married." My stepmom chimed in.

"I'm not getting married no time soon, I'm too young."

"How young do you think you are? I had three kids and a wife by your age."

"Yes and you were divorced not too long after. I'm only getting married once."

"Time is ticking." My stepmom said.

The mood was killed, so Tracy and I left not too long after. Tracy was holding her breath, here we go! "Time is ticking you know." She said lowly.

"We haven't been back together long enough to know."

"It's been over a year and we're not strangers."

"So this was the plan, pressure Steve night?"

"No, but it's like they were speaking my thoughts."

"You know better than to ever think you could live without me. I love you, you love me. We're going to be together stop the nonsense." Tracy drove silently. "Give me a little more time. I want to do this right."

****

I was walking slowly to the Bart station, trying to decide which way I was going. Tracy the QUEEN OF ALL DRAMA Queens has been working my nerves. Acting all sad and depressed cause I've stood her up a few times. Kamony too, but that doesn't phase me none. Topaz and I got into it real bad one night. He gone try to say if Tracy was unhappy that meant I wasn't doing my job as a man. I'm so sick of him and his philosophies about my life. Like he don't know some women are just depressed and it don't matter how good a man is to them, that woman isn't going to be happy because of the things going on in her life. He tried to say that wasn't the case with Tracy. So I pointed out her weight loss, and he pointed out that another man got that going for me, I just reaped the benefits. That's when I cursed him out real bad. We almost came to blows cause I went in so badly on him. Topaz and I have been best friends since we graduated from high school. He brought up every possible child I could have and all the people who've come here looking for me. It pissed me off that this was the first time I was hearing about it. I needed to move out, but where was I going to go? If I moved in with Tracy, she would definitely put pressure on me to marry her. With Toya on the roster I know I'm not ready to marry anybody. I could move in with Kamony, which might even buy me some time until I figure out my next move. I only go over Toya's when I know her son isn't there. I'm not trying to mess up anything with Pretty Ricky for her. Shoot it serves me well for him to take care of her like he does.

"Why you walking so slow?" Shirley said walking along side of me.

"Hey Ms. Shirley." I gave her a hug. She held on to me longer than I thought she should've but it's whatever. "What are you doing still out here?"

"I had to kick in a little over time. How are things?" She smiled at me.

"Ok." I figured Tracy told her something for her to be fishing like she is.

"You two were doing so well, I thought for sure you were the next ones to get married."

"Married? I'm too young to be thinking about marriage right now. But I do feel like I need to step up or I might lose her. She's not happy right now is she?" I needed to know whatever she's told this woman. Shirley was so happy to have someone listen to her she'd tell me everything I wanted to know.

"I'm not going to lie to you, you should know she's not happy. She feels like you're pulling away from her. She doesn't know what she's done to make you distance yourself." I sighed, "have you eaten?"

"No, but I'm on my way home." I said.

"Let's get something to eat." When I hesitated, "my treat. Come on,

I've got to get you two back together."

We went to the restaurant she likes, she spilled everything. I couldn't believe Tracy told her so much about our business. How things have changed and sometimes I'm not in the mood. My mood changes, everything. "I'm just stressed beyond belief. I just got some devastating news and I don't know how to tell her. I mean I know she's going to freak out on me, she might even run." Shirley's eyes got big as she leaned in. "I just found out I have a daughter. I have to pay $500 a month in child support and I can't afford that. This is my mess that I created while Tracy and I weren't together. I can't expect her to pay for a child that isn't hers. We can't get married."

Shirley sat back looking stressed. "Tracy would definitely freak out."

"What am I supposed to do Ms. Shirley? I don't make money like both of you do. Tracy deserves better than me. Maybe I should try my hand at selling to earn a little extra money."

"Street prescriptions?" She leaned in with big eyes. "You can't be that desperate, there has to be something that you could do legally?"

"Everything else will interfere with the time I need for Tracy and my daughter."

"But it's illegal."

"Look I know weed will sell. I can't be hustling no stolen merchandise. For one it might not sell and the risk is worse if I get caught with stolen stuff verses a little weed on a first offense."

"You go to jail and Tracy will be done with you. She will not date a Street Doctor. She still has her Christian morals you know." She was quiet for a minute. "How about I give you the money, just until you think of something you can do legally."

"How?"

"Meet me for dinner on the first each month and I'll give you money in cash that way it can't be tracked back to me. You can deposit it, and then write your baby momma a check. Or pay it to the courts, however you have it set up."

"Why would you do that for me? For us?"

"I love Tracy like a daughter, and I don't want to see her hurt anymore. I want you two to finally get married and be done with all the dumbness."

This idiot is too easy! "Oh thank you Ms. Shirley!"

Then my phone rang. It was Tracy she was drunk off her butt. She asked me to come pick her up cause she was too tipsy to drive. She said they were going to take cabs home but the drinking bill got out of control. I ran to the Bart station, caught a train, got to my car and then drove to Tracy and Marie. Her cousin was very cute and silly just like Tracy, they kept laughing then crying. It was driving me CRAZY! I wasn't in the mood for this scene. All the way to Tracy's place I was going off, this was ridiculous. She needed to stop drinking so much cause she was adding unnecessary calories to her diet. Tracy started crying and accusing me of not loving her anymore. She said we were moving backwards instead of moving forward. She mumbled that maybe we should just cut our losses now before it was too late. Panic flashed through my entire body hearing her say that in her drunken state means that she's only thought about it constantly when she's sober. I grabbed her, "you can't leave me! I will kill you! Do you understand me?" My words weren't registering with her. Last time I said something like that she got scared and freaked out. I kissed her; I needed her to feel me. Tracy was completely gone. I took her, completely raw. I pushed her legs back and plunged in as deep as I could. She didn't have her thing in and I was winning. Just in case she remembered my awesome moves last night I took the garbage out so she couldn't freak out. I hoped I did what I needed to do. Cause once she remembers she's going to freak out guaranteed.

****

"I'm going to get you. Roar! Roar!" I chased Richele around the park as she laughed and laughed. Toya was on the phone with her new friend. Some guy she met, that I could care less about. As much as she pants after me, I don't care what she does.

Toya stormed over, I got to be home by 7, Drew's bringing the baby home at 8." She looked mad.

"Why are you mad? You barely have the baby."

"He just wants to stick me with the baby so he can go out and meet somebody new. Why I got to be stuck with him? He don't want him, what makes him think that I would?"

"UM! Cause you're his mother." I pushed Richele higher in the swing.

"If this guy doesn't pan out, I think we should move."

"What?"

"Maybe I could try my luck in New York, or Atlanta, or some place where I can catch a big fish."

"That doesn't explain why I have to go."

She looked at me, no jokes in her face. "You go where I go, I need you."

I scratched my head, "um... You got something you want to tell me?"

"Don't go getting big headed." Then she folded her arms and walked away from us.

I kept pushing Richele and I was confused as all get out. She was leaning against my car watching us. Richele was no longer laughing or having a good time. So we cut our park time short and we went back to Kamony's place. Toya said she wanted to meet my baby momma. When Kamony answered the door her eyes went straight to Toya and then she stopped smiling. "Who is she?"

"This is my cousin Toya. Toya this is the baby momma."

"Cousin? How come I never heard of no Toya?"

"Don't worry about it, you know who I am now." Toya shot at her.

"She wants to take my daddy away!" Richele cried.

If looks could kill, "what happened baby?" Kamony took Richele's jacket off of her.

"She said she wants my daddy to go with her."

"What kind of family member takes a man away from his child?"

"The realistic kind. You know you not hurting for no $200 a month. That's chump change."

Kamony stared at Toya for a minute. "Baby, go in your room and turn your movie on. I need to talk to this *cousin* of yours."

"Ok, bye daddy. Please don't go. Please!" Richele said one last time.

I gave her a kiss on the forehead then I watched both of them size each other up. "BULL! This ain't none of your cousin! There's not a drop of your blood running through her veins."

Toya smiled, "you're so sure?"

"I'd bet my life on it." Kamony moved closer, "I know exactly what kind of female you are. Steve is mine! We have a family and he's not going anywhere with you. I'll make his life so crazy, you'll want to release him to the wild." Kamony moved closer again.

"Oh so you want to fight." Toya opened her arms to tell Kamony to come on. "I'm a kick your butt, and I'm taking your man."

"Wait a minute! Wait a minute! Nobody's taking me nowhere. I don't belong to neither one of you. You both need to calm down." Both of them turned on me and started fussing. I turned on my heels and walked out the door. Toya ran up on me, she hit me in the back of my head and I lost it. I grabbed her and snatched her up by her shirt. I flung her body into my car. Toya didn't even look scared; Kamony's eyes on the other hand were big as she watched from the doorway. "Don't you ever put your hands on me. If you hit me I will hit you back! Do you understand?"

Toya smiled, "Steve. Your momma issues are showing. You can't handle a little tap on the back of your head. You would think working out would make you tougher." She almost giggled.

I was still gripping her clothes pushing her into the car. "You would think being a hoe you'd know better than to fall in love with the guy you're gaming."

Toya's smile dropped and she started crying immediately. "No I didn't!"

I looked at Kamony, "go back inside. I'm sorry, and I'll call you later."

Kamony smiled widely as she did as she was told.

Distorted Mirrors

****

I blinked my eyes, nope I'm seeing correctly. Tracy has gained a little weight. I was about to be irritated and then I looked at the calendar. I hadn't been on lock down at all this month. Tracy refuses to open her legs on her period. Sometimes I mess with her just for the joy of seeing her freak out about it. That girl is so worried about smells and being clean, one time I almost got her in the bathtub. Then she remembered she didn't have that thing in. Then she thought of the mess and she refused to go through with it. Well that song and dance hasn't happened yet. Maybe it was getting ready to happen and that's why she was slightly going the wrong way. Her moods have been impossible though. I know I started this, but now I'm rethinking it. I'm not ready for this to happen. I like our setup exactly as it is. I'm the baby, what if she has a boy? She won't need me anymore! I told myself to calm down and to wait it out. Everything will be fine.

****

I was sleep when I heard Tracy grunt in the bathroom. I looked at the clock and it was still somewhat early. I laid there for a minute trying to figure out what that crazy girl could be doing in that bathroom. Then she came and tried to quietly slip back into bed. "What's wrong?"

"Nothing," she said as she got back in the bed. I watched the drama queen's face like it would reveal what I already knew in the back of my mind. She was just catching on, but I already knew. I could feel it. She went back to sleep and I laid there trying to calm my heart down. I got up and went to the bathroom. I washed my hands and as I was about to walk out the bathroom I noticed the cup in her garbage. I moved the cup and there were pregnancy test in the garbage. I felt so betrayed and I immediately felt angry. I'm her baby, she can't have a baby. I laid there trying to calm myself as she slept. My mind kept bouncing between waiting to flip out and being excited. This is the first time I've ever done this on purpose. If she had to have a baby I wanted a little girl. I need to be the King of my castle; I didn't need some young prince competing with me for first place. But then it didn't matter what she had, she was going to be overly concerned with that baby and it would take up all of my time. When would she have time for me? And don't get me started on the weight gain! Toya learned that you don't snap your fingers and pop back into place. She's still struggling and I consider her someone who's concerned with her appearance. I was screaming at Tracy in my mind when she opened her eyes. "Stop staring at me."

"Tracy you know I don't want any kids right now right?"

She sucked her teeth, "yes."

"So when were you going to tell me about the test?" I tried to hold back my wrath.

"What test?" She turned over with her shoulders hunched like she was trying to keep it together.

"I thought I could at least trust you to be on the same page as me."

What?" She sound like she didn't understand.

"Are you trying to trap me?" This is still her fault.

"What?" Now she's playing dumb.

She knows my financial situation, I can't afford a child. "Why every time you take a chance and try to trust someone stuff like this gotta happen. I will not marry you!"

I could hear her tears. "What are you talking about?"

"I don't have time for this. I saw your test in the garbage. I wondered why you were making so much noise in there. I'm not ready to be a father, so let's be clear on how we're gonna proceed."

"Trapping you???? You????" She tried to look confused as if she didn't know what I was saying.

That did it I went completely off. I told her she was a scheming, plotting, evil female like all the rest, she was stupid for even trying to trap me, her momma should've taught her how to catch a real man by cooking and cleaning and being a supportive partner. I didn't let up because she was crying. I kept going and going. Eventually I got up and left, I was so annoyed. I went to Kamony's place where she was just happy that I was there. There were no hassles about anything.

****

Every time I think about her being pregnant I get mad. She was going to get heck of fat now! She was going to lay down and eat cause she's "*depressed*". Depression is such a cop out. *Oh she doesn't feel well, her world is coming to an end cause Steve is mad at her*. She needs to love herself, shoot. If she don't love herself what am I supposed to do with her? Every time I talk to her, she's crying and falling apart. Trying to make me feel guilty, like I'm wrong or something. I want to hold her and apologize, but she won't let me come over which makes me mad all over again.

Shirley was eyeing me as she walked towards me. Great! Now this old lady going to be tripping. "Hey Ms. Shirley." I stood to hug her.

"I'm hearing things, what's going on?"

"Tracy's pregnant and losing her mind."

"Why isn't the baby bringing you two together? I'm so confused."

"She took the test and started freaking out. She kicked me out of

Carey Anderson

her place, when I came back to talk to her she threatened to call the police on me. She keeps picking fights with me, she's being unreasonable."

She stared at me for a minute. "I know she's emotional, but isn't that one of the things you love about her?"

"Not when she uses it against me. You haven't told her about my daughter have you?"

Shirley looked surprised, she touched my chin. "Of course not. I would never betray you like that." Then she handed me the envelope. "I'm on your side."

****

We were laughing and catching our breaths. Toya was kissing all over me. "I love kissing you." Then she nuzzled her head into my chest. "Um, Steve why do you have stubble on your chest?"

"Tracy likes smooth skin so I used to nair the hair off. But since she's acting like such a baby I don't feel like keeping up with it."

She licked my chest, "I accept you as you are. Let it grow in, the fat girl has been overthrown."

"I love her Toya," I said honestly. "We're getting back together. Tracy doesn't deserve to raise my kid alone. Unless it's a boy, I'm not dealing with that."

"What's wrong with boys?"

"He's going to be competing with me for her heart. I'm not trying to go to jail for killing a kid."

"So that's why you don't come around when I have the baby?"

"Dang Skippy!"

She was quiet for a minute. "Madam Creole tried to reach out to my father to tell him he was a grandfather."

"That was nice of her."

"Every thing is a game with her. She was trying to get some money. He told her I wasn't his daughter. When she tried to argue he told her I was his ex-bestfriend's kid. He told her the guy confessed that he slept with her. She came over here and beat me up like I was responsible for who she opened her legs to."

I looked at her like she could've been putting me on. "Why did you have the baby?"

"I thought Drew was going to marry me. I wanted a family with him. I thought he'd be moved to marry me when he found out it was a boy. I had to get out of her house. The things she says to me..." She looked off, "who talks to their child like that? I never thought Drew would leave me hanging. Until that fat girl his heart has always been with me. I hate her so much!"

"So is all this with me and you pay back for Pretty Ricky?"

"It was at first." She backed away from me. I pulled her back; I had her against the ropes. "No!"

"Tell me!"

"No!"

"Toya, tell me." I grabbed a fist full of her hair. I pulled her down on the bed, "tell me!"

"No! You can work the fat girl. I know you! I am you!"

I smiled, "what does that mean?"

"You get off on hearing someone genuinely profess their love for you. You're in love with the fat girl and it makes you feel vulnerable. So you find fault with everything about her. I did the same thing to Drew. Just like I thought he was going to marry me, you're dumb enough to think she isn't fed up with you right now. When a woman is pregnant normally she wants to be with the father. She needs to feel loved. She's shut you out cause you keep hurting her like I've done to Drew."

"You're tripping Tracy is going to call me like she always has."

"You said your last argument was different. She was done with you."

I was about to get mad, and then I smiled. "You're trying to change the subject. Tell me."

She started kissing me; I'm supposed to see Kamony later on. Toya's sucking me dry, on purpose. Right when she was climaxing I made her admit it. She surrendered and admitted that she loves me. I love her too, but we both know it's not the same.

|Chapter 6 Like A Thief In The Night

I kept looking at the door. I was at the right apartment? "Can I help you?" A middle aged cat asked me as he sat down his box."

"Excuse me." Two guys said moving a big bookshelf into the apartment.

There was nothing seen from the doorway that said Tracy ever lived here. At this moment I regret never accepting her invitations out. At least then I'd know where to find her. "Tracy Thomas lives here?"

The guy looked at me like I was an idiot. "No, my lease begins today. Check with the office."

"Thanks," I hurried down to the leasing office as I quickly tried to think of a sob story to get me in their hearts and get a forwarding address.

I walked into the lobby and it still smells brand new in there. A male leasing agent was trying to handle a disgruntled tenant professionally. Then a girl came out the back, inside I sang YES! as she smiled at me. "May I help you?"

I pointed with my thumb behind me. "I'm desperate, there's a guy moving into my sister's apartment. We have a family emergency and I'm at a loss."

Her eyes took me in as she sized me up. I tried to keep the telltale signs that I was lying through my teeth to myself. "Why don't you call her?"

I wanted to scream at her that I tried that first. I took out my phone, "this is a new phone I lost all of my contacts." She didn't believe me. Now I wished I could've started over with the guy. At least maybe with him I could've had a brotha to brotha level conversation.

"Our tenant's information is confidential."

"I understand that, but this is a family emergency." I was desperate and my chest started to ache.

"I understand that but there's nothing I can do." She said like it's irrelevant.

"Please help me, I'm desperate! You're my only hope." I pleaded.

She looked right through me. "Privacy Act! Sorry, I can't help you." Then she turned and walked back in the office and shut the door behind her to show this conversation was over. The guy and the tenant watched me. I took a step in the direction of the office and the guy stood up quickly. He said I couldn't go back there unless I was invited. The tenant had her phone out threatening to call the police if I didn't leave.

I turned and walked out, it felt like lightning was striking my soul. How could Tracy abandon me like this? I started breathing heavy and labored. She left me? She really left? I started to take another step and I felt dizzy and out of control. I told myself to get a grip, now I was acting like Tracy. "You alright man?" The guy came out.

"Yeah, I need a minute."

"Truth?"

I shrugged, "truth." I shook my head. Everybody wants the truth. "She's pregnant with my kid and she packed up in the middle of the night and ran away. Who does that?"

"A woman who's trying to protect herself and her child. You've got some serious anger issues, you need to check that before it gets you in trouble."

"With all of this... I'm gone. She did this to hurt me, what did I ever do to deserve this. I love her?"

"You ever hit her?"

"Never! I said I love her."

"Were you cruel?"

"I wasn't always nice if that's what you mean." I shook my head, "I never thought she'd leave me. She didn't even say goodbye, she just left." I felt so empty. "Thanks, I'm good." Then I walked away.

I drove on autopilot to my place. When I walked in the door Topaz looked like he was on his way out. "It's about time you showed up.

I've been waiting and waiting for months. I'm moving out; I already put in the thirty-day notice. You got two weeks." He started to walk towards the door then he stopped and actually looked at me. "Tracy finally kicked you to the curb for real didn't she?" I didn't speak, I looked at him. "You don't listen, I warned you." He shook his head then he walked out.

****

"If you don't stop acting like a girl, keep carrying on like you have been and you're going to lose your job too." Toya said walking around my room picking up clothes and cleaning my room. "Good riddance, now you can be free to love me with her out of the way."

"That's big talk for the woman who's still in love with her baby daddy."

"That might've hurt if I wasn't expecting you to say it." She stuck her tongue at me.

Her comfort in Tracy being gone was bothering me. I needed to bring her down to my level. "What are you doing?"

"Cleaning up, so we'll know what to pack and what not to pack."

"Oh, you know how to clean cause your place is spotless huh?"

"You could eat off the floors." She smiled with pride.

"In every room but your son's room."

She started moving faster, "I don't know what you're talking about."

"You always keep his door closed, so I opened it out of curiosity. The smell was the first thing to hit me in the nose. You ain't got no sheets on his crib, clothes everywhere. I thought I opened a door to another dimension. How can your son's room be a pigsty but the rest of the house be immaculate? Your son who can't do nothing about it, has to live in that disgusting room?"

Toya stood there staring at me tapping her foot like that was the only thing keeping her calm. She looked like she said, "forget it." She dropped the basket and charged me on the bed. "YOU'RE MAD BECAUSE SHE LEFT YOU! DON'T TURN ON ME! I AM THE ONLY PERSON YOU'VE GOT! YOU'RE ALL I GOT, DON'T MAKE ME HATE YOU!" She said as she tried to hit me, kick me, scratch me, and bite me. You name it, she was coming after me.

"Alright! Alright! Calm down!" I backed up off the bed.

Toya walked to her purse and got a hair thingy out of it. She smoothed out her hair and then she put it up in a bun on the top of her head. Then she looked at me with cold calculating eyes. "This is what you're going to do. Go move in with your baby momma. When the baby is gone you can come hang out with me. We've got to think of a plan B meanwhile." Her voice was too calm and scary almost.

"You think she's going to let me?"

"Of course she will, she's too dumb not to. Don't ask just go and don't leave." Then she tilted her head at me. "Who's the old lady?"

"What old lady?" I was looking around the room at my stuff.

"The old lady in the city."

I rolled my eyes, "I don't know who you're talking about."

She picked up my drinking glass off the floor and threw it at my head. It conked me in the temple, and bounced into the wall. It shattered. As I yelled in pain, "don't try to play me. I was being nice to you, but you want me to unleash the crazy I see."

I felt warmth on my face, she cut me. I ran over the bed as she reached in her purse again. She pulled out a inhaler looking tube. "Stay back Steve or I will Mace your behind!" I moved another inch, "don't tempt me! I'm not playing with you."

I acted like I was going to walk away and then I grabbed her arm which made her hold the bottle up. She sprayed and I turned my head. I felt every drop as it hit my skin. I screamed in pain as I threw Toya on the bed. "Oh my God! Did you really just mace me?" She dropped the container and she rushed to the bathroom to wash her hands that I assume were on fire.

Topaz was standing in the hallway with more boxes for his room. He had a smirk, shocked, grin on his face. "Oh Steve, she's so FINE!" He laughed sarcastically, shaking his head as he went in his room.

I stripped in the bathroom and stood under the water. My skin was raw where she pepper-sprayed me. When I came out of the bathroom with my clothes in my hands she was rubbing lotion on her hands and laughing. "Why would you pepper spray me?"

"Don't mess with me Steve. I'm trying to help you. I'm not the one who's homeless. Who's the old lady?"

"Tracy's coworker, she puts money in my pockets."

"How she do that?"

"At the end of the month, she gives me an envelope with cash in it to pay my child support."

Toya was thinking, "you sleeping with her?"

She insulted me, "NO!"

"Listen, I think you should."

I grimaced, "come again?"

"She's paying you like she's putting you on layaway. Why should she care about your kid? Your daughter ain't nothing to her. She's trying to show you she cares about you on the under."

I made a wounded sound, "sleep with an old lady?"

"Pussy is pussy Steve."

"Yeah but that's old and dried up stuff."

"Get creative, besides women do it all the time. Like those young girls actually love those old rich men? Please, they open their legs for a place to stay and money to spend. Find out where she lives, check out her place." I wasn't speaking I was thinking. "How you meet her?" She eyed me.

"I met her one day on lunch. And the rest... lunch, became dinners, dinners became talking. The next thing I know she volunteers to help me out."

"She's paying the whole time?"

"Yep!"

"She's going to be our plan B, turned A."

****

Kamony was so happy to have me in the house. The first week I was there, she took Richele to daycare, and then she worked from home. So she saw me off properly and then she greeted me when I came home. It was actually kind of cool at first. Then she started tripping about me coming home late from my dinner with Shirley. I told her I was working late and that was all that mattered really. Then she started asking me to pick Richele up from school. She wanted me to fix dinner, which I did one time. It wasn't spectacular but I was proud of my dish.

Then she started nagging me about coming home late or the next day, or at the end of the weekend from Toya's. Kamony assumed I was still seeing Tracy. She wasn't crazy enough to disrespect her in my face but you could see it in everything she did. Yeah, this wasn't going to work. I needed my own spot, not more roommates in my business. Something I could afford. Toya and I argued about it, cause she wanted me to concentrate on saving my money in case she decides we need to move away. Saving is not something I inherited from my father. My sister is more like him when it comes to that. I spend until it's gone. I'm not giving a red cent to Toya to hold for me. I could give money to Tracy and know she wasn't going to spend it. The thought of her threw me backwards. I wondered if she was showing yet, how far a long was she? When she'd find out what she's having.

I was inputting mortgage loan data on autopilot when the girl from the mailroom gave me an envelope with handwriting on it addressed to me. It was Tracy's handwriting. My mouth suddenly filled up with saliva as I turned the envelope over and over. Imagining her hand being on it a day or so ago. I figured this was her explanation about where she was, and she was waiting for some huge romantic gesture. I didn't care what it was I was going to do it. I used my letter opener to open the top of the letter. I could've sworn I smelled her peppermint scent pour out. When I saw the one sheet of paper I knew it wasn't good. Tracy's always longwinded trying to explain everything to me so I understand. I still have some of the old letters she wrote me, declaring her undying love. Those were at least two to three pages front and back. I unfolded the single sheet of paper and took a deep breath.

Dear Steve,

I'm sorry for being such a source of pain in your life. I thought you should know that I lost the baby. I didn't want you to think I was keeping the child that never was, away from you.

Have a good life,

Tracy

I turned the letter over like there had to be more. There was no return address, no apology! NOTHING! I started breathing hard again. I struggled to catch my breath. I walked away to the opposite end of our office floor where the empty offices were. Where Tracy and I made passionate love once shortly after we resumed our sexcapades. It can't be over! How could she do this to me?

****

"Ms. Shirley is it true? Did she lose my baby or is she that mad at me that she would lie to me?"

"Shirley, its just Shirley. I'm not that much older than you." She touched my arm. "She says she did. She's been off work, Becca our boss can't share what's going on with her."

"Can't you call her?"

She shrugged, "I don't have her new number yet. I think she's disconnected from everyone." She rubbed my arm, "I can't believe she wrote you a letter and mailed it. I had no idea that Tracy was such a coward. You deserve better than that." Then she opened her arms to hug me. As she released me she put her lips on my neck.

I acted like I didn't notice. "I'm in love with her, I've got to get her back." I meant every word.

"You don't think it may be time to move on?"

"Move on to what?" I was getting mad? "Move on to who? Can't nobody love me like she can! Nobody ever will! I'm alone in the middle of a crowd without her." I stood up, "you don't understand."

People were starting to look at us and she was getting embarrassed. "Steve calm down, I'm here to help you." I sat down, "what's wrong with you? Why are you so tightly wound up?"

I surprised myself with how upset I was about this whole thing. I had to switch gears. "I thought we were going to move in together. I put my notice in, we had a fight. When I go to make up she's gone like a thief in the night. You know how much money I don't make, I've had to move in with my baby momma." I sat back in my chair shaking my head as I looked at the table. "I'm happy to see my daughter every day, but her momma drives me crazy. I need Tracy back. I'm sorry for everything I said. I was freaking out. If she really lost the baby we could try again. I'll do whatever she wants."

"Even marriage?"

"Yes! Whatever it takes!"

Shirley looked disappointed, "but you're so young. Why does everyone have to get married? Tracy may think that's what she wants, but marriage makes anyone rethink life altogether. You've got plenty of time to get married."

"That's what everyone except Tracy and my parents think. In the end it matters to me what she thinks. I just need to talk to her. Please tell her to call me."

"What are you going to do meanwhile?"

"Suffer in the shadows, what can I do?"

"Move out," she smiled.

"Where am I supposed to go?"

"I got room you could stay with me."

"How would that work when Tracy and I get back together? She would hate you."

She hadn't thought of that. "I'll help you find a place."

"What?" I frowned, "no. You've done enough."

"Hush, I insist." She said as she put the envelope in my hand.

****

"You look very pretty." I smiled at Toya.

She smiled, "thank you. My mark is at three o'clock."

"My three or yours?"

"Duh! Mine." She smiled again as she played shy.

"Why doesn't he think you're with me?" I felt the jealousy rise in my throat.

"Because your friendly act with those females showed we weren't together." She smiled bigger, "hook, line, and sinker. He's coming." She looked at me, "be cool."

I looked over as mister Jet Magazine glided over in his suit. "How you all doing this evening?"

"Good," Toya smiled real big.

"How you doing brotha, I'm Will." He stuck his hand out to shake mine.

"Steve," I looked him up and down. "Nice suit."

"Thanks, you know how we all come down to the watering hole after a long day. What brings you out?"

"My cousin told me about the day he was having so I told him I would buy him a drink. Would you like to sit?"

"Is that ok with you?" Will watched me for an answer.

"Of course, matter of fact excuse me for a minute." I got up to give them space and check my attitude.

I went back to the ladies I was talking to earlier. I went back after awhile and Will seemed fine. We had an okay time; he bought our rounds of drinks. On the way to the Bart station I asked Toya if she liked him? She said he was square enough to serve his purpose.

****

BANG! BANG! "STEVE!" Toya yelled out.

I looked at the clock and it was just after nine. Kamony jumped, Richele was sleep on my couch. Kamony and I were about to get into it when Toya started banging. She's supposed to have her kid this weekend. I got up quickly, snatching open the door. "What's wrong?"

Toya had fighting clothes on and her hair in a bun. She was crying hard and her eyes were red. She completely disregarded Kamony. "I TOLD YOU! YOU DON'T KNOW A WOMAN'S HEART! YOU ARE SO STUPID! I CAUGHT THEM TOGETHER!"

I fell into the wall, "NO!"

"YES!" She said pacing the floor.

"NO!"

"Steve?" Kamony said with big eyes because I was becoming unglued.

"Kamony you gotta leave! I'm sorry, it sounds like I'm going to jail tonight!"

Kamony moved quickly and took sleeping Richele out to her car. I watched out my front window until they drove away. I closed my curtains then I looked at Toya. She was crying a heartbroken cry. "FORGET HIM! I GAVE HIM A SON! I SACRIFICED MY BODY FOR HIM! HOW'S HE GOING TO CHOOSE A FAT GIRL OVER ME?"

Her comment sent me over and it seemed like she knew it would. We started fighting. I threw her on the couch and she kicked me. We tore up my living room. Neither one of us hurting each other like we could've and wanted to. Everything I thought I knew about Tracy felt like a lie at this point. Toya's shirt was shredded and her bra was hanging off of her. Toya ripped my sweats, when she looked at me her angry eyes made me come alive. She jumped on me and connected us before I could grab a condom. Toya went for broke as if she was trying to get pregnant. I didn't fight it, it didn't matter anymore. As we laid there catching our breaths Toya started crying again. "I knew something was up. I could feel it in my bones. I went where I figured he would be."

"How did you get there?"

"Bus. We were arguing and that he/she tackled me to the ground. He walked away towards her with my son! MY SON!"

"What he/she? Who are you talking about?"

"The girl who thinks being a man is going to stop her from loving Drew!" Then she started mumbling. "Acting like I'm crazy and I don't know the truth! OH! I KNOW THE TRUTH! YOU CAN'T REPLACE ME!"

"You saw them together?"

"He was there, she was there... They were there together."

"You saw them together?" It felt like my heart was going to burst.

"Are you really going to play this game? He was there, she was there. I didn't need to see him with his tongue down her throat to know they were together."

"Was she pregnant?"

"Everything was happening so fast I didn't see."

No matter who tried to pop up in Tracy's life she's always chosen me. I just need to see her, to talk to her. Once I talk to her everything will be smoothed out.

|Chapter 7 Where There's A Will

We just finished working out in Toya's gym. She's been getting on my nerves cause she's stressed out about her place. Pretty Ricky is trying to get full custody of the kid she doesn't even want. She's more concerned with the money she's not going to be getting to pay for this place that she turned her nose up to at first. We've been hitting this gym pretty hard. Her anger and frustrations have helped better than any supplements ever could. We were fooling around in the gym. Covered in sweat and stickiness, I pulled back and told her we could wait until we got to her place. We walked out of the gym in all smiles. Toya ran into Will cause she was looking back at me. Her eyes got big, as she plastered on a smile. "Mom!" She said nervously, "what are you doing here?"

"You've been quiet lately so I decided to drop by. How come you didn't tell me you had a new boyfriend?"

Toya looked at me, "cause it's new."

"Who's here?" Her mother stuck her head in the door. Toya looked almost exactly like her mom, except Toya was dark chocolate and her mother was caramel almost yellow. Her hair was long too, but it was brown. She burned me with her eyes. "Who's that?"

I put my towel over my head and came around the corner. I pushed the towel back after I came around the corner where Will could see me. "Auntie it's me Steve." I smiled and gave her a kiss on her cheek.

"Oh right," she looked at Toya.

"Hey how you doing?" Will greeted me with a smile and a firm handshake. "Toya you've been hitting the gym hard these days."

Toya smiled, "you like?" She modeled her new form.

"I love!" He drooled.

"Steve's been training me, he motivates me to go even when I don't feel like going. His workouts are hard, but nothing I can't handle."

Madam Creole looked at me, "but you've been working out since you were..." She snapped her fingers.

"Since high school, so I've learned a few things."

"I need a workout routine too." She pointed her eyes at me.

Toya looked like she wanted to die. "Of course Auntie, anything for you." I mean what was I supposed to say?

Toya started walking towards the elevator, "what brings you over? Without calling might I add." She playfully hit him.

I turned my eyes while Madam Creole stared at me with hatred in her eyes. Whenever Will looked in our direction she would put on a fake smile. Will and Toya kissed and then she sent him off with a smile on his face. Toya didn't look at her mother as she hurried to the elevator. I stood next to Toya while her mother stared at us. She hit Toya in the shoulder as she told her to hurry up. Toya looked like a little kid who was about to get a whooping. The door barely closed as her mother went off. After she cursed both of us out she wanted answers. "Who are you?"

"Steve."

"He's my boyfriend mom." Toya admitted in defeat. I hadn't considered myself as her anything.

"What happened to Drew?" She screamed at Toya.

"He don't want me. He got his son and he's got the judge telling me he has custody. I'm losing my place."

Madam Creole started smacking Toya everywhere, "that's what your dumb behind get messing with that hustler's son. They're too basic for us anyways. Now what you going to do?"

"I've got Will, but it's too soon to move in with him."

"He got any money?"

"He's got a suit job, he's probably on the same level as Drew." Her mom started hitting her again. "He's the best I could do for now."

"Where are you going cause you can't come home, my new guy don't think I have any kids."

"But I'm grown." Toya cried.

She sucked her teeth, "he thinks I'm your age."

Toya didn't mean to but she started laughing over her tears. If I didn't know, they could've passed for sisters. Toya's laughter hurt her mother and she knew it. "Drew's mom could pass for his sister.

You wish!"

Madam Creole kept hitting Toya and she kept laughing at her to hurt her. I walked out the room into the kitchen. I filled my bottle with water. I drank and then I refilled, I wasn't even listening to them and their nonsense. I was going to miss this view of the Bay. I stared at the buildings and houses below. I wondered if she was down there somewhere thinking about me. Of course she was thinking about me. I know she's confused and over reacting as usual. I told myself to be patient and I will see her again. The thought of holding her again and feeling her love for me is what I hold onto. The hands on my chest pulled me back to reality. I looked down at the hands and jumped hard when they were too light brown to be Toya's. "Since you don't have a problem with being a side piece when you gonna come see momma?"

I swallowed, "uh. Gina? Why?" I took her hands off of me.

"Give me your phone." She said through clinched lips. Then she took my phone out of my pocket. She opened it and punched in her number. Then she called her phone. "Come see me when you're done here."

"Huh?"

She walked in my face, "you need to pay for my silence or I'll blow your cover with her boy toy. Can you afford to support yourself and Toya?" I looked at the floor, "like I thought."

"Mom?" Toya said in the entryway of the kitchen.

"Your boyfriend is coming to see me."

"Mom!" Toya exploded.

Madam Creole opened her phone and rattled off a number, "or I could call Will and tell him the truth."

"WHAT KIND OF MOTHER ARE YOU? WHO DOES THIS?"
Toya screamed out of frustration.

Madam Creole started laughing, "I'm not Amber that's for sure."
Then she kissed my lips. "Hurry up!" I didn't know what to say. I
was stuck like, *is this really happening?*

Toya stood there cursing her mother so badly all I could do was
stand there with my arms crossed. Is it bad that this is so wrong
that I was in? Toya's momma don't look like Shirley and I'm sure
they're about the same age. I didn't really care, but I knew it was
wrong so I waited to see how this was going to play out. They
exchanged swears back and forth then I heard Madam Creole tell
Toya we were now doing it in her bed. Toya picked up a knife as
she went off walking towards her mother. Madam Creole still hit
her in the face, which made her drop the knife, and then she
dropped her. She hit Toya so hard she had no choice but to fall.
Her mother kicked her a couple of times then she grabbed my hand
to tell me to come on. I didn't move, I looked to Toya to tell me
what to do. She cried as she told me to go. Madam Creole kissed
my salty neck and chest. When she pulled down my sweats she
looked at me standing there at attention. She looked at my face,
"are you hard?"

Irritated I said, "yes."

She scoffed at me, "what am I supposed to do with that? Little boy
please! Put your clothes back on!" Then she snatched the door
open. She screamed at Toya then she left.

Toya rushed in the room sobbing as she threw her arms around me.
She kept kissing my cheeks and my neck as an apology. We stood
there silently for a long time.

****

"So... She lives with you now?" Kamony was trying to pull her attitude back.

"It's temporary."

"What does Tracy think of your *cousin*? She better not be dumb enough to fall for this!"

I didn't like hearing Tracy's name in her mouth. "Shut up!"

"Why hasn't she asked to meet me? After all these years she has to know Richele has a momma."

"Shut up Kamony, I'm not in the mood for your mouth."

"If I don't shut up you gonna hit me again?"

Kamony was on my nerves today. I didn't hit her. I shook the mess out of her though. "I didn't hit you."

Kamony stared at me for a minute. "I love how you rewrite history. You came over mad about something with Tracy high as a kite. You..."

I cut her off; the memory came burning back to me. "Shut up!" I remembered now. I slapped the mess out of her for flapping her gums like she is right now. Toya and I were supposed to be spending the evening in when Will popped up. I didn't know what was going to come out of my mouth so I left. I was missing Tracy like crazy. The calm and peacefulness of her place. Laying my head in her softness as she ate it up and we watched a dumb chick flick that secretly amused me. No random guys popping up at her house, calling on her phone. She was all about me and what made me happy. Being high gave me a false sense of that feeling. Only I knew it wasn't real but I needed it. Toya provides me with understanding about the things I hid from Tracy, but that girl is crazy and she got it honestly. Her mom sends me naked pictures of herself followed with texts about how I'm too small to ride that roller coaster or something like that. Toya said she's exaggerating cause I'm not that small. She said I'm about average and her mother must be used to huge monsters. Anyways, I went to Kamony hoping to feel some sort of love from her, but she was nagging me. It felt like a dream when I slapped her. The shock and fear that spread across her face made me angry. Immediately she started apologizing. Next thing I know she's serving me up the best head I've ever had. "You act like I got pleasure out of that."

"You never apologized."

"I thought I was forgiven." I watched her eyes.

"I was scared, I needed you to calm down." Then she looked past me. "Who is she?"

I turned around to look Shannon dead in her face. My mouth dropped open, she was looking at me with so much hurt in her eyes. Her son was with her oblivious to the fact that I was there. I wanted to run away, he looked like me. She looked like she was debating then she approached us. The boy followed his mom, when he set his eyes on me it was like he knew without anyone saying anything. "Steve." She said with pain in her voice.

"Shannon."

"Who are you?" Kamony spit looking her up and down.

"I'm his mother." She pointed to her son. Kamony was about to say something like so what when she looked at the boy. "Baby," she turned towards her son. "This is your father."

"WHAT???" Kamony screamed making everyone look at our table. "I have his ONLY child!"

"Shannon you shouldn't bring him here telling him that without proof." I looked at the kid, he frowned at my words. "Your mother and I were never together."

That little bastard punched me! I didn't even see it coming.
Kamony gasped covering her mouth trying to pull back her
laughter. Shannon grabbed her son and struggled to pull him back.
"MY MOMMA AIN'T NO HOE! IF SHE SAYS ITS YOU, THEN
ITS YOU!"

I stood up, "IF SHE WASN'T A HOE YOUR REAL FATHER
WOULD BE IN YOUR LIFE AND WE WOULDN'T BE
HAVING THIS CONVERSATION RIGHT NOW!"

The boy cried angry tears as he tried to get around his mother. "IF I
EVER SEE YOU AGAIN, I'M GOING TO KILL YOU!"

One of the busboys helped drag the kid in his preteen body out of
the restaurant. Kamony was now crying, "you lied to me!" She
tried to catch her breath. "You may not care about your health, but
I care about mine." Then she stood up and walked out.

****

Toya was frustrated, she was trying to excite me and nothing was
working. The anger I projected on that kid, ran through him and
jumped on me. My mood was unshakable; I missed the one person
who made all this pain go away. "You're not even trying!" She
charged.

"I told you I'm tired."

"Lately you're always tired! Stop making me feel like this!"

"That just means more fun with Big Willie for you."

Toya threw herself around the bed. "He's not fun! He goes in
missionary and a minute and a half later he's done. I break more of
a sweat washing clothes."

I smiled, "it's that bad?"

"Yes, he better be happy he's cute and pays me."

"I'm fun then?"

"You're a blast, I can have fun with you and you don't hurt me."
She smiled.

It just came out, "I miss her!"

"Sometimes when you're sleep I wonder if I stab you just right if I
can stab her out of your brain. I mean I know her breast are big,
but does it matter that much?"

I laughed, "not physically. Emotionally, my world is crumpling
around me. She was good at helping me through even if she didn't
realize she did."

"Let's have a baby." She was staring at the ceiling.

That snapped me out of my trance. "WHAT?"

"I go see the baby and I feel nothing. It's not even like he's my kid.
All I see is his father. The face and eyes of a man who doesn't love
me anymore. We are in our version of love and it's so perfect. You
see me and I see you. I want us forever Steve. Even if you and the
fat girl get back together, nothing will change what we have.
Nothing changes us right now."

"Except that I can't afford nor do I want a baby right now."

She kissed my neck, "it's not your baby. It'll be mine. Please
Steve!"

"Yeah until you got to feed and clothe it."

"Big Willie's gonna pay. He's even going to marry me."

"That's what you said last time." I laughed.

"I'm not blinded by love with him this time. Will is too easy, and so in love with me. Please Steve," she started massaging me.

It was different knowing that I was willingly giving her life. It was even better than the night I got Tracy on purpose.

****

Toya screamed from the bathroom, "ARE YOU SURE YOU'RE NOT SHOOTING BLANKS?"

"My sperm don't want to create your demon spawn that's all. Stop trying to force it. It will happen when it's time."

"These test are supposed to be able to tell you right away. Like days after."

She walked into the living room gesturing with her hands, I pulled her into my lap and I kissed her. "This is weird."

She smiled, "I know but I want it. Give Toya what she wants and she'll give you what you want."

"I've already had you in every way possible."

She raised her eyebrows, "not every way."

The room fell silent as I took in what she was offering me. I swallowed air, "you're in to that?"

"I'm into anything that will satisfy my man and make him think about me all day. Give me a baby and it's on!"

I moved her to the couch and I went to the bathroom. "You're using generic, this won't do. You need name brand quality results. I'll go to the store." Toya giggled, "if I can prove you're pregnant today, we can do it tonight?"

"Well, well, well!" She stuck her butt out, "aren't you eager." She smiled seductively at me. "As soon as you prove I'm pregnant, you can have me ANY WAY YOU WANT ME!"

I jumped around, "this is the first time I..." I couldn't even finish the statement cause I knew it was a lie. I held on to my smile for dear life. I hurried out the door. I sat in the parking lot of the drug store. I ran my hand over my face, what was I doing? How is a baby a fair exchange for back door exploring? Toya say she loves me, but I think she's still rebounding from Pretty Ricky. Heaven knows I'm rebounding from Tracy. I needed to smoke to get out of my own head. Suddenly I didn't care about going in this store anymore. As if she could hear my hesitation my phone rang it was Toya. She wanted to know what brands I was looking at. I went inside and got the test. I saw the brand Tracy had in the trash that fateful morning. I knew to skip those, we discussed the other options and I came home with three different ones. Toya was all ready to go, and I told her it's only been three weeks and to wait one more week. Tonight I just wanted to smoke and relax. She didn't like my answer; I got high before her bratty ways drove me crazy.

A couple of days later she took the test and they all said positive. We celebrated for a day, and then she went back to Will's place. She got him so drunk he didn't remember whether they slept together or not. She waited a few weeks then she told him she missed her period. Will's excitement about the baby caught her off guard. He didn't ask her if she was going to keep the baby or even consider an abortion. She said Pretty Ricky never wanted her to have any of the abortions she's had. She said the last one she had; she figures he knew the baby wasn't his. He was willing to walk away from his girlfriend that he was serious about to save the baby. She started crying saying she didn't know how to be now that he doesn't care about her. She said there's no love in his eyes when he looks at her. No kindness or tenderness in his tone when he talks to her. She said he talks to her like she works for him, he's very direct. She said she's not in his heart anymore and that hurts her. I understood. She said Will's blind love for her is a lot like Pretty Ricky's used to be especially in the beginning. I asked her if she felt bad for tricking Will. She looked in my eyes with seriousness and evilness in hers, and then she said NO!

|Chapter 8 Stepping in the building and I'm feeling myself

"Why are you avoiding me?" I stood on Kamony's porch trying to understand what was going on.

She came out the door and folded her arms. "How many kids do you have?"

I backed up, "where is this coming from?"

"Shannon," hearing her name made my insides turn. "She was still outside when I left. Her son was still trying to get back inside to get to you. The poor girl sweated her hair out exhausting herself to restrain him. I mean you look the little boy in the face and you see it clear as day. Just like I knew Richele was your child, I know this child is your son." She exhaled, "so I told them about Richele." I took another step backwards. "Turns out there's one more according to Shannon. She said they keep in contact to keep the kids together." Kamony took a step forward, "how many women have you had unprotected sex with? How many times did I jeopardize my life just to satisfy you, or to be satisfied? And you just let me... You got a death wish or something? You should be happy that all they or you got was pregnant. HIV is real, and I'm not trying to die even if you are."

"You're judging me? How you going to pin some kids I don't know on me?"

"Shannon's son is your son. I haven't met the other one."

"Since when you care about another woman's interaction with me? You've been trying to take me from Tracy all these years. You even got pregnant on purpose."

"I didn't know it was your routine to raw dog random females."

"So you called me over and I never covered up? That's what you think of me. How long had we been messing around before there was nothing between us?"

"Yes, but..."

I cut her off, "you don't care! Can you stop with this act? Did Shannon get in your head? You don't even know her and you jumping on the bandwagon. Why? Because her kid looks like me? You think she wants to be your friend, you all going to create some kind of support group against me? Shannon likes to try to manipulate people. She'll play nice with you to get to me. Next thing you know she's asking how you get child support. Then she's taking me to court, even though I know that kid's not mine let's say for argument that he is mine. You know I don't have no money. The little $200 you whine about will be cut even smaller and her kid is older than ours. First-born rights would shift and now you're only getting $50 a month. Be stupid and team up with them if you want to."

Kamony was quiet holding herself and rocking. "Steve do you love me at all? What has all of this been?"

"Kamony don't do this."

She burned me with her eyes. "Do what?"

"How did you think a love connection was supposed to come out of the way we hooked up? I'll admit that I got caught up with protecting the both of us from pregnancy."

159

"Does Tracy know about me?"

"To an extent."

"When is she going to meet Richele?"

"Never for as much as I can control it."

"Never?"

"She's focused on the baby right now. She...."

"SHE HAD A BABY!!!" She screamed then she walked inside and slammed the door.

She didn't let me finish, although I don't know what I was going to say next. I laughed to myself Kamony is forever competing with Tracy and I don't know why. Then I thought about it, they all were. It's like they couldn't believe that I love Tracy as if they are supposed to be superior choices. All they can comment about on Tracy was her size. They never got to know her, to know how amazing she is. Especially Kamony and Toya, they manipulate people and treat them like they're supposed to be valued for being pretty. I do value them, but once my erection has been satisfied I'm still longing. I guess there is more to a woman than just her size, and at this moment I'm hoping Tracy hasn't blown back up. But I know how she is when she's missing me. She's sad, and depressed. She's probably blown back up to her old size, but I tell you I would welcome the warmth of her full figured size right now. I want to put my hands in her hair and live in her peppermint smell. Kamony can be mad all she wants; I know she's going to be calling me again. It's only a matter of time.

****

"STEVE! GET HER OUT OF MY HOUSE!" My stepmom yelled in a tone that made the hairs on the back of my neck standup.

"All I was saying is that maybe if you had kids of your own you'd..."

"Little girl! If you know what's good for you, you'll get your tail up and walk out that door. Don't ever come back to my house. Matter of fact I better not find out you were down the street from my place or else I'm not responsible for what happens to you!" My father threatened.

"Can everybody calm down for a second?" I yelled.

"WE'LL BE CALM WHEN YOU LEAVE!" My stepmom yelled as she got out of her chair.

Toya smiled wickedly, "honey we didn't get a chance to tell them about the baby."

I froze, and then my stepmom came after me. "NO YOU DIDN'T! WHERE'S TRACY?"

I ran, "probably sitting in the corner somewhere stuffing her face. Steve upgraded to a better make and model. Now we're having a baby, deal with it!" Toya spit.

"Let's go!" I told Toya.

We were almost to the car when my father came out, I told Toya to get in and to stay in. Then I met my father half way. "Son please tell me she's not carrying my grandchild?" His eyes pleaded with me to say it was a lie.

"It's complicated."

"What happened to Tracy?"

I deflated, "she left me."

"What did you do?"

"I got her pregnant then she left me."

"You acted ugly?" I looked away, "you're talking to me. I had three kids; you think it was music to my ears when your stepmom told me she was pregnant. I took care of business immediately to avoid any more mishaps. It's not like I knew she'd lose the baby. I regretted every horrible thing I said."

"Tracy sent a letter that she miscarried, but I don't believe it. I need to talk to her."

"She probably left you because of that one over there." He nodded towards the car.

"I didn't..."

He cut me off, "don't. I'm your father, I know you. That child is pure evil, I don't know how you got it up."

"This is the most honest relationship I've had."

"That doesn't make it right. Do me a favor, introduce her to your mother, and keep her away from me. I don't ever want to see her again." He hugged me then he walked away.

When I got in the car Toya smiled at me, "nice parents."

It was coming and I couldn't stop it, before I could tell myself not to, I slapped the mess out of her. Shock, surprise, and evilness flashed across Toya's face in a matter of seconds. "How dare you talk to my parents like that! As crazy as your sex-crazed mother is I do not disrespect her and say half the things on my mind." Toya sat there looking at me not speaking. I started the car and started driving. She kept staring at me; I got on the freeway still going off. As soon as I hit the middle lane she punched me in the jaw. She kept hitting me and trying to poke my eyes out. The car was swerving and swerving, until I finally hit the brakes. I threw on the hazard lights and Toya jumped out the car in the middle of the freeway. I sat there for a minute trying to focus my eyes. This female is crazy! She was now on the side of the freeway walking on the shoulder. A car let me over and I slowly drove behind her. Then I stopped the car and waited for her to realize that any minute now the police were going to be coming behind the incident. She's the one with a warrant as she's quick to remind me whenever I want her to go with me when I buy from her connect. She got a little ways then she ran back to the car. She tried to open the door and it was locked. "That doesn't sound like an apology!"

"Drew! I mean Steve!" Then she started cursing and screaming. She kicked my car. "You know the police are going to be coming. Open the door."

"Apologize!"

"I apologize that your parents are so weak and pathetic, that's why you are the way you are." I stepped on the gas and the car jerked forward a foot. "Steve stop playing! You are being very childish!"

"RESPECT MY PARENTS! I DON'T KNOW WHAT PRETTY RICKY LET YOU GET AWAY WITH! MY PARENTS ARE OFF LIMITS! DO YOU UNDERSTAND ME?"

"YES!"

"NOW APOLOGIZE! OR I WILL LEAVE YOU OUT HERE TO EXPLAIN TO THE POLICE WHY YOU'RE WALKING ALL THE WAY BACK TO RICHMOND!"

Toya cursed! "I'm sorry Steve Dang! Why you so sensitive about your parents?"

"Your mom screams at you and you melt down, but no one can say anything about that. You think it's ok to insight my stepmom to want to fight you when she's not a violent person? You were out of line!"

Toya looked at me and then she started crying, "I'm sorry Steve." She was about to start cutting up.

"Shut up! I know the difference between when you're putting me on and when you're sincere. Don't ever try to get over on me with those fake tears."

Toya's eyes got big. Women! Will I ever understand them? Why would that be a turn on? I unlocked the door and she quickly got in the car, and I drove home like a model citizen. I kept watching my rearview mirror looking for a highway patrolman to come and pull me over. It's a wonder no one hit us with all the madness. When we got to my place Toya was swimming in her juices. I wouldn't let her touch me, which drove her even crazier. I smoked to relieve my stress, and then I slept on the couch. When she tried to come in the living room with me, I kicked her butt back to the bed. Will popped up early in the morning, and I was happy that everything was consistent, and I was so happy to see her go. I stayed in all day relaxing. Mid-Afternoon Kamony came over like a fiend being pulled in for another hit. I had her all over that bed, and I made sure I got her smell in the sheets real good too. Kamony had to get back to her kid, and I had more smoking to do. Toya came home looking dissatisfied with life; she gave me a heartfelt apology. I just looked at her, when she went in the room she snatched the door open and then she stared at me. I continued to watch my movie that had me cracking up. She brought the dirty sheets and blankets in the living room and put them in the middle of the floor. She kept making a big production about getting the fresh linens and blankets for the bed. She told me I was cut off, as she marched towards the room. I laughed and I asked her when was she going to see Will again. Toya cried herself to sleep while I stayed on the couch laughing at my movie.

****

"She won't discuss you, what am I supposed to do?" Shirley was irritated.

I did my best to chew back my irritation; I put my bud down in the ashtray. I got up, opened windows, sprayed air freshener, and went to the kitchen, "you want some juice?"

"Sure," She answered back. Then I heard Toya's key in the door. I could hear Will's goofy laugh before they got in the door good. Toya hasn't been on my favorite person's list. At first she tried to hold on to her anger about me slapping her, but eventually she bent. She's been trying very hard to get on my good side, and all I can think about these days is getting Tracy back. "Hello..."

"Oh, this is my boyfriend Will, Will this is Steve's friend Shirley." Toya was in polite mode.

I could hear Shirley's smile in the kitchen, "it's so nice to meet you." When I walked into the living room Shirley was standing and looking Will up and down while he smiled at Toya.

I handed Shirley her glass, "would you like some juice?" I asked Will.

"No thanks we just had dinner."

I moved my folded blankets and pillow to the floor. "Have a seat, get comfortable." Shirley pulled back her disappointment. Just before I got up she kept inching closer and closer to me on the couch. I hope she wasn't planning to make a move on me. I haven't warmed up to the idea of her.

Watching Toya behave in front of Will was always amusing and hilarious. She had the good girl act down and he was eating it all up. Toya went into the bedroom and when she came out she was in a shirt that revealed her small growing belly. "I didn't know you were pregnant."

Will motioned for Toya to sit next to him, he rubbed her stomach and said, "YEP!" proudly. "I'm hoping for a little girl." He kissed her cheek.

"Do you have any names picked out?"

"Junior if it's a boy, and we seem to argue about girl names." Will said.

"He likes some of the most crazy names." Toya smiled at Will.

"You know some couples wait until the baby is born to choose a name. They choose a name based off the baby's face and personality." Shirley smiled.

"I guess, but that's how you end up with weird names out of frustration." Toya said.

"Yeah like Latoya." I interjected.

"Latoya is a beautiful name for a beautiful woman. I love the name." He kissed Toya's cheek again, while she shot me a look. "How about either way we have a junior, boy Will, girl Latoya?"

"My name is not weird!"

"What did you two do today?" I changed the subject.

"Oh you know, I was hanging out with my love. We spoke with my family over the phone briefly. I'm trying to arrange a visit so she can meet everyone. It would be easier if we could go out, but her doctor said it's not a good idea for her to travel right now. So everyone will either have to wait until the baby is born or come out for a visit."

Toya know she don't want to run the risk of someone seeing right through her. As I walked Shirley to her car I thanked her for visiting with me today. She smiled weakly then she said she wanted to have me over for dinner. I hesitated, as I couldn't think of a response. Shirley hugged me and got in her car. I was starting to feel bad, but then I thought of all the women who do the same or worse. Will was leaving as I walked up the stairs to my place. The door barely closed, "how long are you going to be mad at me?"

"I'm not even mad anymore." I walked in the bedroom to take my shirt off.

Toya closed the bedroom door behind herself, "prove it. You haven't touched me since we went over your parent's."

I chuckled, "having sex with you doesn't prove anything."

Toya jumped on me and went for broke. Even with her belly she still commands my body for at least two rounds. I was knocked out as she tried to wake me for another round. I told her I needed to eat. She offered to order a pizza and I didn't want to wait an additional hour. I told her I would be back, but she pulled on sweats cause she said I wouldn't come back all weekend. Before I opened the door she pulled me in for a kiss that went on and on.

"Will opened a checking account with me on it today. He's going to propose any day now, the jeweler called him while we were in the car earlier. He was fumbling to tell them he would call them back."

"You sure you want to marry him?"

"For now, I haven't found anyone better. I'm going to open a savings account. I'm going to give you the ATM card, so you'll have what you need. Shirley seems like she's panting, why haven't you done it yet?"

"I guess I'm not as cold blooded as you are."

"Yes you are, if you could sleep with my momma you can do Shirley."

"But I didn't sleep with your mom."

"You were going to. But you know what it doesn't matter cause I don't want to think about it." We pulled up to the closed grocery store. We exhaled, "you feel like a burger? My treat!" She held up a new card, no doubt from Will.

"Fine," something told me to go home.

When we walked into National Burger I looked up at the menu when Toya kissed me again. She kissed me like she was trying to go right in the middle of the floor. I was about to turn my attention back to the menu when Toya took off into the dining room. Here goes nothing I hate when she starts drama and then... It was Pretty Ricky. I was going to tell her to hold on when I saw Tracy. Everything was happening on hyper speed, but in slow motion. I ached for her immediately, and she was standing there looking scared as if I've ever hit her or even raised my hand to her. Pretty Ricky kept getting in my way like he was playing keep away or something. I told him this was between me and her, but he wouldn't move. I got frustrated, Toya looked at me like she was waiting for direction. I wanted to know where my child was and she wasn't leaving until I knew. Frustrated I hit Pretty Ricky trying to move him. Not only did he not move, but also he turned my body into a punching bag. I felt like my insides were twisting and shifting positions. Suddenly he was bigger than me and moving faster than I could. Tracy was begging him to stop; I knew she still loved me.

****

It hurt to stand but I had to walk out of here with all these citations.

Public intoxication, assault and battery even though I was the only person battered. They towed my car and they gave me the information for the impound lot that had my car. They let me call a taxi; I slowly walked out the door. A kid started laughing at me when I took my third step. "You've got to be Steve Turnage." He continued to laugh.

"Who are you?"

"I'm the person amused by the look of your busted up face. Here you go my man." He held out papers towards me.

"I don't want that!" I took two small steps.

"Hey! Hey! Elephant Man, when I offer you something you take it." He was still smiling even his eyes looked crazy.

I wanted to get home and sleep in my bed. "What is it?"

"Guess you gonna have to take it to figure that out." I snatched the papers. His smile became plastered and very fake. "That's you're last pass, irritate me one more time and I'll kill you right here." Then he started to walk away, "oh right. You've been served!" He started laughing, "did you ever see that movie? Com-moe-dy!" I blank stared at him. "Have a nice day. Just cause you got beat up don't mean you gotta lose your sense of humor about life." He laughed as he walked away.

I slowly got to the curb as my taxi arrived. My face and entire body hurt, all I could focus on was Tracy's fear and embarrassment. I stared out the window as the shocking events of Friday night played out in my mind. Tracy still looked good, she didn't blow up. Maybe she had the baby a little early and then she starved herself cause she's missing me. Until I know what happened for sure everything is possible. Pretty Ricky though? Isn't that weird? My head was starting to hurt as I tried to understand this nonsense. I barely made it in the door as I went for my stash. I lit, inhaled, suppressed the choke as long as I could, then I choked, and suddenly the pain lessened tremendously. I stood in the middle of the room exhaling the pain away. The physical pain as well as the mental. Tracy had more of a reaction to Pretty Ricky hitting me than Toya did. I took my clothes off then I got in the bed and slept. I awoke to Toya putting a warm heating pad around my middle, which felt like heaven. "How did you get out? I thought you had a warrant?"

"I went before the judge today. They filed restraining orders against us!" Her eyes were evil. "Since when does Drew hide behind paper?" Her breathing got heavy. "The fat girl is so weak! She's making him into a punk already!"

"Toya stop!"

She started to say something then she looked at me. "He let the police take me away! He let her...." She was too angry.

"You need to calm down before you blow a gasket!"

"I..." She grabbed her stomach and bent over. Toya yelled in pain.

I forgot about my pain and I sat up. "You need to go to the hospital."

"No! I'm..." She grabbed her stomach again.

I put on clothes, I grabbed my keys and then I remembered I didn't have a car. I called Will on her phone. He got to us quickly, and we hurried to the hospital. Madam Creole came in the pregnant people emergency room looking worried. She directed all of her questions to Will, while I sat there watching. Then she looked at me and smiled, "I talked to your momma today."

"Did you now?" I had no idea what she was talking about.

"I was telling her she been divorced and remarried twice, I don't understand why she keeps taking your daddy's name back." Her eyes smiled to tell me she was telling the truth.

"Will, thanks for the update." Then I walked away. How did she know my momma? How did she find her? I mean I cared but then again I didn't care. I went to the men's bathroom, which was one room. I locked the door and looked at my face in the mirror for the first time. I exhaled as I looked at my black eye and bruises. I guess I was going to have to come up with an excuse for work. When I heard the knock on the door I knew who it was and I didn't have any fight in me. I opened the door and Madam Creole hurried in. She locked the door behind herself. I want to say I was shocked but it would be a lie. I guess it was more evil this way.

I flushed the condom then I washed up at the sink. Madam Creole smiled at me; she said it was more fun than she thought. Then she told me if I didn't have a death wish I need to stand down when it comes to Pretty Ricky.

|*Chapter 9 Blind Justice*

I pulled up to her house and I was impressed. Shirley's house was pretty big and on the hill in San Leandro. I parked in the driveway like she told me to. Shirley opened her door with the biggest smile. She gave me a big hug when I entered her house. Shirley proudly showed me around her palace. She had four bedrooms and two and a half bathrooms. An upstairs and downstairs with a nice sized backyard. She had my cocktail ready and waiting on the coffee table next to a fat blunt. "I thought you didn't smoke?" I picked up the blunt and inhaled it's wonderful aroma.

She brought a lighter to me, "I never said I didn't, I just refuse to drive under the influence. When I'm home for the evening, I tend to let my hair down."

We smoked then we ate. I had to ask her where she bought from cause it was potent. She smiled and said she had a card. I kept getting stuck, stuck in that nothing space. Nothing hurt, nothing was wrong, and time passed. I don't even know how we ended up kissing. I guess it was better this way cause I know I would've ran from this. I kept imagining Madam Creole. All except Shirley is a screamer. I could tell it had been a minute since she's had any. She wanted everything and nope, I was done. I finished and was fine. I awoke to Shirley freaking out like she didn't mean for this to happen. She's a HORRIBLE actress. All she wanted to hear was that I wouldn't tell Tracy. Tracy wasn't going to hear about this from me. When I sobered up I got ready to go home. Shirley was disappointed that I wanted to leave but she let me take the rest of the new blunt home.

When I walked in the room taking off my clothes Toya was knocked out. I got in the shower scrubbing every inch of everything. I smoked a little in the kitchen by the window. I wasn't happy about today, it just was what it was. When I got in the bed, Toya rubbed my back. "The first time is always the hardest. It'll get easier."

****

"How come you don't talk about the fat girl?" I didn't even react like I heard her. Toya exhaled, "one of these days you gonna learn to let it go. Why don't you talk about her?"

"I don't have anything to say about her to you."

"Where's she from?"

I looked at her, "why?"

"I'm just curious," she tried to give me a genuine smile.

"You're lying," I shook my head.

"Fine!" Evilness was visible in her eyes. "You know I want to hurt her. I hate her! Watch how she walks in this courtroom like she's the victim. She's gonna have Drew catering to her like she's some delicate flower he needs to protect."

"You're just mad he's not catering to you." Toya didn't respond she stared out the window. "Would you get back with him if..."

She cut me off, "don't ask me that. I'm still in love with him, but I hate him for abandoning me. All those other babies he begged for their lives. When I finally give him what he wants he leaves me and for a fat girl! That other fat girl didn't have him like she got him. He likes her helpless act that much I guess. Shoot! I could've been helpless if I would've known he wanted that." She swallowed hard, "this judge is going to give them what they want. My son without any regard for me, and I'll have to stay away from Drew or risk going to jail. I can't believe he's going for this!"

"You don't want that kid no how. You don't want the one you're having."

Toya delicately touched her stomach, "I love my baby. Why would you say that?"

"You were trying to fight Tracy with your potbelly."

"I was so angry and everything was happening so fast."

I couldn't find close parking so I let Toya out in front of the courthouse. I parked and then I sat still for a minute. *Steve you're going to see Tracy. It's going to kill you that you can't talk to her. You're going to want her to put her arms around you, but she can't. You know how deep her heart runs even if Pretty Ricky doesn't. I am the first man she's ever loved. Pretty Ricky may have money, but he's not you.* I took a deep breath then I got out of the car. I walked casually down the street. A guy got out of a black SUV as I walked past him. He kept staring at my eyes like he could see through me. There was no smile or friendliness to him. I nodded at him and he stared. I kept walking; he looked like he was looking for a reason to be late to his case. I went through the metal detectors and then I looked for the waiting area for our courtroom. Great! Toya was sitting across from Tracy and Pretty Ricky. He was watching me as I approached them. He didn't seem concerned that I was coming and that upset me. Look at my face! He should be worried about my retaliation. I was still bruised some; I told my boss it was an attempted mugging and that I needed to testify today. I sat down and I whispered in Toya's ear, "she's so scared she can't get it together. Stop intimidating her like that it's not fair. You're going to drive her to eating again." Then we laughed.

When Tracy stood up she was all nerves, she was nerved up enough for all of us. My eyes traveled all over her skirt, an attempt at modesty, with those curves demanding to be noticed. Pretty Ricky was dang near drooling and then he looked at me and smiled like he knew where my mind trailed off to. He caught me off guard last time. I didn't care that he was a little bigger than me. I can take this guy... With a weapon of course.

When we sat down I couldn't take my eyes off of Tracy. The past year she's lived in my memory and now here she is. I wanted to talk to her. He's probably making her do this cause he knows she's still in love with me. Toya was all into the drama of other people's lives, she was so focused she didn't see or care about my stare. She looks like the Tracy that made me those cookies the first time I came over her place. The Tracy I laid down on that couch. The Tracy... Pretty Ricky smirked while looking ahead. He knew I was watching, he was getting a kick out of my bleeding heart. Then he put his hand on her thigh and started rubbing. Everything inside me turned to an angry red haze. I couldn't be quiet, I couldn't cooperate. I gladly absorbed the opportunity to get in Tracy's head. I stuck to the baby when it was our turn to speak. I knew this would kill her, I knew she would spend the rest of the day in a depressed state over the loss of the eternal us.

When it was time to leave the courtroom Toya begged me to stay seated. I saw the guy from the street and the guy who served me in the courtroom. Toya begged me to stay put until they were gone. As we walked out to the car she explained that Pretty Ricky's brothers are known killers and how Pretty Ricky always kept them off of her, but she was sure he wouldn't stop them if they got after her right now. Once we got in the car I sat there processing what just happened. Toya was doing the same. When we looked at each other, Toya started screaming; saying Tracy must've cooked Pretty Ricky some red sauce. We sat there for a long time going off. I told her about him having his hands all over Tracy in the courtroom. I drove a couple blocks over by the train station. I needed to smoke cause it felt like my head was going to burst. Toya stayed in the car while I leaned against it. She got out the car and got in the driver's seat while she waited for me to finish. I needed numbness in the worse way. When I got in the car Toya looked at me. "You want to get her?"

"How? She got that paper."

"They won't expect us to come today. I bet I know where they are. Do you want to get her or not?"

"Of course I want to get her, but I'm sure we're not talking about the same thing." I laughed uncontrollably.

Toya was not amused. "Steve if you're going to be so silly on the stuff Shirley's been giving you then you need to cut back. It's go time are you ready?"

"Ready! Steady! Betty!" I laughed again. Toya was talking a mile a minute, as if I cared to listen to her. I didn't want to feel what I was about to feel so numbness was the way to go. Toya pulled me in the door quickly and into a booth by the bathroom. The restaurant wasn't crowded, she was whispering about something and I just sat there smiling cause I had no idea what she was talking about.

There are no words to describe how seeing Tracy walk past me stole my high. All the pain I smoked away was there, and I couldn't stand it. I started to get up and Toya pulled me back down. When I tried to get up again, she pulled me again. I was about to hit her if she didn't take her hands off of me. She told me to focus and to do what she told me to do. I had no idea of what she was talking about. I watched her disappear in the bathroom. I sat there for a few minutes counting backwards, and then I went in the bathroom. All the things I thought I would say, the way I thought I would win her heart back went out the window. She was afraid of me, and I felt some kind of way about that. It was like I was dreaming and those weren't my hands, and I wasn't doing the things I saw myself doing. Then my body went flying and I don't know why. Those fools jumped me and fortunately for me I didn't feel a thing. Only thing is when this high wears off, I know I'm going to be in a world of hurt for sure.

****

"I'm in pain can someone please give me my pain medicines?" I called out from my bed.

The cell door opened and closed, I held my hand out. "Steve Turnage?" A male voice questioned.

I looked at the guy standing in my cell, "yea?" I don't know who he was or why he came. I barely even saw his face. I just remember hair as if he had a lot of it. He beat me up all over that cell. If I thought I was in pain before, my body was on fire now. Brown fist pummeled my body from top to bottom.

"If you're smart, you'll leave Tracy alone. But I have a feeling you're not and we'll meet again." I could only hear his voice, I couldn't see his face. The cell opened and closed again. I didn't even hear his footsteps walking away.

I laid on the ground surrounded by my own blood until I heard casual footsteps towards my cell. They stopped. "What the? Turnage? What happened to you? I need medic help!" The guard called out.

No one saw or heard anything; it was like an invisible man came to get me... or something.

****

"Steve, we like you. You've worked here for a long time. Lately you've been flaky and unfocused. As your boss I need to warn you that you're skating on thin ice. As your friend and completely off the record, I think you need to take a leave of absence. I don't know what's going on with you. I don't want to have to fire you." My boss pleaded with me.

"You're right, I need to take some time off. I don't understand all that's happening right now to even try to explain it to you. I'll see if my doctor can help me."

My boss clicked around the screen, "well you know you haven't taken your sabbatical yet. Is there a reason why?" He asked as he clicked away on the screen.

"I didn't think I was eligible for one. When can I start?"

"Monday if you'd like."

I sighed a sigh of relief; I really thought I was about to lose my job. "I have to start Monday. I have to finish healing."

He clicked away, "Monday it is."

****

"You may kiss your bride." Toya and Will embraced and kissed. We were in a courtroom in the Alameda county courthouse. They were having a quick ceremony at the Justice of the Peace since Will wanted to be married before the baby was born. Even with the pregnant belly Toya made a beautiful bride, Shirley and I sat over to the side opposite Madam Creole as we watched them marry.

Madam Creole forced a smile as she looked at Toya's ring. Again I don't know what's wrong with the women in this family. I know that ring was not cheap, but Madam Creole acted like he got it out of the cracker jack box and put it on her finger. I hugged Toya and I told her I was happy for her and that everything worked out well for her. The look she gave me was child like as she almost pleaded at me with her eyes. I don't know what she wanted, but I didn't want to devote much thought to it either. I needed to get going if I was going to catch Kamony in time.

"Are you coming by later?" Shirley asked.

"Probably not, why?"

"Oh," she was disappointed. "Cause if you weren't I was going to have some friends over."

"I wouldn't hold my breath, I gotta go take this child support and then probably take my little girl out to get something to eat."

"Yeah, but that doesn't take all night."

"Shirley, if you're going to start tripping..."

"I'm sorry! I'm sorry! I'll back off!" She walked away in frustration.

I started to walk in the other direction and Madam Creole was in my path. She was giving me an evil grin. "So you know we have to celebrate right?"

"And what are we celebrating?"

"Our baby is married, we need to celebrate. I'm following you to your house."

"I didn't say I was going home."

"You want me to cause a scene?" She smiled.

Knowing she would do it and not care, I told her to give me a ride to my car. I imagine that Toya knows about this, but some how she's always out of the range of picking up on our encounters. Madam Creole acts like she's doing me a favor even though she comes to me. Demands to be with me, and she still complains about me being too small, so I tell her she's too old to know the difference. We go back and forth clowning each other. It's foreplay for her. I got to Kamony three hours later than I said I was coming and then I was spent. She looked very guilty, but I didn't focus on her I focused on Richele and helping her with her homework. When we laid down and I was completely tired, Kamony rubbed my back and then she whispered, "I'm pregnant!"

I jumped, and then I rolled over. "Please say, *Sike*!"

She shook her head, "I got confirmation today."

"What are you going to do? I can't afford anymore kids?"

"I'm going to have it of course. Richele is going to be excited. Shannon and the other one probably won't speak to me anymore."

"I don't know why you talk to them in the first place. I don't think you should have it. I can't afford it, and if you would've said you weren't on anything this wouldn't have happened."

"Like it matters, you're always high these days. You don't remember half the things I tell you."

"I wasn't high tonight, but apparently you want to drive me to drinking." Not until right before I got in this bed. I exhaled, "look! I don't want to have a long drawn out argument about this. I don't want it; I don't think you should keep it. You're always crying saying you need help with Richele, another kid would make that need greater and I can't help you. I can barely help myself."

"Shannon and her son will probably write me off anyways!"

I stared at her for a minute, "this is about competition isn't it? That is not my kid when are you going to believe me?"

"Never! I've got eyes and I can see. He looks just like you. Sounds like you, talks like you, walks like you, he even thinks like you."

"Good night Kamony!"

She blew air, "you're going to sleep?"

"Yes. I'm tired and you just turned me off."

"When did you and Tracy begin? Cause Shannon act like she don't know her."

"Goodnight!"

"Play dumb if you want, but the moment I catch you lingering in Berkeley we're going to have problems."

"Save your threats for someone who cares." I was about to fall asleep.

"Look I'm not stupid! I know Tracy bought a house in Berkeley."

"How do you know?" I turned over and looked at her.

"I ran a search on her name at work."

I needed to know everything she knew. "Yeah right!"

"She's over there by the Claremont Hotel. I know exactly where to find you."

Then monstrous growling noises came from my phone. I thought I turned the ringer off. That was my ringtone for Madam Creole. I got up and answered my phone. "Hello?"

"Toya's in labor, I figured you should be there for the birth of your child."

She gets on my nerves, "we've got hours. Can't I sleep?"

"We need you to run interference when they ask her questions. Besides, second babies come a lot faster. Get your butt over here now!" Then she hung up.

I started getting dressed. "You're leaving? Should you be driving in your current state?"

"Don't matter, I got to go."

"Steve," Kamony said above a whimper. I went in Richele's room, kissed her warm cheek goodbye. Kamony was blocking the doorway, "Steve!"

I exhaled, "can't you just rewind the tape to what I said the last time we had this conversation? I didn't want a baby by you then, and I don't want a baby by you now."

"Why is Tracy's kid so special? Why her kid get to have you, but ours gets denied. You know how many guys wanted a baby by me and you try to act like you're too good."

"So why don't you do this. Pen that baby on the guy who's here when I'm not." Kamony's eyes got big. "You know the one that Richele calls daddy too." Kamony stood there looking stupid. "The guy that thinks he's got a good woman and that you all are a family." She dropped her eyes, "I've been as patient as I can be with you. But I'm not going to play this game anymore. You got him you don't need me! Matter of fact..." I gently pushed her out of the way. "I'm not breaking my back to pay you no more. I'll see Richele when I can, and if you don't come when I call you or give me grief about anything else I'm calling Marvin and telling him the truth. I still have my DNA results, do you?" Kamony's face dropped and all she could do was cry. I smiled so big to myself as I walked out to my car! YES! In her face! I've been holding on to that for a minute for the perfect moment to slap her with it. I saw Richele first then him in Wal-Mart walking around like a father and daughter as she drug him to the toy section. She convinced him that she needed a new Barbie, and he surrendered to her request. In line at the register he was telling the older woman how proud he was of his daughter. Toya was coming from the other side of the store. She saw me staring, when she saw Richele she walked over to the guy. "Dupree?"

He smiled real big, "no."

Toya flashed her smile at him and he blushed. "Dupree stop it," she playfully hit his arm. "Tell your sister to call me."

"My name is Marvin, but I'll gladly tell anyone of my sisters to call you."

"Marvin? Are you sure?"

I couldn't believe Richele wasn't recognizing Toya. That or she's been trained not to say anything so well that she remained silent. Toya got him to tell her that he was taking his daughter out to dinner to reward her for having such a good week at school. Poor sap was a good guy who was in love with Kamony and honestly believed that Richele was his daughter. Toya even said, "your daughter must look like your girl." To which he replied that she did. Toya wanted to go blast her, but I'm so glad I waited.

When I got to the hospital Toya was walking around the room cursing with her hands on her hips. She had on a little skirt that let her stomach hang out and a sports bra. She was sweating and going off. She was asking herself why, and then she cut her eyes at me like I did something. "YOU KNOW I WAS CLOSE TO DELIVERING! WHY WEREN'T YOU ANSWERING YOUR PHONE?"

I raised my eyebrows, "I was celebrating your nuptials my way. Apparently you were celebrating your way."

Will chuckled, "that is love for family. I promise my family would be the only ones I'd risk my life for when I'm high."

A big contraction hit Toya and she squatted down and grunted. "STOP THAT TOYA! You're not a dog for crying out loud!" Her mother yelled as she went to the door. "Can somebody come check this girl, she acting like she's about to push out her litter."

The nurse came in as Toya was squatting, she asked Toya to get on the bed so they could check her. Toya got on the bed on all fours and she refused to lay down. The doctor came hurrying in, and they started moving stuff around in the room. Will looked at me like he thought I should leave, so I started to the door, but Madam Creole grabbed me and told me to stay put. I wanted to leave and then Toya's voice went real low and she grunted hard and deep. I saw juiciness and then the doctor caught something grey as it fell out. The doctor asked Will if he wanted to cut the cord and he happily cut it. Toya laid down and they put the baby on her chest. They wiped a lot of the gross stuff off the baby. Will was so excited he started snapping pictures and kissing Toya. Telling her how happy he was, thanking her for doing this for him, and telling her how much he loved her. Toya was crying as she looked down at the baby. I walked over to where I could see his face as Toya kept kissing him. The baby looked like Toya, but he was definitely my son. I looked at Madam Creole and she grinned evilly at me. "Oh my goodness Toya he looks just like the men in our family."

|Chapter10 The Bad side begins this way

Watching Will love the baby, and seem so happy makes me so mad. I don't know why it does cause I don't want that baby. I mean I thought I didn't. I can't tell you how I feel these days. Thinking just makes me hurt, oh and THEN! I keep having nightmares about hitting Tracy. I finished my community service for my violation of her restraining order and everything. I keep seeing the fear in Tracy's eyes as I struck her, as I hurt her. Something I swore I would never do. I can't be high the next time I see her. I need to clearly tell her everything and make her understand. Not that I understand all that well myself. Nobody else lost their baby as far as I know, why did Tracy lose hers? Why do I feel anything when I look at Toya's kid? I know when he was made and I went in knowing he was going to come. That's my son carrying on some other man's name. Toya's fine with that and I don't get it. She claims she loves me, tells me she's still in love with Pretty Ricky. Plays good wife to Will, runs around all the time when she should be home resting.

Toya honked from the parking lot. Will bought her a car as a wedding present. She was too happy about it. When I came down the stairs I whistled. I ran my finger along the door of her Lexus. "He pulled out all the stops didn't he?" I sat in the passenger seat.

"You like it?" She was so proud.

"Call from Will..." The car called out. Tracy's car has that same feature. "Answer," Toya said smiling. "Hey babe, I just picked up Steve."

"Steve," he sounded irritated.

"Hey, what's going on." I smiled.

"Can you talk some sense into your cousin? She's supposed to be at home resting."

"I'm sitting in the car. We're going to walk to the table. Sit, eat, then I'm going to sit in Steve's place for a while. Then I'll come home."

"Latoya, you are doing too much! You need to rest and heal."

She cut her eyes at me, "can we talk about this later? I don't want to start my day off arguing with you. Tell me you love me and we'll continue this discussion when you get home."

Someone said something to Will in the background. "I gotta run into a meeting. Sit your tail down somewhere and rest. I'll see you this evening."

"Ok babe, luv ya!" She blew a kiss at the dashboard. She smiled at me, "I forgot what it's like to look into your eyes and see clarity. How you doing?"

"I'm fine."

"You miss me?" She smiled.

"I guess." I smiled back.

The baby made a noise but he was fine, "he looks just like us. That's amazing huh?" She looked so proud.

"Call from Drew..." The car called out.

Toya got excited like the captain of the football team was calling. "Answer," she said too happy. "Drew."

185

"Why are you sending messages to me?" He sounded completely irritated.

"Oh I guess you forgot that your little girlfriend has paperwork to have me put in jail if I come anywhere near you or our son. You know, at first I thought she was stupid, turns out she's very smart and got you eating out the palm of her hand."

"And out of her lap." Then he chuckled while Toya and I gasped at the dashboard. "What do you want?"

Toya was squeezing the steering wheel. "You must want me to hurt her!"

"Now you must want to piss me off! I've got work to do, what do you want?"

"To see my son!"

"Your son? Thought you said he was my son and you didn't care anymore?" He mimicked her voice.

"Pregnancy brain! I don't recall saying anything like that."

"Hold on," you could hear a door close. He exhaled, "no Toy! I'm not putting Andre through your mood swings. You are not stable and you're not going to use him as a pawn in your games like you've been doing with that crackhead. You ran out and married the first guy who couldn't see through you. You're all over the place."

I looked at Toya, "Steve is not a crackhead!" She protested.

"Ok, ok. Maybe he doesn't realize all the stuff he's been getting high on. Weed don't get you that high. But you're in love with a crackhead, that's ok. No one's judging you Toy. It's ok." Then he laughed.

"Says the guy laying with the fat girl!"

"Hhhhmmm! Big! Beautiful! And just how I like my women! Happy and satisfied with who they are. I love that woman proudly regardless of what size she is. A good woman is a good woman. Every time you point to her size as something she or I should be ashamed of it shows how insecure you are with yourself."

"If you don't care, then why she lose weight?"

"Cause she wanted to, I honestly don't care. You see you got to work hard to try to hold on to the mirage. You're as...." He caught himself. Then he exhaled, "you can't see Andre! I'm not subjecting my son to your manipulations. When are you delivering, you need a do over."

Tears were streaming down her face, "I'm not ugly!"

He laughed, "that's all you heard?"

Toya was falling apart, "stop being mean to me Drew. Why? You don't love me anymore?"

He was quiet, "don't turn on the water works. I...." Toya erupted into tears. They weren't the fake ones either. They were the tears after her mom came after me, the tears when she thought I was done with her, the tears when her mother wouldn't tell her who her real father was. They were her real emotions, real hurt, real pain. I know I've said meaner stuff to her and he gets real tears that easy? "Toy! Stop!" She kept crying, he growled lowly into the phone. "Stop trying to make me choose. I will not choose you! You turned your back on our son. You acted a complete fool, and then you're having more kids? You are toxic, we are getting older. When are you going to settle down? You're making me side with Malcolm and you know how much I love to do that! Leave me alone and you'll live. Don't make me choose."

Toya blew air until she caught her breath, "you better hope I don't find that fat pig! I'm gonna gut her like the hog she is!"

His voice got even deeper, "remember that you chose this." Then he hung up.

Toya parked the car then she sat there screaming to the top of her lungs. I looked back at the baby who remained sleep like this was normal behavior. "What did you just choose?"

Toya started beating the steering wheel. "I'm first! I'm first!"

Um! Does she remember I'm right here? "Toya?"

"WHAT?"

"Who's Malcolm?"

She immediately stopped her fit and looked at me. Her eyes were puffy and completely red. "Malcolm?" She wiped her face. "Did he mention Malcolm?"

"Who is he?"

Toya wiped her face, "I need to lay down. Can we go back to your place?"

"Fine."

I carried the baby seat inside staring at my son. Toya looked around with a smile. "If only you had money, we could've been happy together."

"What's wrong with Will?"

"I fired the housekeeper, and now I see why he needed her. He grew up all proper; he's not up on anything. You know like the fat girl." I put the carrier on the couch then I walked away. I went in the kitchen. She came in the kitchen and threw her arms around me. "I'm sorry." She said as she bit my ear.

"What are you doing?"

"I'm ready." She sucked on my neck.

"Huh?"

"I'm not bleeding anymore. I'm ready."

"I'm not! Seeing you give birth was disgusting! I have no desire to go in there."

Toya looked me in my eyes, "Steve I'm going to say this with love. You need to slow down on you're smoking. You about to be Pookie in this piece."

"Funny how you're only concerned with my smoking when you're not getting your way."

"I care Steve! You're all I got, well you and the baby. We're a family even if it's all messed up. That's just for now. I'm going to figure everything out."

"Whatever, I'm hungry."

"Take my car, money is in my wallet."

"You want something?"

"Bring me whatever you get."

As I drove down the street I smiled. Tracy never gave me the keys to her car. She acted funny about me having a key to her place. I went over to the El Sobrante cafe and got omelets for us. As I was walking out she was walking in with a group. "Steve." Shannon said staring me in my eyes.

"Shannon."

"We'll save your seat." A girl in their group said as she went inside.

"Steve how could you?" I blank stared at her. "You know you are his father, how could you deny him right in front of his face like that? My child hasn't been right since that day."

"Is my response supposed to be different because he's standing right there? You know that you had a boyfriend when you hooked up with me. You cheated on the idiot repeatedly with me. You can't turn a hoe into a wife."

I know my words wounded her, "regardless of what your opinion was of me at that time in my life. I was young and dumb, not thinking about consequences or anything. He's still your son, but you've made such a mess of everything you can't meet him."

"Good cause I don't want to. He's not my kid."

"What about the others? Kamony's kids aren't yours either?"

"Why are you questioning me behind what some other females told you? You are not my woman. You are somebody I got lazy with, you took that and ran with it." I got to go, my food is getting cold. Then I walked away. Shannon stood in the doorway watching me. I chirped Toya's car and she looked pissed.

When I came back Toya was feeding the baby and smiling at him while he ate. I put her food in the microwave, and then I sat at my table watching them. I don't know how she was with the other baby, but she was showing my son love. The way she was looking at him how could he not feel loved. When he finished she burped him, loved him up and then she gently laid him back in his carrier. "You weren't like this with the other one?"

"No," she heated up her food then she sat at the table. "I didn't even hold him right away. Drew was so matter of fact; there was no love in the room when he was born. Even though you were high you were there. You cared! You showed me love," then she smiled at me. "In your way of course. We won't ever be the stereotypical kind of family, but you get me and I get you."

"So what was that earlier with Pretty Ricky?"

She tried to hold on to her smile, "I still love him. I was his first real everything. He's done so much dirty work for me. I can't believe he's just washing his hands of me like this, and over her. A fat girl."

"Toya, did you hear anything that he said?" She blank stared at me, "he's not concerned with her weight. She's a good woman and he sees that. He wants her for who she is."

"You ok with that? Just because he wants her he gets to have her?"

My stomach flipped, "I don't know what happened the last time I saw her. I was too high, I never hurt her before. It was like something came over me and I wasn't doing it. I think about her everyday, and as much fun as you and I have. She took care of me, she protected me. You're about me until Pretty Ricky comes around. You are out for Toya."

"Answer the question."

"No, he doesn't get to have her. But I know she loves me, I just got to be straight when I see her."

Toya huffed, "you're never straight anymore."

"You're right." I smiled then I went out on my balcony and smoked. Toya stood there watching me through the glass.

When I came back in the door she was still standing there. "Feel better?" I smiled, "make love to me."

My mind was telling me no, but my body was telling me YES! I'll have to test the theory when I'm not high, but breast milk tastes really good.

As I was falling asleep I know my mind was playing tricks on me, I could've sworn I heard Toya saying that she wanted Tracy dead, but I know I didn't hear her right.

****

"You look nice." Shirley said looking me up and down.

"Thanks." I walked slowly.

"So, don't be mad ok." I looked at her, "Tracy has been working out here over the last couple days." I gasped, she put her hands up. "I was trying to get her to talk to you, she's so against the idea. She said you're trying to kill her." She searched my eyes as if that could be true.

"Shirley you know how much I love that girl. I may have said some mean stuff to her out of frustration, but how could I show her how much I love her if she's dead?"

"I know, I know. You know how dramatic she gets sometimes."

"She left already?"

"I think so, how was work?"

"They're talking about layoffs again. They already cut all the short timers, the redline is getting closer and closer to me."

"Where will you go if they lay you off?"

I exhaled, "I don't want to think about that right now."

"Are you coming over tonight?"

"Probably not, I need to unwind."

"You could do that at my place." She smiled helplessly.

"I want to go home and relax."

She sighed, "she will be here tomorrow too." Everything in me perked up, "I'm going to try to get her to talk to you. Make sure you dress nice, but I'm not promising anything she's very cold when it comes to the idea of you. Be good Steve!"

"I will!"

****

"Sir are you ok?" The paramedic asked me.

Everything in my body hurt, "yes." I said slowly as I allowed them to sit me up.

"Do you know your name?"

"Yes."

"Can you tell us what happened?"

"I guess I was walking too close to this guy and he turned around and zapped me." My entire body ached.

"Can you stand?" They got me to stand and then slowly walk. They asked me if I could call someone. My car was at the El Cerrito Bart station. I should've stayed on the train.

I called Toya and without a full explanation she said she was on her way. When she pulled up Will was driving, and she looked annoyed. "Bro, what happened?"

"I got zapped by some guy. You know how territorial these West Oakland and Berkeley fools be. Knocked the wind out of me for a minute." I looked down at the baby who was quietly looking around the back seat. "Did I interrupt a family moment?"

"Naw, we were trying to decide on dinner when you called. I keep telling this woman she got a family now, and she can't keep running out the house by herself." Will looked around, "you hungry?"

"Naw! I just need a ride to my car." I looked at the baby, "I saw my ex at the Bart station."

Toya slapped down the mirror so she could look at my face. "Really? What happened? Tell me everything!"

"I was with Shirley and she was with some guy with long dreads." Toya looked like she wanted to explode. "I guess she isn't as good as I thought if she's cheating on her man with this guy. He was all territorial about her like he was her man or something."

"Brown skin?" I shook my head yes. "Solid build?" I shook my head yes. "I think I know who you're talking about, and if that was who I think it was he's completely crazy! He seems all nice and calm, almost like a push over, then a switch flips and out of nowhere he almost kills you. He's crazy, was his name Jeremy?"

"That wasn't the name they used. It was something unusual."

She sat there like she was thinking about it. "Oh well, maybe that wasn't... no it couldn't have been him cause you're cool."

"You know the guy his ex is with now?" Will interjected breaking Toya's train of thought.

"Oh yeah, I went to school with his ex's now boyfriend. It's such a small world."

I kept flexing and unflexing my hands, they hurt. The paramedic told me to go home and relax, right now I feel like I was in a fight all over. "Steve come out to dinner with us." She watched my eyes in the mirror.

"Fine!" I surrendered.

"Honey, let's go to Juan's right out here in Berkeley. "Toya directed him to the restaurant. When Will went to the bathroom, Toya leaned in with a smile. "If you don't stop trying to be nice to that girl I'm going to kill you myself. You could've died today and for what? Just because you're trying to talk to that girl who is strung out over my man!"

"Your man?" I frowned.

"You know what I mean! It's over, it's done! There's nothing you can say to her to make her come back. Drew has turned her out and she ain't coming back. Got it?"

"You don't know her like I know her."

"You sound like some love sick female who don't know how to leave well enough alone. It's all right there in front of you and you want to sit over here acting simple."

"You still think Pretty Ricky is coming back to you."

"The difference between you and me, is that I had his virginity. You did not pop that fat girl's cherry. I know what she's getting and she's strung out. You wouldn't want her back afterwards anyways. Once I take care of her, he's coming back. I am all he knows."

"And I'm supposed to be doing what when he comes back to

you?"

"The same thing you've been doing." And there was my point, I want what I had back too.

|*Chapter 11 Going Down*

"I didn't come over here to argue, I could've stayed home for that." Toya snatched her shirt on.

"There's no argument to be had, you come over here thinking you're going to pump me for information about Tracy, but you're extremely tight lipped about Pretty Ricky. I ask you questions and you don't answer. You think I won't notice when you don't answer me?"

"Steve, I love you. I really do, but I don't want you to get hurt thinking you could ever be a match for Drew. He may seem all white collar, but his family's not."

"He a drug dealer or something?"

"No, he's never sold. But his family is full of hustlers. The most successful one is his mother. She had this high profile boyfriend for a while. I thought for sure she'd get him to the alter, but she couldn't keep him. She been on TV a few times as the date of a few people here and there, but it's not like anyone is talking about her. Who the fat girl run with?"

"Nobody really. Ever since her friend got married she was pretty much lonely."

"Pretty much is not entirely."

"Yeah," I sat up. That's when I noticed the evilness in her eyes. "What is wrong with you?"

Toya threw her body around. "YOU'RE STILL IN LOVE WITH

HER!" Then she jumped on me and started clawing me. She was killing my high. "I HATE HER! I WANT HER DEAD!"

I slammed Toya on the bed. "What is wrong with you?" I held her down. "You don't have a right to say nothing! You're married to who? You're in love with? And you're getting out of my bed!"

"She took my man!"

"Who are you talking about when you say that?"

"You, Drew, I'm sure she'd take Will if she met him."

I smiled, "you ever think if she didn't meet me or Pretty Ricky. You think she was supposed to meet Will and live a boring life with him?" Toya screamed, "you have to admit he's more her speed out of the three of us."

"SHUT UP! HOW COULD YOU SAY THAT TO ME?"

"You know this drama is supposed to be you, me, and Pretty Ricky. Somehow they got caught in our web of lies." Toya was losing it, and it tickled me.

"I saw Topaz the other day." She waited for my reaction.

"SO!"

"Were you two supposed to be good friends?"

"We were roommates, what do you think?"

"You still see him?"

"We workout together."

"He didn't tell you we hooked up?" She smiled at me as she stood up.

I came across the bed and I threw Toya against the wall. "You're just mad! Pretty chocolate drop Toya may be married to a guy with money, he still regulates your spending. He's whack and stupid for you. You want Pretty Ricky and he can't stand to hear your voice. Then there's me, I ain't got nothing but love for you! Not the kind of love you want either. You're mad cause Tracy's better than you and you know it. All you got is pretty, once that wears off you have nothing. So what if you just reminded me that you're a whore not to be trusted. I've already gotten my payback, over and over again. At this point you're only playing catch up."

"Pay back?"

"Go home Toya, you're boring me." Then I walked in the bathroom.

Toya was thinking hard as she left. I watched her struggle with the baby carrier and diaper bag as she got in her car.

I waited as long as I could, then I called Topaz. He started laughing as soon as he realized it was me. I asked him what was so funny. He asked me what did Toya tell me. I told him to tell me what happened. He said she tried to come on to him and he left her standing there looking stupid. I asked him why he didn't tell me, he said he was going to tell me when he saw me. I asked why he didn't call me immediately. He said it wasn't that big of an issue to him. He said she's always stared too hard or tried to brush up against him. Toya was messing with my high. Once I was cool I made my way to the gym. Topaz was there he looked at me hard then he asked me to spot him. "I know your life is none of my business, but when has that ever stopped me from speaking on it?" He chuckled, "what are you smoking? Your weight is all over the place. Depending on when I talk to you I may catch you when you're coherent. Is that girl keeping you high so you don't pay attention to the things that are happening?"

"No. It's just been a lot going on."

"Right, a lot has been going on and you're not present for any of it. She got you wrapped up in her games and you're never coherent. Are you even thinking for yourself anymore?"

"Of course I am! Toya thinks she's got me wrapped around her finger." I exhaled, "prepare yourself." I looked at him, "you were right. You were right about everything. Tracy got a restraining order against me. I miss her like crazy and then when I see her she acts like she's scared of me. I..." I lost my breath when a flashback slapped me in the face. "I was high. I... I... I choked the mess out of her." Topaz frowned at me. He sat up and then he stood up looking at me like he was about to snap. "I was high man, part of the scene seemed like a dream. Her pretty boy boyfriend put me in the hospital. Someone broke into the jail to re-injure me as I was healing. Now it seems like people are always watching me. I think I'm paranoid these days. Toya's momma is blackmailing me; I gotta break her off whenever she feels like it. I'm going to move in with my suga momma cause I got my pink slip the other day. Women seem like they get more scandalous the older they get. A couple of her friends are on rotation too. Kamony is due any day, it's mine but you know me. Oh but she got this guy on the hook thinking that my kids are his. So I only see her when I feel like it. I don't know whether I'm coming or going these days. All I think about is when things were calmer and the worst thing happening was Tracy and her dramatics. Toya is crazy, and I can't figure why or how I could love her but I do."

"That's not love, that's Lust. Toya is beautiful. Hands down, everyone knows it. You're still stuck in high school, in a place where someone like her wouldn't have looked at you. That girl is toxic. You need to get away from her. Imagine if you would've believed that I slept with her? Why would she lie and say I went for that anyways? Good thing you know me better than that."

I looked at Topaz, "right. Good thing I know you better than that."
I know he likes to rub my nose in a lot of things. Toya lies to them,
she doesn't lie to me. A moment of weakness is understandable,
but I just need him to be honest.

"Why are you looking at me like that?"

"Because if you did *fall in*, I might be upset but I'd respect you for
being honest with me. It's just weird that you didn't call me but you
knew why I was calling. Toya doesn't lie to me."

"Steve, as your friend I'm going to tell you that you need to stop
smoking. You're talking to me. **ME!**"

"Yea, and you didn't call me." Then I walked in his face. "You did
it didn't you?"

"We've been boys since we were kids."

"Yep, and you've been judging me for that long too. You were
feeling Tracy the whole time we were together. You ain't been
right since we broke up either." Topaz turned his eyes from me full
of guiltiness. "You were feeling Tracy?"

He took a step back, "I was feeling how good she was to you. I
never pushed up on her or said anything to her. Until I met my
girlfriend I was a little confused about that cause I wanted
someone like her. You know she would've told you if I stared too
long."

"And you didn't think Toya would say anything so you went for it.
I don't deserve to have a woman that fine huh? Steve Urkel can't
have someone like that? Huh!"

"Urkel? You're tripping man, calm down."

"I'm not tripping, I can see you. Just admit that you did it. Either way I can't trust you no more any ways. You might as well go out like a man telling the truth."

Topaz picked up his bag. "You are tripping! We've been boys since we were kids."

"And you've always considered yourself above me. You respected me with Tracy cause in the end she was a fat girl. But Toya's beautiful and downright sexy. You can't even admit it!"

Topaz walked away and got on a machine. He couldn't even look at me. If Toya wouldn't have told me would he? I couldn't even workout anymore. I grabbed my stuff and walked out the gym. I called Toya, she sounded sad but I didn't care. I went in on her. I asked her if she was telling me the truth. She promised on everything that she was telling me the truth. She even offered the birthmark on the inside of his thigh as proof. I had never seen it, but we've talked about it before. I sat there over an hour watching people leave the gym. Topaz walked out with his towel over his head as usual. There was a car coming in the opposite direction. As soon as he was almost to the middle of my lane I stepped on the gas burning rubber and everything. Instead of moving backwards he ran forward right into the other car. He bounced off that car and hit the trunk of my car then he fell on the ground as I drove away. The other car stopped. I went to the gas station and inspected my car. I pushed out the slight dent on the top of my trunk. I got gas and paid cash for a car wash. I drove around not letting myself think about Topaz. I found myself in downtown Oakland at a little burrito shop off of 16th and Franklin. I found myself looking at each person within sight. Shirley said Tracy works somewhere down here, and I come down here once in awhile in hopes of catching a glimpse of her on the street. "Ahem!" A voice said from behind me. I looked up at Karen, "where did you disappear to?"

I smiled, "where did you disappear to?"

"I didn't disappear on you. You disappeared on me."

"So this is what we're going to do? Go back and forth over who disappeared on who?"

"Well I'm waiting for you to stand up and give me my hug." She smiled seductively.

We sat in the burrito shop catching up. I told her I had a girlfriend and I laid low for a while. I don't remember how, but when I mentioned Tracy's name Karen got a funny look. She asked me what Tracy's last name was. I hesitated for a minute, when I said Thomas she lost it. I sat there watching her. Why does everybody react this way to that girl? Karen asked me if she was first and when I said no she looked like she wanted to cry. Now I was confused when she said she met Pretty Ricky while Tracy was pregnant. When was Tracy pregnant outside of me? She told the judge she didn't have any kids. Karen said that everything came out at her brother's place. She said Tracy hit her and then hurried out. If I didn't know for a fact that Tracy and Kamony fought I might not have believed her. So I asked Karen about Pretty Ricky. The way she gushed over him made me sick. She had stars in her eyes as she talked about him. She said she met him at a club, and he hangs out at the club all the time. Or at least he used to. She said he slowed down a lot on his clubbing, she said she rarely sees him out anymore. I didn't understand why thinking about him made her sad. I asked her if she needed to get back to work and she said she was done for the day. I suggested we drive over to the lake and walk around it. It was a nice day out in Oakland; Lake Merritt would provide a lovely backdrop to the day. Besides incase I needed to I was hoping that this time spent with Karen would provide a lovely alibi for me. Karen and I walked around the lake; initially Karen was looking at me like she remembered me. Once Pretty Ricky came up, she got that same lost and distant look that Tracy used to have once they broke up. She wasn't even thinking about me as a viable option anymore. I suddenly felt like I was teleported back to high school when girls only wanted to be my friend while they acted like I was a nonsexual being. We exchanged numbers and then I went home. When I got home there were no sirens waiting for me. I didn't smoke anything to make sure I was on point when they came. Toya called me still upset, about the day. We talked it out, and then I went to bed.

In the morning no one was looking for me. I called the office and my boss told me to come tomorrow to clean out my desk. He said I was definitely being laid off and that the entire office was being shut down. My boss was so angry, he's been with this company for years and he felt he was being release as if he was nothing. We talked for a while. Then I called Shirley, the first thing she wanted to know was what was happening with my job. So I told her, she was too excited to ask me when I was moving in with her. After talking to her I needed to smoke, but I was still waiting for them to come.

I went over Toya's; she was playing with the baby and playing the roll of a good wife and mother. She may have loved Pretty Ricky, but she didn't love his son. She has my son with her all the time. She's always kissing on him and showing him love. To the point that Will has said at times he feels neglected. At least I know she's not just doing it for show. "I hit him," I watched her face.

"You punched Topaz?"

"I hit him," I gestured like I was driving my car.

She picked up her phone. "You better get anything you need out of that car."

"Why?"

"Just go!" Then she dialed a number. I went out to my car and got a few things out. When I came back inside she was getting off the phone. "You can't hit someone and then expect nothing to happen.

You gotta get rid of the car. Did you hurt him?"

"I don't know."

She put the baby down then she jumped on me. One day I'm going to ask this girl for a list of turn ons. "How did you get me back?"

I looked her in her eyes, "you already know."

Toya's face turned so hurt, "no I don't. How?"

She was about to flip out on me. I got up and pulled my clothes on as fast as I could. "You already know."

Toya put her clothes on equally as fast. "No I don't!"

"Why did you sleep with my friend?"

"He was drooling, I was curious. You're always protecting the fat girl and he was singing her praises, I wanted him to like me better." She looked at me like it was my turn to share.

"She was going to out us if I didn't do it."

She grabbed her chest, "my mother?"

"You had to know there was a reason she was cooperating."

"Yes, because I've been paying her to keep her mouth shut. Not because!" She waved her hands like she was disgusted. "You like it don't you?" She looked me in my eyes.

"Yes."

She grabbed her stomach, "my mother? Who does that?"

"Toya shut up! You'd do my dad if you had the opportunity to seduce him."

"Dads are different!"

"My dad is to me what you're pretending your mother is to you. Dads are not different." Toya waved her hands like she was trying to get it together. "Did you try to seduce my dad?"

"Yes, but that's not the point!"

It seems like every time I say I'm going to stop snatching this girl up something dumb comes out of her mouth and I can't even stop myself. When I came after her she ran, I chased her. She ran in the kitchen and pulled a knife. I touched my heart, "stab me right here! I'm tired of living! THIS IS NONSENSE TOYA! WHAT DID I EVER DO TO YOU? WHY?"

"Don't tempt me, my mother Steve? Really? My mother?"

"You already knew! She's just like you, I know she told you."

"I didn't know that's what she was talking about! Steve! You can't!"

"What am I supposed to do? She calls me demanding."

"Tell her no! Tell her you're with me!"

"She's going to tell!"

"If she does she won't be getting paid no more. The money is worth more to her than laying with you just to hurt me."

"I don't think so."

"Oh because my mother loves you so much? Steve wake up! I'm the only one who loves you! All those other females just want to win. They don't love you!"

"This is what you call love? Sleeping with my best friend, my dad!"

"I didn't sleep with your dad Steve come on." She said like I was being ridiculous.

"The only reason you didn't is because he turned you down."

"Details!"

"This is not love Toya! Love is when you want only that person, and even if you could you don't hurt them because you want to protect them from hurt. You..."

She started waving the knife as she cut me off. "You're going to stand there and try to tell me what love is. I was faithful! I played the good girlfriend, and you know what it got me? Pregnant by someone who didn't care! Thrown to the side like I was ugly or FAT! For an ugly fat girl! I..."

"Tracy is not UGLY! And she's not FAT! You are so limited in your perception of someone that all you can do is harp on the one thing you knew about her. And so what if she was FAT she LOVED ME! She was good to ME! And SHE NEVER WOULD'VE HURT ME LIKE YOU DO JUST BECAUSE YOU CAN! This is not love Toya! This is some sick twisted way of existing! I don't want to do this anymore! I'm tapping out!"

"Steve!" I kept walking. "Steve!" I picked up my shoes, "STEVE!" She screamed my name in a blood-curdling scream. I looked at her and she had the knife resting on her wrist. "I'll do it!"

My heart sped up cause that evil, crazy, and determined look was in her eyes. "Toya, what about your son?"

She cried, "I'll do it! Take one more step!"

I put my hands up like she told me this was a stick up. "Toya, don't! I'm sorry!"

"You are my only pleasure! My only joy! I only love that little boy because of you! I get up because of you! I'm in love with you! If you leave me I will have no one! I don't want to exist alone anymore. If you want to kill Topaz, that's fine. I can help you with that. I'm trying to kill the fat girl, but you can't leave me."

"I don't want Tracy to die."

"SHE HAS TO! SHE TOOK EVERYTHING!"

"I want to sleep with her first."

"Fine, whatever! Kiss me!" When I got close to her she sliced my arm. "DON'T EVER THINK YOU CAN LEAVE ME!"

It wasn't a deep cut, it barely bled. I took the knife from her. "You are crazy!"

"Crazy for you!"

|Chapter 12 Guilt

My car was gone when I walked outside. I was sitting on the couch playing with the baby when Will came home. He asked me where my car was. I walked out to where I parked my car. The glass on the ground was the only sign of my car's previous existence. I was in shock for a minute too much has happened in the past two days. I wanted to smoke so badly, but I needed to get out of here. Will called the police and I filed a report. Will drove me home after he and Toya got into a fight about it. I was impressed that he put his foot down. Toya was pissed, but there was nothing she could do about it. Whether someone came tonight or not I had to smoke. I was starting to feel sick. I called Shirley and we made a plan to move me in to her place in two weeks.

****

It was after four in the morning, I was watching a movie. I couldn't sleep, I didn't want to move in with Shirley, but I didn't have a choice. I heard a car pull in to the lot downstairs. I looked out the window and Toya parked all crooked. She was stumbling as she got out of the car. She looked up at me in the window as she tried to walk to the door. I was startled by her tears. Toya started fussing in between her tears. She said she went out with Will and he insisted that they go to the club that Pretty Ricky manages. She tried to come up with good arguments but again he put his foot down. She cried as she said she sat helplessly watching Pretty Ricky and Tracy grinding on the dance floor. She said she couldn't have a visible reaction otherwise Will would've asked questions. She said Drew's brother came over to their table hurling insults at her. She said Will was defending her when the brother flashed his gun. She said he had an expensive bottle sent to their table. Will wanted to send it back but she drank it. Then she stood there crying about Pretty Ricky being all over Tracy. She was messing with my high. I asked her how she got out of the house, and she said she put Will to sleep then she came to me. She sat on the floor holding herself as she cried. After I smoked a little more I sat on the floor next to her. I put my arm around her while she cried. She started kissing me and she was on me before I could blink.

Although I was disgusted my body released before my Johnson got the message that this wasn't cool. As soon as Toya got off of me I got up and got in the shower. She was standing in the doorway still tipsy with her arms folded. She wanted to know what was wrong with me. "You're killing my high! How you gonna come here without washing yourself?" I proceeded to go off for about thirty minutes. Toya hurried to the toilet and emptied everything in her stomach. She sat on the floor with vomit in her hair and on her shirt. Toya is losing it, I never thought someone so beautiful could look so... so... **Gross**! She was dirty, covered in sweat and vomit.

My stomach turned looking at her. I backed up against the wall and I slid on the floor. Everything is so crazy; all this thinking was messing with my high. What have I become, what happened to me? Everything inside me hurt, Toya sat over there crying like she was thinking the same thing.

She slowly stood up, that's when I went off again. I told her to have the decency to wash up before she came to me. I promised I would choke her out if she ever did that to me again. Toya got in the shower while I scrubbed myself again in the sink. She got in the bed a little more sober than she came. She put her mouth on my ear. "She has to die!"

****

Toya said Will went off so badly on her when she came home the next afternoon. She went home hung over and in my T-shirt and her pants. She said Will wouldn't let her get a word in edgewise. She told me she was going to lay low for a bit which was fine by me. I didn't tell her that I was moving to Shirley's the next weekend there wasn't a point.

I needed about four more boxes and then I'd be all packed up. Tonight I was packing up all my boxes and things in Shirley's truck that she rented for me.

As I walked into the rental and moving supply place in the direction of my future boxes, someone paused when they saw me, which caused me to stop. Indigo was looking stuck standing next to a little girl. The little girl looked just like her, I didn't see any traces of me in the kid. It's a shame that now every time I see an ex I looked for myself before I do anything. "Steve?" Indigo looked me over.

"Yes, how you been?"

She looked at her daughter, "he used to be a friend." Then she looked at me, "I'm good. What's happened to you? Are you sick?" Her eyes floated over me.

"Do I look that bad?" I felt self-conscious.

"You're skinny and dried out looking. What's going on with your hair? What are you wearing?"

Indigo and her daughter were kind of over dressed for a moving truck rental office visit. They had designer sweat suits and J's on their feet. Indigo's mini-me even mimicked her mothers side swept ponytail that hung neatly out of shiny hair thingies. "I'm moving, this is not a dress up occasion."

"Don't get defensive, I just figured maybe you were in the hospital or something like that."

"Look! I know I've lost some weight, but it's not a crime to lose weight."

"No, but I was thinking the hospital would be the only excuse or something that could or would hold you back from being there at Topaz's funeral." I grabbed the shelf but I still fell like she hauled off and punched me. "Steve! Do I need to call for help?" She grabbed my arm.

"What? When? Where? How?" I didn't even try to get up.

"It was a hit and run. No one got a read on the car that hit him. The driver probably didn't see him until too late. I knew for sure someone would've called you." Her eyes turned sad, "I'm sorry Steve. I thought you knew. Baby go wait for me at the counter." She told her daughter who held the same sad look for me. Her daughter did, as she was told, Indigo bent down so I could hear her. "What are you smoking?"

"Don't bother me with this nonsense right now."

"Are there any other addicts in your family? Are you the only one?" I frowned at her. "Stop playing dumb! You know this is probably the last time I'll see you. I need to know what I'm dealing with." She gestured towards her daughter.

I got up off the floor, "that's not funny."

Indigo looked annoyed. "I know I never told you but I wasn't sure. It was between you and my now husband. We found out when she was a baby. He knows, she doesn't, and from the looks of you it would be useless to ever tell her."

"You just disappeared, one day we're fooling around and then you're just gone."

"We weren't in love. Plus your eye wandered too much for me."

"Diabetes runs in my family staying healthy and active will help her. Everything I am, she will become." Then I picked up my boxes and walked towards the front.

"Um! Steve! This is my store, just take them and go." She looked annoyed. That explains the expensive clothes.

"So why did you tell me now if it doesn't matter?"

"I never thought the health nut would end up like this. It doesn't look like you'll be around too much longer a few years tops."

I frowned at her, "not only will I be alive. I will be healthy and happy. When you decide you remember that you care about me, reach out to Toya. She'll know how to find me."

Indigo's face turned angry, "you and Toya?"

She could try to hide it all she wanted to, I knew she was hurt. "Yes! The most beautiful woman any man could have."

She grinned at me, "you're stupider than I thought. Toya is toxic and your whole appearance makes perfect sense now. When you talk to her tell her that I won on the boyfriend swap. I married the football player and she got you." Then she smiled and walked away.

When I walked into my apartment I heard the backdoor close. I dropped everything and ran back there. I opened the door and looked around. I couldn't see anyone. I felt like someone had been in my place and to mess with me everything was almost the same as I left it. Maybe the FBI was after me because of Topaz. I kept trying to get back to packing but I couldn't do it, my nerves were shot. I needed to smoke in the worst way. I sat on the floor and looked at my blunt after taking a puff. This one was different and my lips felt numb off one hit. One of these days I need to find out where Shirley buys from. The stuff Kamony had did nothing for me. Shirley's stuff keeps getting better and better. I know there's a ton of things I should be doing right now. However, all I can do is sit here and smoke away my guilt. Try not to think about my friend that I meant to hurt, but not kill. As the thought crossed my mind to turn myself in, I fell asleep.

****

She's a little taller than Tracy. She's barely brown, shoulder length brown permed hair. Slightly freckled, I could go on and on about the things about her that are nothing like Tracy. She even talks in a light almost child like voice that I actually don't care for. But her curves, her body is what got my attention at first. Her shape made me think of Tracy. She was top heavy just like her, and the moment I laid eyes on her I wanted her to hold me just like Tracy used to. I thought I was getting over Tracy, but Raven made me miss her. I don't talk to her much over the phone cause I can't stand too much of that. I normally hang out with Raven while Shirley's at work. Shirley takes care of me, but it's not the same. Whenever Shirley buys for me she asks me if I'm sleeping in her bed that night. If I want the stuff no is not the right answer. If I want something from her I have to give her what she wants. I sleep with her as payment for services rendered. Now she's telling me she loves me. I let that ride on the air, I don't feel loved.

I haven't spoken to Toya in a minute. Last time I talked to her over the phone we got into a big argument because she was talking crazy again. She plays too much talking about Tracy. She called me in the middle of the night screaming about some girl named Karen and Pretty Ricky messing around while she was pregnant. She was saying she killed her and that Tracy was next. I almost believed her but something told me there was no way. Shirley came in the guest room where I was sleeping after I hung up. She asked me if everything was ok. I told her it was fine. My cousin got into it with a girl at the club. Shirley asked me to come to her bed lowly. I lit up; once I was numb I went to her.

****

"How long has she lived here?" I looked at the paper.

"A couple years, not exactly sure. Why don't you know this?" Kamony asked.

"She was coming to my house or we'd meet up somewhere randomly." I looked at the pictures of Tracy's house. Immediately I was angry, how could she build a whole happy life without me? But how happy could she possibly be without me? Shirley says that Tracy has been acting weird with her since that time at the Bart station, acting like she's too good for everybody. She says that she thinks Tracy is messing around with that guy. I know I'm not crazy, but I know I see him everywhere. Every time I see him it's like a flash though. He'll be watching me and I'll see him and then in the blink of an eye he's gone as if I wasn't just looking at him. Most times it happens when I'm downtown in Oakland when I'm hoping to get a glimpse of Tracy. When he disappears like that it makes me nervous. I keep imagining him creeping up on me and electrocuting me out of nowhere. "She live here alone?"

Kamony smiled, "I don't know. You lost control of her didn't you?" She was too happy.

I looked down at her carrier, "what did you have?"

"A girl, her name's Sarina. She looks just like Richele did at this age." She pulled back the blanket she had over the carrier. It was another version of Richele's face.

"Richele happy to be a big sister?"

"Very, she thinks Sarina is her baby." Then she swallowed, "so Shannon and her son didn't take the news too well."

I blank stared at her, "you're not that dumb. Why would they be happy about your open stupidity? How many kids am I supposed to have?"

"Sarina makes four."

I shook my head, "that's ridiculous!"

"How many kids does Tracy have?"

"She doesn't have any." I stared at the pictures trying to memorize the look of the house.

"You're lying! You told me she had a baby."

"No I didn't!"

We argued back and forth for a while. When I had enough I looked at the baby again then I said goodbye.

****

"I TOLD YOU! I'LL GET HOME WHEN I GET HOME! KEEP CALLING ME AND I'M NOT COMING HOME AT ALL TONIGHT!"

She cried, "please calm down Steve. I'm sorry. I'm sorry! Please calm down!"

"IF YOU WANTED ME CALM YOU WOULDN'T KEEP CALLING ME!"

"Do you need me to come get you? My cousin did me a favor last time, by not giving you a DUI. We can't afford for you to get caught up."

"STOP CALLING ME! I'LL BE HOME WHEN I GET HOME!" I slammed my phone close. She's so clingy and needy, Shirley drives me crazy.

It was cold out; I could see my breath on the cold air as soon as I stood up. I locked the car, and then I started walking. My heart started beating fast as I got close to the corner. I crossed the street and looked down the block at Tracy's house as I walked a block up. It was completely dark in her house, there was a car in the driveway, and it was a nice car. I didn't see Tracy's car though. I walked a block up and then I walked around that block to the opposite corner. As I started walking down Tracy's block I saw two other guys walking towards me. I crossed the street and they crossed the street and continued walking towards me. The guys were looking at me but they didn't raise their heads where I could see their faces. I stopped walking and they stopped walking as well. One of the guys raised his arms and asked me what was up. I said I was just passing through. The other guy asked me where I was from. I turned around and started walking away. The last thing I expected up here was to have to identify what set I'm from. The guys stood there for a minute like they were talking. I walked normally. Then they suddenly started chasing me. I started running, but they were faster. I threw my head back and begged my legs to move faster. I ran across the street and then I doubled back. Anything in my path I grabbed and threw it behind me in hopes that it would buy me a few seconds. I flew past Tracy's house where Pretty Ricky was standing on the porch with his hands in his robe watching me run. A hustler's son? How did he know I was here? I heard him tell them to get me. I ran so hard that each stride projected me up. When I hit the corner of Ashby, I ran across the street. This street is busy during normal hours, at this hour it was vacant. I grabbed my keys out my pocket. I got the driver's side door open and almost closed when the guy grabbed my door. I put the key in the ignition and started the car. The guy busted out the window and grabbed me. I stood on the gas as I threw the car in gear. The other guy shot out the back window as I barely got away. Ok so walking down Tracy's street was a bad idea. Were they going to shoot me for walking down the street? How did Pretty Ricky know I was there? I pulled into the Berkeley Bowl grocery store parking lot up the street. I cursed as I looked at the car. How was I going to explain this? It was quiet and I was the only car in the parking lot. I was looking in the trunk for anything that could help me. I normally give Shirley such a hard time about all the things in her trunk, but this time I was thankful and rummaging through everything looking for my salvation.

Suddenly lights were on me, high beams were coming at me from every direction. My eyes hurt as I tried to shield them. All the lights turned off and the cars stopped after they had me boxed in. I kept blinking trying to focus my eyes. Pretty Ricky got out of one of the cars like he was supposed to be running something. He said I had to be the stupidest somebody he knew. He said he's been trying to be patient with me and that other people have died for less. Each car had two guys in it. They all stood looking at me with serious faces. I know I couldn't have been the only person who was cold.

Pretty Ricky was still in pajama pants, house shoes, and a silky robe, like the bay chill wasn't bothering him. Pretty Ricky walked up on me, I thought he was going to say something else but he punched me. My body immediately went limp. Everything hurt, and I can't even tell you where he hit me other than I heard the hit more than I felt it. I guess my adrenaline was still going. He looked disappointed that I didn't even try to fight back, but I couldn't get my arms and legs to cooperate with me. He kicked me a few times, and like I said I couldn't feel anything at the moment, but I knew in the morning I was going to feel everything. Someone told him that they would take care of me and it was time for him to go back home. Pretty Ricky reluctantly got back in one of the cars and they drove away. Someone picked me up and put me in the backseat of Shirley's car, which was covered in glass. They drove the car, parked it and got out. I was in severe pain all over my body and I couldn't pinpoint the origin. I needed to smoke, but my stuff was in the glove compartment and my body wouldn't cooperate with me. When Shirley came out in the morning to go to work, she stopped herself from screaming by covering her mouth with her hands. She called 911 and they rushed me to the hospital. I had cracked ribs, and a concussion. I swear he only hit me once and kicked me a couple of times. Next time our paths crossed I was getting my revenge and I was bringing a weapon. No ifs ands or buts about it.

My room door opened slowly and Toya walked in. I had forgotten how beautiful she is. Worry and concern were in her eyes. When Shirley walked out the room she quickly asked me what I did. I told her I tried to walk by Tracy's place. She got angry as she said that Pretty Ricky had the place locked up. She said someone sent a kid in who actually made it to the backyard, and then the dogs took bites out of his legs. I asked her who sent a kid. Toya cut her eyes at me and said I needed to talk to my baby momma.

|Chapter 13 The News... Again!

I can tell when she's lying! Kamony was stammering like crazy.

"Yes or No?"

Little sweat beads popped up across her forehead. "Your cousin set me up!" She fidgeted.

"How?"

Kamony was trying her hardest not to cry. Her cheeks and ears were bright red. She said she was with Marvin and her girls out to eat when she saw Toya, her baby, and her husband. She said she wanted to ask her about the little boy who looked like me when Toya asked her when was the last time she spoke to me. She said she couldn't believe she was going there with her in front of their men. She told Toya that she hadn't spoken with me in awhile. Toya smiled and said it looked like you and Tracy were getting back together. She said you didn't come around anymore because you were always with Tracy. Then Toya smiled and said she heard wedding bells. Kamony said she caught herself from going off like she wanted to. She said she could tell Toya was getting a kick out of watching her squirm. Kamony cleared her throat and said that Toya's baby looked just like me. She said Toya didn't flinch as she said the baby actually looked like her Uncle Steve who was my father. Kamony said she took her baby out of the carrier where Toya could see her. She said Toya stopped smiling. I asked why they were hollering across the restaurant like that. She said Toya started it.

She said she couldn't stop thinking about it and she snapped. She asked her cousin to go get Tracy. I asked what she meant by *get*, and she said "GET!" As she ran her pointer finger across her neck, as if she was decapitating herself. She said he went through the neighbors below Tracy's backyard. He scaled the wall and once he thought he was sure there was no dog he went in the yard. Kamony started crying. She said her little cousin said there were so many guns on him and then the dogs chewed him up. She said the officers who took him away beat him up real bad and told him he better never even drive through upper Berkeley ever again.

I sat back cause I understood the feeling. All I was doing was walking down the street and I got my hat handed to me. Kamony said that's when she realized that Toya set her up. I asked her why would she shoot Tracy? She looked at me and said she **HATES** Tracy. I thought about it for a minute. "I'm going to be as honest as I can be with you right now." Kamony looked scared like she didn't know what was about to come out of my mouth. "I love Tracy and all this distance between us is temporary. Now that I know how far you will go behind being a jealous and manipulative female, if Tracy trips over a crack in the sidewalk I'm calling the police and telling them you caused the crack. I don't love you, I never have and I never will. Leave her alone!"

Kamony got angry, "after everything I've done for you!"

"What have you done for me that no one else has?"

"I've forgiven you." She wiped her tears. "You know what, forget it. You not about to have me up here crying and feeling rejected like I'm some ugly fat girl. I stuck by you even through this cracked out look you've been sporting. You really need to sit down and eat a meal. Do something with your hair, find some clothes that fit. You look homeless and tired. Stay away from my girls and leave me alone." She stood up.

"You act like I've ever cared about those brats! Those are your kids, you never have to worry about me even remembering them." I turned in my seat.

****

I stared at her stomach. I know she was trying to talk to me, but I couldn't hear her. "Who's is it?"

"Like you care! Can you please try to focus on what I'm telling

219

you!" Toya said through clinched teeth.

"You're messing with my high!"

Her eyes glazed over, "Steve PLEASE!" She grabbed my hands. "I need you to focus. I'm trying to tell you my plan. We gotta leave here. That detective turned on me and is trying to ask me questions about an attempted murder."

I laughed at her, "what happened to your plan to bring Pretty Ricky to his knees? Aren't you supposed to be putting his father under the jail?"

"STEVE FOCUS!"

"Who's baby is that Toya? I can't keep having babies! Every time I turn around someone's telling me they're having my baby. Did you know Indigo had my baby?"

Toya sat up, "she did what?"

"Yep, that kid don't look like me but she said she was my baby. Oh and she told me something about a boyfriend swap and that she married the football player."

Toya screamed and started slapping on me. I sat there laughing at her cause I know she didn't want to create a scene. She had to get herself in check and all I could do was laugh at her. "You should've smoked that memory away along with the others." I kept laughing, "I'm cutting you off. Does me no good if you're going to be sloppy."

"Cutting me off from what? It's not like you come see me no more."

She exhaled, "it's this baby. She makes me tired, I can't keep up with too much anymore."

"Why are you having another baby?"

She looked angry, "I didn't do this on purpose. One day my period didn't come. I don't even know if it's yours or his." She rubbed my hands, "baby please focus. I need you to focus for me. They're going to kill us if they catch us. The police are looking for me, we got to move. Will's going to transfer to North Dakota."

"North Dakota? What's out there?"

"Nothing and we can lay low for awhile. I need to get this baby out, she slows me down."

I stared at her stomach, "its a little girl? I like little girls."

Tears fell out of Toya's eyes, "Steve baby please focus. I didn't know you were this bad off. I'm cutting you off."

"Why do you keep saying that? Cutting me off from what? Were we going to do it today? You weren't acting like it."

"No."

"Oh come on Toya. I've been laying with all these old ladies. I need some of your pretty chocolate. I need someone who's going to give it a real go. They so lazy."

"Are they worse than the fat girl?"

I smiled as memories flooded my mind. "Tracy was good, she used to look back at me and twist herself..."

"STEVE!" Toya was about to explode.

"What? What's wrong with you? Why you mad? You asked, and I was telling you."

"I'm cutting you off. If I'm still out, I'm coming for you in a couple weeks."

****

Shirley came home looking irritated. "I told them this is not the same stuff he's been selling me." She tried to touch me; I jumped cause the thought of it hurt. She cried, "there's nothing I can do he swears this is the same thing." I immediately became sick out of nowhere and I vomited all over the floor. "Steve! I don't know what to do!"

It hurt to talk or even move, "call my cousin." I barely got out of my mouth.

I couldn't explain what was happening to me, but I was sure that Toya could. She came over a little later. I heard Shirley explaining everything to Toya and Toya was listening like she had no idea of what was happening to me. She asked Shirley for all my buds. She calmly talked to Shirley like she was in control of everything. After a few minutes I heard her explaining to Shirley it sound like they were lacing my weed with something and they either couldn't get the same supplier or something but I needed to be weaned off of whatever it was. She told her not to let me run through them unless she wanted to go through this again. Shirley came in explaining everything that I heard Toya tell her. Shirley went to put on some coffee for me.

Toya sat on the bed with her belly bigger than the last time I saw her. "You got to get healthy Steve. Mind over matter, you can do this. Work through the withdrawals. You're going to get stronger! We've got to get out of here. Deep breaths, you can do this. I believe in you Steve!" Her hand stroking my head was the only thing that didn't hurt.

Everything hurt so badly, "Tracy!" I said above a whisper.

"What?" Toya stopped moving as her eyes turned evil.

"I need her! I love her! She never would've let this happen to me."

"That fat pig doesn't love anyone! She's the reason why you're messed up like this. Listen to my voice Steve, we are all we have and we're leaving. You've got to get ready to make the trip."

****

It's been tough and painful, but the pain did lessen over time. I ended up in the hospital for a while. I'm not proud of the way I've behaved. I went after Shirley a few times demanding more blunts. That's when she put me in the hospital. Naomi, one of Shirley's friends that I've been seeing on the side and getting money from, tried to come by, but Shirley told them I was sick. I'm sure they were wondering where I've been this month. As I come back to myself, I've started exercising again. Each push up feels like a reminder of who I used to be. How strong I used to be, everything I am.

I keep apologizing for how horrible these past months have been. Shirley says she's just happy that I'm feeling better.

We were sleeping when my phone rang. I didn't recognize the number. I let the call go to voicemail. They hung up and called right back. After the third round of this I answered the phone. "HELLO?"

"STEVE!" Toya was crying. "STEVE I NEED YOU! HELP ME! HELP ME PLEASE!"

I sat up, "what's wrong? What's going on?"

Shirley stopped snoring as she turned to me. "Who is that?"

"It's Toya, I'll be right back." I walked down the hallway, and into the study. "Toya? Where are you?"

Toya was crying hysterically. "Can you come get me?"

"Where are you?"

Toya explained where as I drove to a park where she was shivering at the pay phone in her hospital gown all twisted around her and hospital socks with the rubber soles. I wrapped the blanket around her and carried her to the car. She was pale and helpless. She said they ran into Pretty Ricky and his family earlier today. She said they told Will everything! She screamed as she sat there. She said the police are looking for her and they were going to turn her in. That or Pretty Ricky's father was going to kill her. I asked her why would he want to kill her. She shook her head, and then she said the police have been looking for someone to testify against him, to prove their theories about him as fact. She said they said they would protect her, but now that she has that attempted murder case against her for that minister's son they were treating her like a criminal. I asked her why she was in a hospital gown. She said she gave birth and then while Will was out of the room probably calling the police on her, she ran away.

I asked her what we were going to tell Shirley? Toya said she would take care of it. By the end of everything Shirley was hugging Toya and telling her she could hide with us from Will. She told her that he was abusive and she had to run away right after giving birth. Shirley worked from home for the next week to look after Toya and make sure she was ok.

"She has my son calling her mommy!" Her eyes were evil. "We're getting out of here! There's nothing here for us."

"Ok!" I said in defeat.

|*Chapter 14 The Plan*

"Stop!" I moved away from her.

"I can't touch you now?" She blank stared at me.

"You're fertile and you're not on birth control. I don't want anymore kids." I'm tired of people popping up telling me I got more and more kids. Kamony finally got some sense and she won't let me see Richele or Sarina. I told her I'm clean and she said she don't care. I could take her to court, but I don't feel like fighting. She hasn't put me on the hook for Sarina so I'm trying to be cool. I haven't even seen the last baby Toya had.

"Oh, that little girl was Will's." She said like she was talking about someone else's child.

"How do you know?" I relaxed some.

"I went by his place in the middle of the night. I needed to see my babies. Will said he got the baby tested and she's his. He said Drew's momma reached out to him about the whole thing. They're running for saints or something."

I don't know why that was one less thing to worry about. I knew she left the other night, I didn't know where she went but I kept Shirley preoccupied so she wouldn't notice. She's been acting weird lately. This living situation wasn't going to last. "So what's the plan? We gonna mess around and risk getting caught at Shirley's for the rest of our lives?"

"After we kill the fat girl we'll run away for a few years until I think Drew has calmed down enough, and then I'll come back and he'll be the new Will."

"What makes you think you can come back here?"

"Drew will clear everything up for me. It's going to be fine, he's in love with me." She pulled out a condom. "We can't afford to have any babies holding us down right now."

I kissed her, I was glad we were on the same page for once.

****

Shirley slammed her car door. She was home early. I looked at Toya with big eyes. Shirley came storming in the door cursing and going off. She kept asking me how could I turn on her after all she's done for me. She said she didn't want to believe it when her coworker said it, but it was true. How could I sleep with her friends? I frowned at Toya; I didn't know where this was coming from. I got up and I walked towards Shirley who had her back to Toya. She mouthed for me to tell Shirley I loved her. "It's all lies, they just don't want us to be together. I'm in love with you and it makes everyone else crazy to see how happy we are together." I rubbed her back as she immediately relaxed. I bucked my eyes at Toya. She kissed her hand then she made fingers walk. She pointed to the bedroom. She made a circle with one hand and she stuck her finger from the other hand in and out of the circle. I took a deep breath then I did as Toya told me to. I spent the evening lying to Shirley.

****

She tried to keep her voice even, even though she held on to my hand. "Toya the magician!" Pretty Ricky sounded annoyed.

"Drew I'm sorry! You know how I get about you. Everything got out of control. Why didn't you try to protect me?"

"That's not my job anymore, why didn't you have your husband take care of everything?"

"Come on Drew, you've seen him. He probably went to call the police after I delivered the baby."

"Well then you should've asked the crackhead. My days of cleaning up your messes are over. You need to sit your hot headed behind down somewhere and calm down."

"You really are done with me? After everything we've been through? Drew!" She was trying to pull at his heartstrings. "You're going to let Malcolm kill me?"

He was quiet for a minute, "the past is the past. You can't manipulate me anymore. You don't control me anymore. You have dug your own grave."

"Drew!" Tears fell down Toya's face. "What did she do to you? What happened to the man who used to love me? I..."

He exhaled, "stop it Toya." He sounded like he was weakening.

Toya let go of my hand as she got visibly excited but she kept her voice the same. "Can you meet me somewhere? We need to talk?" She took a deep breath, "what about next Saturday? We could..."

"No, I have something to do for work."

"On a Saturday? We could meet in the evening if that's better. I just want to talk to you."

"No, next Saturday I have to go to a work event in the evening in Blackhawk."

"Blackhawk? What are you going to do in Blackhawk?"

"They're having a dinner at the museum, you know what it doesn't matter..."

She cut him off, "I could meet you in the parking lot. That way it's all one event to the fat girl." He didn't respond, "she's going to be there?"

"Look Tra... I mean Toya. Next Saturday is no good for me."

Toya exploded, "MY NAME IS TOYA, LATOYA, OR JUST TOY IF ALL OF THAT IS TOO MUCH FOR YOU TO REMEMBER! I DON'T APPRECIATE NONE OF THIS! YOU NEVER TOOK ME TO ANY WORK EVENTS! YOU NEVER EVEN TOLD ME WHERE YOU WORK! I AM THE MOTHER OF YOUR FIRST BORN SON! I..."

"I'm so sick of you!" His voice was low and controlled. "You fall apart because I'm finally in love, and it's real this time! You never loved me, Toy you only care about winning! You've cheated on me, dumped me, manipulated me, hurt me. You cause so much drama that even when I'm trying to save your dumb behind you can't leave well enough alone. I LOVE TRACY! I CHOOSE TRACY! She's good to me, and she's good to my son!"

"Our son!" Toya said through tears.

"Your son's name is Will jr and he looks like the crackhead. My son just like his father has chosen my woman to love and stand by. Andre calls her mommy because she's the only mother he's ever known. You kept my son in that pigsty of a room just to hurt me. Just for attention! If you can't love my son, who is an extension of me, my most valued possession. What in the world would make you think I could love you? You don't love me; all you want to do is hurt me. What did I ever do to you besides love you? Try to be good to you. Protect you! You've gotten so used to being protected you're messing your life up. Then you turn against my father?"

"YOU HATE MALCOLM!"

"WHY WOULD I HATE MY FATHER? YOU DON'T LISTEN, I'VE TOLD YOU TIME AND TIME AGAIN WHAT MY ISSUES WERE WITH HIM AND I BET YOU DON'T REMEMBER?" He waited for her answer. "You're so mad at the world cause you don't know who your father is. You need to project your anger on your wicked mother! She is the root of all of your anger and you're so busy lashing out at everyone else. This is my last plea with you Toya. Malcolm is looking for you; he has everyone looking hard for you. The police are looking just as hard. One of them is going to find you first. Malcolm will mail you back to your momma in pieces and you know he will."

"But I'm Andre's mother!"

"HE DON'T CARE! You came against him! You came against his grandson! You came against me! You came against Tracy!"

Toya shot out of her seat! "HE LIKES THAT FAT PIG! YOU SAID HE HATES FAT PEOPLE!"

"Just like everyone else including your little crackhead over there, we all LOVE TRACY! Ask the crackhead why he keeps trying to get at her if she's so hideous?"

"He just wants to sleep with her." She stared at me.

"Really, a man risks his life coming by my house for a screw?"

"Risk his life?" She looked at me, "Drew what are you talking about?"

"He didn't tell you about our encounter?" He chuckled, "that fool can't even take a punch. If it wasn't for Tracy he'd have been dead a long time ago."

Toya started screaming. "STOP IT! YOU LOVE ME! YOU CAN'T LIVE WITHOUT ME! STOP IT! WE ARE GOING TO BE TOGETHER AGAIN! I PROMISE I'LL BE GOOD NEXT TIME!"

"There's not going to be a next time. I'm marrying Tracy and she's it for me. I'm done with all the games! I'm going to spend the rest of my life being faithful to that woman! I'm going to give her everything I got within me. Andre barely remembers you, in time you'll be completely erased. Her last name will be Wallace just like ours, Toya who?"

"Drew!" She cried, "baby don't! I love you! You belong with me!" He didn't respond. "I'M GOING TO KILL HER. YOU TELL ME HOW LONG SHE LIKES LIVING IN THE BOTTLE YOU'VE CREATED FOR HER! I DON'T EVEN CARE ANYMORE! YOU BROUGHT THIS ON YOURSELF!"

"Meaning?"

"Oh now you want an explanation! Now you want to talk? Too late!" She hung up the phone. When he called back she kept picking up the phone and hanging it up. Then she paced around the living room going off. I sat there watching her be so emotionally involved in all of this. She wasn't acting in my best interest. Only in hers. She was trying to manipulate things so that she could get back with Pretty Ricky. When that happens, what's supposed to happen to me? I needed Tracy back on my side. In order to make that happen I needed to put it on her one last time. While Toya sat there going off, I wrote down *the museum in Blackhawk*.

****

I was at the international market in Emeryville. Toya wanted a sushi dragon roll, and I was trying to decide what I wanted. "Steve Turnage?"

"Yes?" I didn't recognize this white lady and then she shoved a badge in my face.

"I'm looking for Latoya Spencer, have you seen her?"

"Not in a long time." Twenty minutes counts as a long time. "Why?"

"I need to talk to her about some people. She was supposed to be helping me and then she disappeared. Gave birth in the hospital, named her kid, and then she vanished. Left her husband with a newborn and a toddler." I didn't respond, "you got any kids Mr. Turnage?"

"I have a daughter."

"Only a daughter? Oh I've heard it's more than that."

"Rumors." I shrugged her off.

She smiled at me, "I'm sure you're right." Then she turned to walk away. "If you hear from Latoya tell her to turn herself in to me."

I nodded in agreement, and then I turned back to the board. Jerk Chicken it was going to have to be. A kid walked by me and bumped into me heck of hard. "A!"

"Excuse you! You need to watch where you going!" This thugged out kid barked at me. Pants sagging, and major attitude.

I decided to walk away and go somewhere else. Another kid bumped into me. "Hey old man! You need to watch where you going!" Same attitude.

I started walking in the same direction that the cop went in when the two kids started following me, and then he walked up to me with fire in his eyes. "SO! Tell me again what you had to say about my mother? I'm a bastard right?" I did not have time for this. I looked around as people were looking; a lot of them had their phones out recording waiting for something juicy to happen. He walked in my face. "I told you the next time I saw you I was going to kill you! That was a promise not a threat!"

"Oh Mr. Turnage..." the cop slowed down as she approached us. "Am I interrupting something?" She flashed her badge. The kid mumbled that next time he saw me I was dead. Then he and his two friends fell back, they walked away with five other kids. My heart was pounding cause the look in his eyes said he would do it without a second thought. "That is one angry kid, what did you do forget the bike he asked for?"

"He's not mine!" I said.

"Right! I totally believe that." She said sarcastically. "I realized I didn't give you my card so that you could call me when you talk to Latoya." She gave me her card. "You better walk out with me before you end up getting jumped in this food court."

****

I went online and I Googled Blackhawk's museum, and the Blackhawk Auto Museum in Danville came up. I looked on their upcoming events page and there it was. Cooper Financial's Annual Black Tie Executive Dinner. It said the event was a private event so there weren't any tickets available. I went all over their page looking at everything. I decided I'd see Tracy with a clear mind and body there. The old Steve that she knows and loves would find a moment alone with her. She's going to melt at the sight of me.

I deleted the history on the computer then I told Toya I would be back. She was on the phone with someone trying to get them to do something for her. I didn't even want to know. I walked out of the room, and then I remembered that I left the paper with the museum information I wrote down on it. I caught the door before it closed and then I let it close behind me. "He's gone… I know baby, I miss you too…" Then she started laughing. "He's so little, but he's a lot of fun… I know! I know! I try to make sure I buy the condoms because his magnum joke is hilarious… It slides right off, and I'm not trying to end up pregnant." She laughed hard as the person spoke. "That's why I need you, Drew was too big, Steve is too small, but you… You're just right!" She laughed some more. My heart was pounding; I slid out of the room making sure the door didn't make any noise as I exited. Topaz's words came back to me; she was playing me all this time. I gave up Tracy for nothing! I killed my best friend over a lie. If I had thought about it, I would've asked her who stole my car? How was she making all these other things happen if it was just me and her? Of course she was playing me. My family don't even talk to me all because of her. I'm getting Tracy back. Once I have her back then my dad will come around. I took a deep breath and I told myself to man up.

I decided to go to Sun Valley Mall in Concord, for a change of scenery. I found a black suit and I paired it with an expensive shirt and tie. Being a gigolo has paid me very well. As I turned to walk away from the counter Shannon was standing there looking at me with lost eyes. "Shannon." I said.

Tears came to her eyes. "You look better, how do you feel?"

"I'm doing a lot better. How are you?"

"I wish Terrell would've met you like this, instead of before."

I exhaled, "Shannon how can you be sure he's mine?"

"Steve, I thought we were in a relationship. I was faithful to you. He's your son. How can you look at him and still ask?"

I knew she was telling the truth even though I didn't want to believe her. "Because I saw how you manipulated that kid. How you try to use your body to get over on men. I don't have a job, I can't do nothing for you."

She pointed at my suit, "how are you shopping?"

"Girlfriend."

"One of these days you're going to learn to stop trying to get over on females."

****

I got out of the shower feeling great. Toya and I had a long morning as usual. Toya and I go in the morning about an hour after Shirley leaves. Then I rest and wait to see if Shirley's checking for me in the evening. Toya's been so busy plotting that she hasn't noticed a change in me. She's so used to me being out of it that she doesn't even watch half the things she implies when she talks to me. I was in the bedroom dressing when Shirley came in the door cursing and screaming. She said police came to her job asking her questions about Toya and they told her that Toya was wanted for attempted murder. She said the police were coming to search her home. Toya and I grabbed all of our stuff in record timing. Shirley screamed asking me where I was going. Toya told her that I was her boyfriend and I was going with her. Shirley stopped screaming as she plopped on the couch. She asked me if it was all-true. I kept walking out the door. We caught the bus with all of my bags. We caught Bart to Downtown Oakland. We got a room at a hotel to lay low until we came up with our next move.

|Chapter 15 The End

"What's the suit for?" Toya stared at me.

"Why are you going through my stuff?" I pushed past her.

"Steve! Don't play dumb with me! What are you doing? What's the suit for?"

I walked into her face. "All this is so that you can get Pretty Ricky back. Once you have him back what's supposed to happen to me? What about my happiness? What about what I want?"

"What do you want?"

"Tracy!"

Toya took a deep breath, "you are so stupid! Why on earth would she want you after she's had Drew? I'm the only person dumb enough to want you. She..."

I started laughing, and then I walked back to my lotion. "I used to try to tell Tracy the same thing. That nobody would ever want her and I was the only person crazy enough to deal with her. Pretty Ricky sure made a liar out of me huh?" I laughed again, "if the long line of women all claiming to have my baby doesn't tell you anything it should tell you that EVERYBODY wants Steve! You come in here parading your beautiful chocolate around promising to be this delicate bite that I've never tasted. Yeah I fell for it, cause I never tasted poison before. I'm not letting you take Tracy from me ever again."

"That's just it, Steve. I didn't take her from you. She left you just like Drew left me. I didn't break you two up; I had nothing to do with her leaving you. I simply love you and she doesn't."

She was right, she had nothing to do with our break up that was all me. Tracy has been in love with me since the first time she baked me cookies. Love doesn't turn off and on for her. "She might be mad at me, but she loves me. You can't understand the type of love she gives. You aren't capable of loving on the level she does. She loves me and we will get back together." I started snatching on my clothes.

"Where are you going?" She said as she cried real tears.

"To pick up my rental car, get my haircut, and to get my woman!" I said irritated.

Toya threw herself on the floor and grabbed my leg. "No! Don't leave me Steve you're all I got."

"Like you said you're still in love with Pretty Ricky. You don't care about what happens with me."

"I'm in love with you Steve, please don't go. Tonight feels like a bad night to go out."

"That's because you are stranded to this room. It's too dangerous for you to go out. I'll be back later!" I shook her off my leg and I walked out the door.

I rented my car and then I got my hair cut at this shop on International Boulevard formerly known as East 14th street. I stalled as long as I could, then I drove to Danville. I sat at the Blackhawk museum watching time pass. When I saw Pretty Ricky pull up Tracy looked beautiful. Her hair, the dress, I told myself to be cool. I touched her flowers and I told them I would be right back.

****

When I woke up it was dark and my head was killing me. I was laying on the floor of a commercial van next to a box. The windows were blacked out in the back and there was a cage that was too dark to see the front of the car through. We weren't moving and I was cold. My suit was dirty, I touched my head and there was dried blood. I groaned as I sat up, then the box started making noise. I stared at the box for a minute. If I opened it, was a poisonous snake going to strike me? I kicked the box and then I recognized the whimper. I opened the box and Toya was all bound up inside. Her hair was wild and sticking to her from all her tears and sweating. When I took the tape off her mouth she kept saying Malcolm was going to kill us. I freed her from her bondage best I could. My head was pounding and I was getting dizzy. Toya moved for the door then she stopped. I asked her what was wrong. She said something wasn't right. Why would we just sit in a van? She said there could be vicious dogs waiting to attack, or she could turn the knob and the whole van blows up. Toya told me not to touch anything cause it could all be a set up, it had to be. She touched my head then she told me she was sorry.

We sat quietly for a while trying to hear anything outside. There was no movement or anything. Toya asked me where they found me. I told her I don't know what happened, everything went black and I woke up here. Toya said she broke down and went to her mother's. She begged her mother for a name or anything for her father. She said her mother was still trying to convince her that the other guy was her father. Toya said she looked up the man that her mother has always tried to say was her father online. She surprisingly found his number and she called him. She said he was very matter of fact about the whole thing. He told her that Avis Le'on was her father. She said right after she left him a voicemail she went back to our room and that's when they came.

We sat there not moving for a long time. Suddenly the van started rocking, and it rocked real hard. Someone blew the door off and they ordered us out of the van. There were guns everywhere and three guys stood calmly by a car. "Daddy you promised that I would be able to shoot her!" One guy said with fire and disgust in his eyes.

"So!" The man in the middle said.

"Once we deliver her when am I supposed to be able to do it? You promised daddy!" I guess he was supposed to be funny.

"Don't kill her." The man in the middle with the deep voice said.

Before I could respond he had his gun out and he shot Toya. She spun around and hit the van. She screamed so loud and I screamed as I ran to her. "Again daddy again!" The guy said.

"Don't kill her." He repeated.

The guy lowered his gun and shot Toya's leg. She screamed again, but there was no blood just a hole in her pant leg. "WHAT ARE YOU DOING? STOP IT!"

"Keep your panties on, they aren't real bullets.... this time!" Then he threw down his gun and walked straight to us. He looked so crazy; I knew I've seen him before. I just couldn't remember from where. He pulled out a big knife. "I have always hated you!" He put the knife up to Toya's throat. "Nothing would make me happier than to slice your neck right now. Then I'd sit and watch you bleed out to make sure you died so there'd be no accidents where you somehow made it to the hospital and survived and I'd have to kill you again."

"Wait a minute..." I tried to talk.

He grabbed my face, and then he threw the side of my head that had been bleeding into the van. "Shut up! No one was talking to your punk, sell out, whipped, and sorry excuse for a man self."

"He's the idiot!" The guy who hasn't said anything until now said.

"He's the one who put his hands on my daughter in-law?" The main guy said raising his deep voice.

"Yeah daddy he did just like this!" Then he started choking me. "I can't make my eyes crazy like his was, but he was high as a kite when he did it." His demonstration of my actions amused him. I tried to move his hands but they were too strong and something told me he could squeeze harder if he wanted to. All my years in the gym, and in this moment I felt like a helpless female.

"Darryl you're about to kill him." The first guy said unamused.

"Daddy can I kill him? He wasn't part of the deal." He said as he continued to choke me.

"No, let him go. Toya's already gotten him back for everything he's done to Tracy."

When he let me go I gasped and gasped, then I threw up. My vision blurred and I couldn't see, my head was pounding, this kid said something else to me then he started laughing. Toya said nothing, she was shaking in fear. Two police cars pulled up and that woman approached us. The dad told the woman that I was hiding Toya and I was her accomplice. They put handcuffs on us.

****

"Mr. Turnage, we have a problem." My public defender said looking at paperwork. "You gave us the names of family members of your friend Topaz Rockwell as character witnesses. Do you know who Eunice Brown is?"

"Topaz's girlfriend."

"She named you as a possible suspect in the hit and run murder of her boyfriend." I was speechless, he flipped through papers. "She claims that you two worked out together normally and it was odd that you were nowhere to be found when the incident occurred and you never called to inquire about his whereabouts. The gym shows that you did come to the gym that day after Mr. Rockwell. We have video footage of you at the gas station messing with your car and then going through the carwash. Then your car was mysteriously stolen, stripped, and burned. Mr. Turnage I need your side of the story..."

****

I took a deep breath, and then I picked up the receiver. "What?"

Her eyes looked all over me like she was searching for something. "What happened to you?"

I was annoyed with her dumb question, "obviously I fell on hard times. What do you want?"

She took deep breaths, "what did I ever do to you? How could you be so cold? So cruel? I loved you, and I thought we were in love. You walked away from me like I was nothing and you deny our son."

I exhaled, "I'm going to be honest with you. I hate you!" I said so matter of factly. "I could never trust you. I saw you manipulate that guy. Talking to him on the phone while you stroked me. Seeing how cold blooded you were with him, what makes you think I would've ever taken you seriously?"

Shannon dropped her head as she cried; "he can forgive me but you cant?"

"He'd be stupid to forgive how down right evil you were to him, no respect for his heart. And then as if I'm an idiot or something you think I'm going to fall for that? I saw how you operated, played the good girl. Got him hooked on you just because he busted you out. Did you forget I was right there watching?"

"I thought you understood that things with you were different." She shook her head. "You know what, it doesn't matter now. That was long ago. I'm here because of my baby. He's in so much pain. He used to be this sweet and loving kid. Now he's full of hatred and pain. I'm begging you Steve! Please! Please reach out to him! Please help him! You're his father!"

"I'm not his father Shannon stop lying to him!"

"I'M NOT LYING! YOU WERE THE ONLY GUY I HAD BEEN WITH FOR YEARS AND STILL YOU WON'T BELIEVE ME!"

"Like I would EVER believe you. Don't forget I know how you are. You are a manipulative skank! I don't know why you waste your time trying to convince me when you know you know who his real father is."

Shannon cried, "you are unbelievable!"

"Oh and he tried to jump me! Did your little bastard ever tell you that?" I exhaled, "I have more important things to do with my time than worry about your kid. He hates me, that's fine, cause I've never had any love for him!" I stood up, "leave me alone Shannon. I don't have any love for you or your kid. You can sit up here and claim you've change all you want, but I saw how you manipulated Kamony. You turned on her the moment she told you I accepted our daughter. You are so jealous and still the same gossipy and messy female. You and Kamony can fight it out for all I care, I've got no use for either one of you." Shannon was crying so hard her whole body was shaking. "Shannon why do you press this so hard?"

"Cause I'm telling the truth and when you deny me it hurts. You reject our son! You'll never know how badly this hurts."

"And I'll never care, that's what's wrong with females? You try to tell them something, educate them and they don't listen. You, Kamony, Toya, and even Tracy. None of you listen and then you want to act like the victim. I'm tired of all you helpless females! You're useless! Got me locked up behind something I had nothing to do with, but I was being a nice guy. I will never take responsibility for that, that, that illegitimate excuse for a boy! I…"

Shannon stood up and dropped her receiver, she was crying so hard. She started to walk away, and then she came back. Her skin was glowing red. She spoke calmly, but I could tell she was shaking. "You listen to me! There ain't nothing you can do for me or my son behind these bars. You are miserable and unfortunately I didn't have the good sense to keep my mouth shut before you plagued my son with your evilness! You have not only ruined your life you ruin my son's. I hope all these females you were chasing were worth what you've done to me, your son, shoot to yourself. I may have tried to run game on my ex, but that was at the encouragement of you. You were the older guy coaching me on how to handle my young boyfriend. Turning me out and then acting like I was stupid for falling for it. I was a little girl who didn't know any better. I hurt my parents and my ex all for a smile from you. You can try and tell the world until you're blue in the face that my son is not yours. She reached in her purse with her free hand and pulled out a picture. BUT YOU KNOW THIS IS YOUR SON! He looks just like you, acts just like you, he even has your mannerisms and walk. I was working with him on his insecurities, the same ones you have until you tap danced all over that. You are poison! You never appreciate anyone good in your life. You're always turning out people for the worst and then you try to play victim. You are in jail because you are unfit to be around good hearted people. They put you in a cage cause that's exactly where you need to be. Away from good people who could actually be of some good use to this world. Your problem is that you know you're nothing. You know you're worthless, and you try to break others down before you know for a fact that they know the truth about you. Everybody knows! Everybody can see your insecurities! They tried to love you anyways! You're so stupid that you don't even get it. You don't even see all the people who have tried to help you. You may feel one way about me, whatever! You may feel one way about Kamony! But whoever the girl is who landed you here, was she a victim of you or what you deserve? From the look of things you got exactly what you deserved. You're going to rot in here, and you better be thankful! Maybe at some point you'll think about all the evil that you've done and find a way to be remorseful about it." She switched hands, "now what you need to be worried about is how many family members I got in here willing to kick your butt on the daily. You may be able to talk all big and bad to me, but I know you're the KING of getting your hat handed to you. You ain't never really been a fighter, a bully, but never a fighter. **WATCH YOUR BACK!**"

When I returned to my cell my mail was on my bed. All of my letters to my father and stepmom came back return to sender. There were multiple letters from the different District Attorney's offices about the child support cases accruing arrears. Kamony for sure, Shannon, and the others filed their cases. I got DNA test results to show all five of the other kids shared my DNA. Kamony then pointed everyone to my father and stepmom. My mother responded to my letter going off about the things I said to her. Then she went off about Madam Creole torturing her about me landing her daughter in prison. My mother is always the victim she can never see what she's done wrong. She always looks at other people's faults like she's better than them. I decided to cut them all off. My father and stepmom turned their backs on me, fine. I'll do my time, read up on some law books and try to figure out how to get myself out of here.

Then the only envelope I didn't touch shined at me like a beacon. I picked it up and it had female writing on it. It was from Raven. She gave me her number and told me to call her as soon as I could. I called her collect the next day. She asked me what happened. I told her that my cousin got me caught up, and now they're trying to pin a murder on me. Raven was crying and telling me that her cousin was in law school. She said she'd have him come talk to me to see if he could help me. I thanked her, and then I told her I missed her.

****

Raven has been my only joy and the only person to care about the fact that I'm in this hellhole. Call me romantic or just caught up in everything she's done for me while I've been in here. We got married yesterday; her cousin has been working hard on my case. There is a light at the end of the tunnel. I will not spend the rest of my life in this place. Raven said she moved to Modesto, so when I get out our plan is to start our family right away.

Every so often I think about Toya, something inside of me aches for her. I don't understand it, but I think it's best if I stay away from her. I just hope I can do that.

When I think about Tracy, I find myself so angry about the way she abandoned me. They try to teach us forgiveness, but she did me so dirty. I didn't deserve to be treated the way she treated me. She ran away from me, she didn't even breakup with me before she moved on. Just forget me, forget my feelings, she didn't even care. It's all her fault that I'm in here, she hyped up her man to get him to overreact every time he saw me. I should've done more than just choke her. I try to tell myself that the Tracy part of my life is over, but it's hard. She hurt me when she left me like that. She can't just hurt me and think there's nothing I can do about it.

****

"Turnage! Letter for you!" Then he dropped the envelope in my cell.

There was no return address on the envelope and the address was typed. I opened the letter; the letters were cut out of a magazine:

StEvE!

yOu BeTtEr NeVeR gEt OuT! yOu'Re A DeAd MaN iF yOu Do!

LoVe,

ThE bAsTaRd!

MORE FROM THE AUTHOR

Thank you for allowing me to entertain you. I hope you have enjoyed reading this Beyond The Wallace's story in the Wallace Family Affairs Series. If you have not read Volumes I - VIII, please do so. Checkout my Author Page and stay tuned for more to come shortly.

Volume I Tracy's Complications (Click here)

Volume II Part 1 Sometimes Love Isn't Enough (Click here)

Volume II Part 2 Love Is Just Enough (Click here)

Volume III Invisible (Click here)

Volume IV Look Beyond Your Eyes (Click here)

Volume V No Regrets (Click here)

Volume VI First You Laugh Then You Cry (Click here)

Beyond The Wallace's ~ A Heart That's Taken (Click here)

Volume VII At Last (Click Here)

Volume VIII Just A Friend (Click Here)

Beyond The Wallace's ~ Abandoned (Click Here)

Beyond The Wallace's – Distorted Mirrors

Beyond The Wallace's ~ Last Words (Release TBD)

Once you've enjoyed all of the background stories for our lovely Wallace's and Latour's. **Please tune in to the "Together We Are Strong" Wallace & Latour Family Episodes (Release TBD) on Amazon.**